STATEMENTS

Statements:

NEW FICTION FROM THE FICTION COLLECTIVE

A VENTURE BOOK

GEORGE BRAZILLER   *New York*

This book was assembled by Jonathan Baumbach with the aid
and advice of the other members of the Fiction Collective. The
introduction was written by Ronald Sukenick.

CONTENTS

STATEMENT

If you want to pick the fruit, someone has to cultivate the orchard. There is an ecology of culture which, like that of nature, may not be as inexhaustible as once was thought.

    Statements: New Fiction From the Fiction Collective was edited by the Fiction Collective, and the pieces were brought into the anthology by its different members. It represents an attempt by the Collective to bring to its appropriate audience that proliferation of fictive forms which now flourishes, sometimes within and sometimes without commercial publishing, but always oblivious to commercial demands. *Statements* does not represent any one school or esthetic. It is not another collection of "experimental" fiction, a term which, in any case, serious novelists abhor as the label the commercial establishment uses for fiction it too often chooses to ignore as "risky." We embrace the concept of risk in the belief that it is only through risk that fiction breaks away from cliché and attains real distinction.

    Statements presents a selection of previously unpublished fiction in a wide range of styles. These stories are not easy to categorize, a fact which is symptomatic of the new scene in fiction. Not only are the new fiction writers working in a great variety of styles, but these styles bear the mark of individual expression rather than of an avant garde with its militant ideologies. One might almost say that these stories represent temperaments rather than esthetics, except that they demonstrate a sophisticated awareness of the formal options and techniques available today to those fiction writers who know their business. And it is precisely this freedom, this destandardization, this educated individualism that is so different about such fiction. While it often ignores old forms, dispenses with plot, characterization, and verisimilitude, blurs the distinctions between prose and poetry, between fiction and autobiography or history, makes use of collage, employs new means of narrative order and even redefines the relation of print to page, it communicates the sense of an exploration to discover new forms that better suit the individual artist.

At the end of the sixties there was an idea in the air that fiction had become impossible. Fiction was, after all, only a product of the imagination and not the "real fact" of journalism. In any case, Philip Roth had told us that reality had become more incredible than fiction. One heard a great deal about "the literature of exhaustion" and "the death of the novel." In a curious turnabout, writers in the seventies—those in this volume among them—have learned to profit from what is by definition an impossible situation. If everything is impossible, then anything becomes possible. What we have now is a fiction of the impossible that thrives on its own impossibility, which is no more nor less impossible these days than, say, city life, politics, or peace between the sexes. To paraphrase Beckett, it can't go on it must go on it goes on. It becomes increasingly apparent that reality is not merely a given but, within limits, to be invented. When reality becomes incredible, fiction, the art of the credible, comes into its own, always starting from the blank page to imagine the unimaginable and to make the impossible seem possible again.

Taken together, the stories in this collection, which run the gamut from social realism to Surfiction, emerge as reexamination of the premises of fiction, and a possible renewal of its forms.

WALTER ABISH

Born in Austria, I spend my childhood in China, seeing an incredibly corrupt society slowly disintegrate. It was as if all the life processes were accentuated and crowded into the period of time I lived in Shanghai.

I have always thought that all the life networks that enable us to proceed wherever we are going, or prevent us from doing so, are predicated on a system called language. This awareness undoubtedly influenced my approach to writing.

My work has appeared in five *New Directions* anthologies, *TriQuarterly, Paris Review, Fiction, Extensions, American Review* and other periodicals. In 1972 and 1973 I was the recipient of grants from the State Council on the Arts and the Rose E. Williams Foundation.

Books: *Duel Site* (Tibor de Nagy Editions, 1970), a collection of poems. A novel, *Alphabetical Africa* (New Directions, 1974), and a collection of short fiction, *Minds Meet* (New Directions), to appear in 1975.

Life Uniforms: A study in ecstasy

I've come to depend on Arthur more than I care to admit. Almost daily we discuss the most recent disaster. Almost daily we also discuss Mildred. I enjoy talking about Mildred. Arthur has a probing mind. A relentless mind. He is not convinced that I understand Mildred. He wishes to broaden my understanding. In a sense the people he brings to the apartment are there for that purpose. To broaden my understanding. Arthur has also mapped most of the unsafe buildings in the business district for my benefit. I do my best to avoid them. Some weeks as many as three buildings collapse in a single day. Because of the alarming rate at which buildings are caving in, it may take a year or longer before the rubble is cleared away and the site is turned into another parking lot, an amusement park, or simply left vacant. Still, the high mounds of rubble have little effect on the people. Life seems unchanged. There is, however, a certain broadening understanding since Arthur was hired by one of the city agencies to document these disasters. By now, determining which building will disintegrate next has turned into a fine science. Some of the best minds sit in a room in City Hall and feed facts into a computer. Once agreement has been reached on a site, Arthur is sent to photograph it. He uses an old German camera. Sometimes the camera is mounted on a tripod. Quite a few of the photographs Arthur takes make the front page of *The New York Times*. It is a grim business.

I met Arthur as he was focusing his Leica on the building I was about to enter. I hadn't noticed the thin cracks in the wall . . . those ominous cracks. Hold it, he shouted. Somehow the urgent note in his voice made me stop in my tracks. Less than a minute later the fourteen-story building caved in. Almost gently, floor by floor, it lowered itself to the ground, while raising a huge cloud of dust. A few people jumped out of windows. Arthur kept taking photographs. I never interfere with the larger scope of things, he later explained. You stopped me in time, I reminded him. But I recognized your face, he said.

The people at the electric company do not visit the disaster sites. They have no need to. They can tell what happened from merely looking at their instrument panel. They can determine the number of kilowatt paying customers they lost on each floor, as the needles on the instrument panel flickers. There's much to be said for electricity.

I carefully screwed the 200 watt lightbulb into the socket. I did it on the advice of Arthur. I did it also to better illuminate what I was doing. In the past year Arthur had lived in eight different locations. That kind of experience is not to be dismissed lightly. Structurally, he said, the building in which I was staying seemed sound. He pounded on the floor with a stick to demonstrate its soundness. However, the elevator was too slow in responding, and the lighting was inadequate. Personally, being aware of the trouble the electric company had taken to bring electricity to this building, and above all to this apartment, I was less critical of their somewhat sluggish performance. After all, the work had entailed laying miles and miles of electric cables, most of them underground. Hundreds and hundreds of man hours. I kept thinking of those hundreds of man hours spent laying cables. All the same, following Arthur's advice, I did not inform them that I had screwed a 200 watt lightbulb into the fixture. It was quite conceivable that the socket was not made to carry anything as large as a 200 watt lightbulb. There may be something written on the socket to that effect. The man who comes to read the meter was here this morning. My heart was pounding as he stood beneath the 200 watt lightbulb. He glanced fleetingly at the most recent enlargement of Mildred. Except for the pile of photographs on the table, the table was bare since I was afraid that any additional weight might be too much for it to support. How did I arrive at such a conclusion. Years of experience, that's how. The meter man briefly placed his flashlight and ledger in which he entered the kilowatt hours on a conveniently close-by chair and studied the ecstatic expression on the topmost photograph. I had not invited him to do so. But given the bareness of the table the photograph on top of the pile was extremely conspicuous. Gravely, for a few seconds the meter man focused his full attention on the ecstatic expression of Mildred. He struggled with some undefinable emotion, but finally left rather abruptly without saying a word. I can understand his difficulty. His training had not prepared him for such an eventuality.

Everyone who has seen Mildred under the glare of a 200 watt lightbulb has found the information Arthur has been able to elicit from her most appealing. Everyone was quick to agree that Mildred had a pair of marvelous legs. White sensuous legs. Needless to say, Mildred is not completely unaware of the effect her legs are having on some of the occupants of this apartment. Similarly I was given to understand that her husband, Mr. E. Batch, is not totally unaware of their effect either. However, he doesn't have a single 200 watt lightbulb in their home. This deficiency is further aggravated by his lack of awareness regarding the existence of the remarkable group of photographs. When he does hear of it, it will doubtlessly come as somewhat of a surprise. He will be gratified that none other than his wife Mildred has been chosen for this study.

Mr. Batch works in an office in the city. From his desk he can see an occasional cloud of dust envelop a tall building. Much time is wasted in the office by everyone standing at a window watching the tall and by now familiar shaped clouds that after an hour subside, revealing a fresh vacuum. Mr. Batch believes everything Mildred tells him. Perhaps he believes her out of a fear of what might happen if he failed to do so. But that is hypothetical. He believes that Mildred has a close friend named Paula who lives in an apartment building that is located less than ten blocks away. He doesn't know Paula's second name. He has never bothered to inquire. Mildred, I believe, married Mr. Batch because he is industrious and because he does not ask too many questions. His questions are reserved for dinner. Why aren't we having any veal cutlets, he might ask her. Although it does strain his credulity, after all he is not a complete ass, Mr. Batch believes that his wife visits her friend Paula at least four times a week. You are seeing a lot of her, aren't you? he once remarked. In the evening Mildred gets on the phone to Paula, and in his presence at great length refers to her visit that afternoon. Of course Mr. Batch cannot be certain that it is Paula on the other end of the line. Even if he spoke to Paula he could not be certain since he's never met her. What is she like, he once asked Mildred. Paula loves anything to do with literature. Paula is dark and has a Slavic accent, said Mildred firmly. Mildred's firmness is a wall erected by her to prevent Mr. Batch from casually exploring the inner recesses of her daily pleasure.

In the electric company an employee jots down on a chart that I have broken a company rule by screwing a 200 watt lightbulb into an empty socket that was not designed for 200 watt lightbulbs. It will be some time before the electric company can take any action. They have other concerns, other priorities that will delay any action they may take. Although, in a sense, one can say that the action has already begun with the notation on the chart. The coded notation, by itself, appears perfectly harmless. It may be nothing more than a checkmark. The absence of windows in the electric company prevent the employees from seeing the rising and subsiding clouds of dust.

Everyone has more time to concentrate on the paperwork. The information that exists on paper is not necessarily conveyed by word of mouth, but carried by a messenger. He carries the checkmark to a secretary. The secretary who is seated at a gleaming Formica table doesn't know my name. She types it without properly looking at it. On the windowless walls are large calendars with reproductions of attractive foreign landscapes. Nowhere is there the slightest indication of a cloud of dust.

The secretary who is typing my name is using an electric typewriter with an 18 inch carriage. She sits on a swivel chair. Industriously she is utilizing the electric typewriter with the full cooperation of the electric company. They even know when her slender and quite graceful fingers are pressing the letters on the keyboard, but they do not know what letter she is pressing at any given moment. If she were to press the same letter over and over again, none of the men who are responsible for feeding the electricity into the wires would be the wiser. They are not oblivious of her fingers. Her fingers have a certain hold over them. It is an innately satisfying hold. Like most men they are receptive to certain letters. One might say that they respond more quickly to specific letters. In most instances they prefer the letter F. Fruitful, fancy, and forlorn are only three of the several hundred combinations racing through their minds. Still it can be said that their F preference is a common preference. It is, one thing remains sure, a preference uniting the men who splice the cables, and the man who reads the meter, and the elevator operator in my building. All are practitioners of F. F is a factor in their life, as it is in mine. All the same, unlike them I never use the elevator because it is unsafe, and one rides up and down at one's own risk. These are the words of the management. As the elevator rises the risk increases.

Who are all these men, asks Mildred as she enters the apartment. She sits on my chair without once thinking that at some point in time the legs might give way. She lies on my couch with the same disregard for danger. The letter F rears itself in her head as well. Frequently she substitutes another letter for F out of a misplaced sense of propriety. Yet the letter F is visible on the enlargements. It is visible when she crosses her legs, which she does frequently.

What does Mildred do when she's not visiting us, asks Arthur.

Arthur secretly uses an electric shaver. To confuse the electric company, he switches off every thirty seconds. Since it is not my shaver, I've not informed the electric company about it. They have their doubts. They have gone over the list of all my electrical appliances. Those thirty second spurts of electrical activity continue to confound them. They cannot determine what is causing them.

I have lived all my life in the city. Most worthwhile efforts take place in the city. An indescribable alertness divides the people who live in the city from the people who live in the country. Mildred is a city person. She takes the elevator to the sixth floor. The absence of large tracts of freshly plowed earth does not upset her.

Who are all those men in your apartment, asked Mildred breathlessly. Who are all those men? They're friends of Arthur, I said. When your hand touches me, she said, I break out in goosepimples all over. I took a certain satisfaction in hearing that. I knew that Arthur and his friends must have heard it too.

When I'm not working in the darkroom I am examining my next move. I know my next move may well depend on those guys at the electric company. What made Mildred say: As soon as you opened the door, I wanted to glide into your arms. Is that statement consistent with what I see on the enlargements. I enlarge Mildred. It is work that fills me with a private satisfaction. It is quite gratifying. Enlarging Mildred the better to see her F stop. Everyone who enters stares expectantly at the enlargements on the table. They seem to know intuitively that the woman in each of the photographs is Mildred. They seem to know that the slight smudge on one was caused by my hand. This hand has caressed every inch of the eleven by fourteen paper, I tell Arthur and his friends. In the dark room this hand is always protected by a rubber glove. The length of the exposures is listed in my notebook. The notes represent years of study. They represent a boundless energy and an acute vision.

The doors on either side of my desk are always open. I'm inclined to believe that they can no longer be closed. But I don't wish to subject them to that test. Open as they are, they disclose another brightly illuminated space. The threshold I have noted in my notebook functions as a kind of boundary or frame. Sometimes I cross that frame. Sometimes I find a reason to cross the boundary. Had the door not been opened I would have been compelled to knock or to rattle the doorknob. When Mildred lies down on the couch in the adjacent room I can observe her from where I am sitting. I cannot see her when I am in the darkroom. She knows this. Arthur and the others know this. No one has ever tried to close the door in my face. It would be inconsiderate, this, after all, being my apartment.

I received the invitation to lecture at the Felt Forum by mail. The invitation couched in the appropriate polite form was contained in a legal sized envelope. Most messages arrive in envelopes. Most are dropped in my mailbox downstairs. If I scrutinize the mailman when he delivers the mail, it is not done to embarrass him. It is done to elicit some kind of information . . . The mailman once delivered a package to my door. I did not invite him in. Whenever I look at him I feel that he has not forgiven me for not inviting him into my apartment and showing him Mildred's photographs.

If I am constantly conducting myself with a certain indisputable authority it is because I am describing a phenomenon that is still new. In time the newness will wear off. In the next room a woman is undressing. I can see her quite clearly. Her every gesture is studied. She looks familiar. I have seen her quite frequently. She seems to be deriving a certain pleasure from her present activity. She has a striking figure. The men are also familiar. Only this morning I had a lengthy conversation with one of them. They all appear to show a complete disregard for their safety by wrestling on the bed, despite the creaking floor. Notwithstanding Arthur's assurances the floor could cave in at any moment. The 200 watt lightbulb illuminates the men as they one by one evoke a look of startled recognition on the woman's face . . . the look seems to say: Ahh . . . here it comes again . . . the familiar ecstasy.

The combination of the chlorine and the iodine vapor has greatly increased the sensitivity of the photographic plate. For the first time her emotions could be clearly assessed on the enlargement, but now the process took much longer. Still, I felt it was definitely worth the effort . . . all those weeks spent in the darkroom. It had taken me two years to produce the plate of Mildred. I now somewhat regretted having used Mildred instead of Muriel, becuase Muriel was less outgoing and more resistant to pleasure, consequently the evaluation of her troubled mind would have been more difficult, and as a result my work would have been more satisfying. After all, the conclusions I was able to draw from Mildred's photograph did not radically differ from what I had been told about her. All the same, correctly interpreting Mildred's uninhibited acceptance of F enabled me to eliminate much of the guesswork in the darkroom. The next plate, I surmised, should not take more than six months, one year at the most.

Let us now consider the world open to us, said Mildred in the adjacent room as one by one the men parted her glorious legs. In the beginning the long U shaped corridors outside had completely disoriented them. They had lost their sense of direction as they stared at Mildred.

All this time Mr. E. Batch does not suspect a thing. The white legs that had given me so much trouble in the darkroom were now firmly locked around Arthur's obese body . . . a certain trembling motion was to be detected with the naked eye. The motion improved the shape of their bodies, I decided, since the few minor flaws became less and less evident.

What did you do this afternoon, asks Mr. Batch. Seemingly unperturbed she crosses her legs. Mr. Batch looks at her legs. In the newspaper he has read that a certain lecture will be given at the Felt Forum, and that there is a sense of great expectation amongst the foremost scientists and amateur photographers. Mr. Batch marvels at everything Mildred says. He marvels at her excellent taste whenever she buys herself a dress. He also marvels that she married him.

You are my developer, she says, and he beams happily.

Poor Mr. Batch.

When I entered the large hall of the Felt Forum I was greeted by a standing ovation. With quick steps I made my way to the stage, holding Mildred's photographic plate in one hand. I had, as a matter of fact, anticipated the applause, and kept my gaze fixed straight ahead as I walked to the center of the stage. It was a Tuesday, and it wasn't raining. From the amount of applause I could only assume that the hall was filled to capacity. If Arthur was to be trusted, the Felt Forum was in no immediate danger of collapsing. Somewhere among all those people waiting to hear my lecture was a face I was bound to recognize. I had taken the escalator to the second floor. It was not the first time that I had used an escalator. Naturally I was somewhat intrigued by every innovative mechanical breakthrough. A slow moving staircase. Quite ingenious. In everything that was powered by electricity I saw a future use that could be applied to my photographic explorations. Somewhere in the days ahead I might well utilize the escalator. In the first row sat a very attractive woman. She resembled Mildred. When I took another look at her I realized it was Mildred. I knew so much about her. I could only assume that the man sitting stiffly at her side was Mr. Batch.

The entire world is now open to us, I told a hushed audience.

Mildred's husband has a neat and well groomed mustache. The information available to him at this stage can be said to encapsulate his love for Mildred and his need to be punctual. Every question he has ever asked has been answered to his satisfaction. There were 1855 seats in the hall. They are all occupied. He and his wife occupy two seats in the first row. He has questioned Mildred about the seats. The front row seats seem a trifle conspicuous to him. In the past his seating experience has been a more modest one. How did you manage to get two seats in the first row, he asked Mildred.

She crosses her legs.

She also stood up frequently in order to see everyone seated behind them. Her white teeth are very much in evidence. She is smiling at the entire world.

Why on earth are you standing, asked her husband.

I'm looking for Paula.

Paula. I didn't know that Paula was coming.

Mildred wore a red suit. It was a bright red, and when she stood everyone could see her clearly, although the suit obscured certain parts of her body that could be seen on the enlargements.

As soon as electricity was discovered, the electric company was formed, I said. One of their first actions was to rush a wire to my darkroom.

Why aren't you more pleased with your success, asked a colleague afterward.

Basically I think that Mr. Batch pushes his admiration for Mildred too far. He doesn't even know that certain words he uses at night are now defunct.

Arthur shaved carefully before leaving the apartment at six. Feeling an uncontrollable yearning for F he made a pass at Muriel. She removed her false eyelashes before calmly stabbing him in the palm with a carving knife she carried in her purse. He was transfixed with surprise. Since this happened on the escalator, he disappeared from sight at the top of the second floor. Muriel in a state of shock rushed to the well lit powder room. Luckily her purse also contained the fourth volume of the Encyclopaedia Britannica. She looked up fucking. It was sandwiched between "Fuchsin" and "Fucoid." It was the right book for an emergency. This could not have happened before the advent of electricity and modern photography.

I still can't get over Muriel's legs, said Arthur when he returned to the apartment, with his right hand in a sling. They remind me, he said, of my recent trip to Ireland. The white legs of Ireland.

When I addressed a gathering of 1855 scientists and photographers at the Felt Forum, the photographic plate was on the lectern, but when I returned after a ten minute intermission it had vanished. Two years of research thrown to the wind. But two hours later I experienced my first erection in years. What a relief. I rushed to a phone, but Mildred and Mr. Batch had left for Switzerland. I think you need a new pair of pants, said Muriel when she saw me . . .

Dear Muriel. It's either that or . . .

Or what? she asks as she rushes into my arms.

JOHN ASHBERY

is the author of several books of poetry, including *Self-Portrait in a Convex Mirror* which Viking will publish in 1975. He teaches creative writing at Brooklyn College. He says that *The Vermont Notebook*, shortly to be published in its entirety by Black Sparrow, was written in Massachusetts.

From   *The Vermont Notebook*

They had a good idea when they named this place Plainville. Of course it *is* plain and it sits on a plain, but there are other facets of its plainness. It has a "Poodle Parlor," from which schnauzers are not excluded, nor any dog not downright mad I should think. A table with magazines. Some of them dog-eared. Those who wish to wait for their pet's beautification may sit and read or not read, if they prefer. Or they may leave and come back in about an hour. Get the shopping over with. This is called "theft of services." In the woods to the south of town are certain trees with bits of red cloth tied to them. Sometimes blue. Mostly red. The blue is found only rarely, if at all.

Man dreams of putting penis between girl's boobs. Is all mankind diminished? Or strengthened? What do you want? I want a pair of orange pants and a pair of orange and white shoes to go with them. I know nothing will work out unless I get them, but I also know that if I do get them I probably won't want to wear them to a dogfight.

Now—step back please. Man removes booger from nostril. Man examines booger. Man *relives* booger. All the shame. But could it have been avoided? Whatever has not been avoided probably could not have been avoided. One must learn to live with this possibly greatest of truths like sleeping over a garage.

Most of these buildings have been torn down now.

That shamrock button, t-shirt showing through the short-sleeved tattersall shirt, the way of looking around—not to be taken from behind, and to take, if possible, from ahead. So we call him their "ringleader."

Not to have passed this way in a very long time. And the next time? Places have a way of coming back; the full curve of expectation meets halfway one's pipsqueak pretensions starting out. Something happens out of this to protect it.

Think spring. We do. Slow down.

The waves were amazed.

America is a fun country. Still, there are aspects of it which I
would prefer not to think about. I am sure, for instance, that
the large "chain" stores with their big friendly ads and so-
called "discount" prices actually charge higher prices so as to
force smaller competitors out of business. This sort of thing
has been going on for at least 200 years and is one of the
cornerstones on which our mercantile American society is
constructed, like it or not. What with all our pious expostula-
tions and public declarations of concern for the poor and the
elderly, this is a lot of bunk and our own president plays it right
into the lap of big business and uses every opportunity he can
to fuck the consumer and the little guy. We might as well face
up to the fact that this is and always has been a part of our so-
called American way of life.

Nevertheless, there are a lot of people here who are sincere-
ly in love with life and think they are on to something, and they
may well be right. Even the dogs seem to know about it—you
can tell by the way they stick their noses out of the car windows sometimes to whiff the air as it goes by. Old ladies know
about and like it too. In fact, the older an American citizen gets
the more he or she seems to get a kick out of life. Look at all
the retirement communities and people who mow their own
lawns and play golf. They surely have more pep than their
counterparts in Asia or Europe, and one mustn't be in too
much of a hurry to make fun of such pursuits. They stand for
something broader and darker than at first seems to be the
case. The silver-painted flagpole in its concrete base surrounded by portulacas, the flag itself straining in the incredibly
strong breeze, are signposts toward an infinity of wavering
susceptible variables, if one but knew how to read them aright.
The horny grocery boy may be the god Pan in disguise. Even a
television antenna may be something else. Example: bearded
young driver of pickup truck notes vinyl swimming pool cover
is coming undone and stops to ask owner if he can be of
assistance. Second example: groups of business people stranded in stalled elevator sing Cole Porter songs to keep their spir-
its up, helping each other recall the lyrics. Third example: a
nursing home director convicted of a major swindle goes to the
federal penitentiary for a period of not less than five years.

Fourth example: you are looking down into a bottomless well or some kind of deep pool that is very dark with the reflected light so far in the distance it seems like a distant planet, and you see only your own face.

*

Some of these tunes hold up remarkably well. So, in the words of the song, I shall "stay on the bus, forget about us, and put the blame on me." Unless you decide to "tie a yellow ribbon 'round the old oak tree." (Corky sees me in the landfill and starts complaining.)

More seagull snapshots. You know they reduce to brownish blobs like old Bible camp photos. The beach is indeed one aspect of the vast Sunday school of the world, waiting for church to be over and go home. It has the look of openness to suggestion and the finished ultimate look that together characterize life. And the humor, is there anything mildly funnier than footprints on a beach? Life comes naturally there, and goes too: no sense worrying about naturalness with so much natural fuzz fuss everywhere, in corners, in bushes, and the aired mystery of the open field Briars come to ask you for ideas, and afterwards your blessing.

The forsythia is now out, marking the beginning of "little spring." In a certain way more of an attitude is possible in the face of winter—smell of boiled coffee and fried clams—because it knows it is on the pathway to nowhere. But to be again settling down like this in a torn silk parachute onto layers of dry half-rotted leaves, loam and anonymous rock outcropping, with here and there a portentous green shoot—does it make much sense to you. The "floods of spring" that are supposed to gurgle and gush impetuously are already sluggish and dark gray. The one comforting thing is all the leftover junk from last season, but this is fated to disappear shortly when Mother Nature starts her annual spring cleaning and "exterior" decoration. Meanwhile an uproar is supposed to be made over the first crocus popups and the like, daffodils that suggest public libraries, violets and the rest of the symbolic crap that is so much eyewash to divert our gaze from the ruthless pageant whose stage is now being hammered together out of raw lumber that will eventually be draped in yellow and green cambric, on which Josephine Preston Peabody's excruciatingly bad *The Piper* or something equally ominous of Percy Mackaye will shortly be enacted by the class of 1919.

Did I know you, split-levels? What it's like to inhabit your dangerous divided spaces with view of celery plantations? The book sits there, alive with pleasure, but there is no more frontage. Fewer than a dozen of the sum of 32 flavors are kept in stock and you have to put a dime into a slot on the door of the men's room to get in. In other times "frontage" meant relief to enjoy, not a nameless dark forced familiarity with things. True, everybody was out then, on foot, on bicycle, or even in a horseless carriage, but this degradation of being forced out and around without thinking about it was only a shadow in the mind. Which gradually lengthened into late afternoon as the skyscrapers grew taller and taller, one by one, so that at present we have a density of blue twilight at high noon. Special vehicles are parked out of sight.

Once, speculators were briefly interested in these parallel bunches of needles. Now the bottom has dropped out from under them. They do move slightly in a metallic breeze that neither parches nor moistens. Many have been declared national park zones. A foreign student stands there, beyond the wire fence. His lips spell out the words: shale cowbarns spread udder mumps.

To the Hard Barn Road Cafeteria

Bev would have loved it here. The rural look of everything, even city intersections. ('Mongst other things, they have the solid old-fashioned traffic lights—red, amber, green, where each color comes on and stays for its allotted due before blinking off, and no green directional arrows.) The landscape is countryish without looking countrified. In fact it looks as though it had its mind on more basic preoccupations, as though if it could talk it would say, "Sorry, I don't have time to think of such things." Up there of course is the subdued glow where McDonald's, Carrol's, Arthur Treacher, Colonel Sanders and Dunkin' Donuts succeed each other at the pace of a stately gavotte. But back here even this close all is already rubble and confusion—the country, in other words. Milk barns with the paint peeling off of them, long pale greenish-blue '66 Chryslers, a sense of gloom and desperation but also of seizing at final solutions. A riotous intoxicating feeling of freedom but so laced across with conditions of terror that one enjoys it as something else, like the one night of freedom enjoyed by Louis XVI and his wife, after their escape from the Tuileries and before their capture at—wait, I know the name, I don't have to look it up—Verviers. Imagine the conditions of such a freedom, of not being able to enjoy a single second of it, enormous as it was, worrying about whether the milkmaid may have recognized you from seeing your profile on a coin. Here nobody is taking any chances on recognizing or being recognized. They all look like faces on Wacky Package stickers or a klutz in Mad Comics, tortured past reason and exploding in a human, all too human display of facial fireworks. This fools nobody but since it has become the unrecognized custom of looking, for these foolish folks who won't bother you and don't you bother them, it has a currency, a legitimacy, both thinner and more extensive than the lumpy look the rest of us have. The scenery looks as though it was painted on cork.

A recent fishing jaunt to the southern Gulf coast of Florida gave me the opportunity to visit with Dr. Jay L. Harmic, the scientist in charge of the long-range research program at Marco Applied Marine Ecology Station. Considerable progress has been made there in the initial three years of operation, and the prospects are excellent for environmental protection and improving the already fabulous fishing.

One of the projects causing a lot of excitement while I was there trying to concentrate on casting for spotted trout and reds, was the successful nesting of a pair of bald eagles in an artificial site. The Marco Ecology Station had moved a tree that had been abandoned by eagles to a new location where it was strapped to a concrete piling in a mangrove thicket. "This gives us the encouragement we need to proceed further in location, saving and possibly relocating likely eagle nesting trees in the area," Harmic commented.

While finding ways to protect and enhance the environment for an endangered species like the bald eagle is making big news these days, it should be only a preview of what we might expect from the $750,000 ecology program being funded by the

Miami-based Deltona Corporation, developers of Marco Island. The ongoing program includes general marine and mangrove island research, monitoring activities that keep a hand on the pulse of the environment, recommendations to Deltona concerning environmental protection, and replacement or enhancement projects.

Of primary importance to fishermen is the program to develop a better off-shore fishery at Marco. The Marine Ecology Station, which has a staff of seven full-time marine scientists and technicians and a half-dozen part-time laboratory assistants, has created two artificial reefs to attract sport species. At a location one mile off Marco, 57,000 old automobile tires have been wired together forming an underwater structure. At another location four and one-half miles into the Gulf, some 5,000 tons of construction debris has been piled along the bottom.

Prior to the artificial reefs, studies revealed that one fish could be caught for every two hours of fishing effort. Right now fishermen are averaging between seven and eight fish per hour, and sometimes the count goes up to fifteen fish per hour. Divers from the Station have recorded eighty-seven different species of fish on the reefs, with the most numerous sport species being groupers and jacks.

Since biologists know the value of the mangrove islands to spawning fish such as snook and tarpon, the Station is now experimenting with the establishment of artificial islands. A large reference collection of marine life is being created, and some extremely valuable records on the dissolved oxygen in the water are being established. Another first at Marco is that no sewerage effluent is returned directly to the water—after three stage treatment it is used to irrigate one of the golf courses.

Marco is an example of how a new community can be sensitive to the natural environment. One hopes there will always be nesting eagles, the mangrove wilderness, and jumping fish. And one hopes that other developments will take note.

This is where we are spending our vacation. A nice restful spot. Real camp life. Hope you are feeling fine.

Some days hell seems very near. As this on-again, off-again

type day, fickle sunshine one moment and deep ugly black clouds the next. At these times you can hear a rustling from the next room, as though hell were about to break its own self-imposed rule of silence and speak, speak up in an urgent, quiet tone, reminding you of its existence and your own laziness, telling you to get on with whatever it is you're doing, even if it's just a crossword puzzle, for your own sake, because all times are getting close and so far there just isn't enough activity of any kind to justify the terribly solemn moment when all four draw near at the crossroads. Not that any justification is required. But it does make it better for them, to feel everything is proceeding according to plan. And it is. Therefore, whatever it is that you want to do, do it, and this way everybody's task will be made just a little bit easier. Though you may well be inclined to ask yourself, just the same, what exactly was it you did. It seemed to be nothing, and the minutes ticked by, cheerful, indifferent—and merely standing still you felt trapped in a sliding scale of a whole universe of judgments, positive and negative, and wondered where you stood to profit in the prearranged woodshed of doubtful possibilities, until a boy detached himself from the uninteresting landscape and came over and tapped on the window, restoring the sense of life's wholeness. That was an apology, but it worked. The lake is no longer restless and the railroad yards are straightened up. There are more cement igloos.

THE FAIRIES' SONG

Clouding up again. Certain days there is a feeling that what-
    ever we arrange
Will sooner or later get all fucked up.
Then there are explosions of a 19th-century, garden variety
    form of intellectual rage.
We have moved too far in the glade, the way this is all about
    harassing.

Sometimes one of us will get included in the trash
And end up petulant and bored at the multiple opportunities
    for mischief,
Screaming like a seagull at vacuity,
Hating it for being what it is.

There are long rides around doubtful walked-in spaces,
Dreaming manure piles under the slop and surge of a March
    sun,
Rivers of reeds, rivulets of webbed mud,
Pale plumes of dullness portentously fixed at the four cor-
    ners of a moment of tearing around only to be caught out.

Thunderheads of after-dinner cigar smoke in some var-
    nished salon
Offer ample cover for braiding two coat-tails together
Around the clumsy arm of an s-shaped settee.
In a screech the occasion has disappeared, the clamor re-
    sumed like a climate.

There are limpid pools of quiet
Offering themselves to the relaxed curve of a pebble,
Baskets of normal occurring, insipid flowering meads,
Wastes of acting out daytime courtesies at night,

Deadfalls of resolution, arks of self-preservation,
Arenas of unused indulgence. Where do we get off
The careening spear of rye? The milk meanwhile is soured
But it all gets mixed up in your stomach anyway.

We dance on hills above the wind
And leave our footsteps there behind
We raise their tomatoes
The clear water in the chipped basin reflects it all:
A spoiled life, alive, and streaming with light.

What lovely antiques . . . (fap, grunt). Isn't it funny the way
something can get crowded clean out of your memory, it
seems new to you when you see it again, although some part of
your mind does remember, though not in any clear-cut way?

Dear Autumn Addict,
    Have decided this bus trip will be good for my spirits. Am
sitting next to a young man I saw in the terminal, who resembles a portrait by Carolus Duran, and whom I shall call
"Oscar." "Oscar" is restless and plainly wants to smoke a

cigarette, although there is a "No Smoking" sign. In some buses they allow cigarette smoking but no pipes or cigars, but this is an interstate bus and so maybe smoking at all is against the laws of one of the states the bus passes through. Anyway, "Oscar" as I call him for want of another name, keeps pulling a rather rumpled pack of Benson and Hedges out of his pocket, turns them over, stares at them or past me out of the window, stuffs them back in his pocket again. Hope that you are now settled permanently (?) in your new home you will pen your thoughts more often. As much as I do enjoy the many new writers, I feel a special bond with those I first started corresponding with when we moved here.

If I don't hear from you again, I shall wonder whether or not you got so wrapped up in your "canning and freezing" that you are either somewhere on a shelf full of preserves with a metal lid on your head or holing up with the frozen peas in your freezer compartment, from life to something else swiftly translated. Be of good cheer.

Beverly

RUSSELL BANKS

Raised in New Hampshire and eastern Massachusetts from 1940 to approximately 1958; after that, attended Colgate University, wandered around the U.S. and Mexico, married, worked as pipefitter, bookseller, display artist, shoe salesman, etc.; graduated University of North Carolina, Chapel Hill, in 1967, returned with wife and daughters to New Hampshire; now a member of English Department faculty at University of New Hampshire. Co-editor of *Lillabulero* magazine, author of a novel, *Family Life* (Avon), a long poem, *Snow* (Granite Press, 1974), and a collection of stories, *Searching for Survivors* (Fiction Collective); stories have been chosen for *The Best American Short Stories* and *The O. Henry Prize Short Story Collection* and other anthologies. At present working on a novel about a plumber.

That

"She says she wanted that she should be the only ideal one, but she is, what else is she but that, she is, and so the human mind rests with what is.

"Yes which it is, that.

"That is what they call it. That."

—Gertrude Stein,
The Geographical History of America

Well, yes, but he ended up helping her along in that. In fact the idea, and then the ambition, the wish, may at first have been his. And his the task of convincing her that the ambition was a worthy one—one worthy of any morally ambitious person, any woman who had said often of herself, "What I want is to be a really *good* person."

He, however, for once, was interested in appealing to some lesser ambition, murmuring, "Why not really make it all the way to the top? Be a Buddha! Buddha, Buddha! Buddha, Buddha, Buddha! You could be happy then, as well as good."

She said yes, sure, it sounded good, but she was depressed again, feeling detached, time to go to sleep, good night, good night, we'll talk some more tommorrow, okay?

"Okay. Sorry."

Actually, this ambition, his first and then hers too (for he was successful, eventually, in his attempt to convince her that it was worthy of her), was only the most recent development in a plot that went back more than a dozen years, across continents, involving hundreds of minor characters and tens of major ones, passing through crises emotional, physical, social, economic and religious, suffering through stages and ages, hormonal as well as psychological, not to say entire physiological changes—a major American novel soon to be made into a major motion picture about to become a modern cultural cliché. That's how long and how much this particular couple had endured together.

This is of course to speak mainly of the manifest content of their life together; the latent content developed, got expressed, was endured—differently. And this is where his ambition for her, her ambition too, gets expressed developmentally, so that, in the course of secret events and rituals in their life together, when placed into chronological sequence, his desire for her to be a Buddha (as he offhandedly phrased it one night over dinner) seems natural enough. But only natural enough if you're willing and able to go back and finger the first bead on that chain of secret ritual and event, groping slowly forward, bead by bead, to this possibly evil moment—"possibly evil," because after all that is what the tale, this tale, is about, the question of the presence of the possibility of evil in actions necessitated by love, self- and otherwise.

Their first meeting—a small and sentimentally shabby hotel in Tangiers, she the high-spirited young American tourist doing the risqué by hopping over from Spain in the midst of her Grand Tour to visit an old friend, a woman, older than she by ten or so years, who had recently bought and now personally managed the hotel, and he the young American Werther disguised as an auto-destructing cynic nightly drinking himself into bitterness and sometimes violence always miraculously survived (probably because of his unavoidable good health, in conjunction with a not particularly pure commitment to achieving his own destruction)—that first meeting was of the rare sufficiency to establish obsession for both, oh yes indeed, sufficient to create for each a whole vision of his own insufficiency and the possibility of another human being for once not providing surfeit, the possibility of another for once merely providing sufficiency.

He packed his duffle and followed her doggedly but whistling—plucky suddenly happy go lucky lad—back to Barcelona where he rejoined her party, which was made up of several female members of her large and considerately protective family. "Don't look now, my dear, but the young man from the ferry, *that* young man, seems to have joined us, though thankfully two tables away. You *don't* think he'll trail us to Florence too, do you?"

He followed them, her, to Florence too, then on to Rome where they could meet in museums and screw standing hard against one another in dark and damp corners. Then Paris, Paris in the spring—it was like that—and on to London, where, in an obnoxious and drunken scene in a suddenly silent restaurant, arguing politics with her father who had just arrived from Alabama to spend the final week of the tour with the family, he shattered her delicate arrangement of feelings and wandered out burly and very drunk to brawl for weeks in pubs and flats—convinced he was content with having been spurned, convinced of course first that he had been spurned, and in a deep secret way convinced that he deserved it.

Later, in a hotel room glimmering with pale New York autumn afternoon light, she forgave him, because she loved him, and also because he explained everything. It's not so hard, she discovered almost to her surprise, to forgive someone almost anything, when you love him and have also been made to understand.

He told her about a mean, dark and sneaky streak of self-destruction, a perverse imp that undercut all his best ambitions and even the most significant of his achievements. She, he told her, was his so far most significant achievement—her love for him, actually, he explained, and by the word "achievement" he really meant the condition for his own happiness, that was what was always being undercut, and just at the exact moment of achieving it, too. The reasons for this annoyance—good god, it was worse that that, it was a plague, a disease, a blight —and the reasons for its presence in his life, which should otherwise have been regarded as gifted, he explained, probably lay in his childhood someplace, probably had to do with his father's impossible high expectations for him, cruelly insensitive expectations that the man had projected all over his young son, he analyzed, that, coupled with his mother's hysterical and unqualified belief in his uniqueness, which had given him his grandiose ambition for earthly happiness. Ergo, he reasoned, he inevitably went for the big fish, the whole hog, the top dog, and just as he was about to grab it, instead he shoved it away. That's what he had been doing in Tangiers— tearing up the few remaining shreds of a prestigious fellowship to study Sufi wisdom tales—and that's what he had done in London—her father had actually *liked* the lad at first, had thought him clean-cut, intelligent, well educated, but after two whiskies, neat, and a few quick jabs, *re:* the War, Lyndon Johnson, the true historical importance of Winston Churchill, after that, why, the fellow seemed to go beserk or something, and five minutes later the old man was sure that he now knew his enemy.

"No, no, he'll come around eventually, don't worry, honey," she reassured him. "Daddy forgets everything if you wait a while and are polite. You'll see. In the end, politeness counts for everything with Daddy. Now lie down here, honey, lay your head back," she crooned to him, and he lay his head back, sank it into the pillow.

It went on like that for a long time, year after year, always with vigorous intelligence and highly developed powers of analysis. The man and the woman loved one another very much, and they treasured their calm returns to lucidity and affection, held them dear, saw them as pacts, covenants, seals. At one point, they came to regard their life together as resembling a chambered nautilus, one chamber opening onto another by way of the same membrane used to seal each new chamber off from the other, until the final chamber, which opened freely out—and they always thought they were situated in that final, outward-opening chamber, reassuring one another almost gaily, in low, intimate voices, stroking foreheads, wrists, fingertips, dropping off to sleep in peace.

But they lost something, too, each time he explained and she forgave him and they talked some more about the future and the promise it still held for them and the new promise he had made to her and she had accepted, believing, he believing it too, because he was nothing if not sincere, and she could not have accepted his promise, could not have believed it, if he hadn't believed it first himself. They lost language—the new explanations always canceled the terms of the predecessors, sealing the old words off, letting them lie in piles in the past, gradually converting there into pockets of stale gas—like the pockets of stale gas trapped inside the chambers of the nautilus, which give it buoyancy. Some of the words and phrases used-up, exhausted of meaning, canceled-out, or otherwise lost, were: *trust, to earn trust, act of faith, leap of faith, father's high expectations, mother's unqualified love, syndrome, pact, covenant, seal, conditional love, unconditional love, pledge, to pledge one's troth, self-mortification, sacrosanct, suspension of disbelief, to imagine a future consistent with . . . , regeneration.*

The image of the chambered nautilus had been hers, first, then his too. They were at that point again, reuniting, sealing off another broken promise (long before, he had perceived that the particulars of the promise were wholly irrelevant; he could have promised her anything—it was the breaking of the promise itself that had become his spasm of destruction), doing it while spending a midwinter week at a semitropical island beach known as "one of the three best shelling beaches in the world." At a gift shoppe that sold only shells, most of them exotic, they bought half a chambered nautilus, bisected longitudinally. In the car, driving back to the hotel, she held the shell in one hand, stroking the cut edge with the fingertips of her other hand. "Look," she said, holding the shell up for him to see. "It's just like us, isn't it?" She asked it rhetorically, in a sad, tired voice, not expecting him to know what she was perceiving, the exact nature, for her, of the analogy.

"I know," he said, not even glancing at her or the shell. "I kind of made that connection myself back there when we bought it, and I was rolling it around in my head when you said it. At least the thing opens out," he added, reaching over to touch her hand.

His voice too had been sad and tired, and he had in fact, she realized, understood precisely what she was perceiving, had perceived the analogy exactly as she had, and that, she knew, was what made it so damned hard to quit—it, him, that.

Clapping her hand onto his bare shoulder, she shook him awake. They were still at the island, the one with "one of the three best shelling beaches in the world." In his dream, her hand had become a brown spider, and he slapped at it frantically, then woke up. "I was dreaming," he explained.

She said she was sorry, but she had been lying there awake, thinking, and she wanted to talk. It was important.

"Sure," he said, biting off a yawn. "If you're going to become a Buddha, I'm going to learn how to be a cheerful disciple," he said to her.

"I know. That's what I want to talk about."

"What?"

She explained to him, as well as she could, without sounding too humble, how she really didn't think she was capable of becoming that, a Buddha, the kind of person he obviously was going to need, he knew what she meant.

He lay next to her silently. The Gulf of Mexico went on flogging the shore.

First of all, she pointed out how it seemed to her that to forgive him properly once again it was going to require that she be a better person, or at least a *larger,* more *secure* person, than she ever had been or actually was, and possibly even larger than she wanted to be—after all, you don't *choose* that kind of resilience, it's imposed on you.

"What do you want to do, then? I mean, regarding me?" he asked.

"I don't know. I don't know. I'll tell you something that amazes me, though. Especially now."

"What?"

"The way we understand one another."

He told her that he was amazed too, and he patted her hand, which had remained on his shoulder where she had placed it to waken him.

"I had always thought it was going to be different. You know. That we'd reach a point where we could relax and just flow along with each other easily, no promises, nothing to forgive, nothing to lose . . . and that at the same time we wouldn't be *stuck* with each other either. . . ."

"Maybe we've reached that point," he offered.

"Maybe." She didn't know, really, she couldn't—she was too busy being the only one, the one with ambition, the ideal one, which of course was what he wanted and needed right now, what he had prayed for, plotted and schemed for. He knew though. He knew. He had to. After all, she was depending on him, for it, that.

They fell asleep listening to the Gulf of Mexico flop upon the sand, the wind rattle the palms, each other's breathing.

JONATHAN BAUMBACH

who helped put together this anthology, is one of the founders of the Fiction Collective. Director of the creative writing program at Brooklyn College, he has published two novels with commercial houses, *A Man To Conjure With* (Random House) and *What Comes Next* (Harper & Row), and a third, recently, *Reruns,* with the Fiction Collective.

His shorter fiction has appeared in such places as *Partisan Review, Esquire, TriQuarterly, Transatlantic Review, Transition,* and *Epoch.* Baumbach is also the author of a critical book, *The Landscape of Nightmare,* and is film critic for *Partisan Review.*

Pagina Man

The baby, rumored to be taking a nap, makes an unanticipated appearance. "Guess what?" he says.

"What?"

"You have to guess," he says.

My mind is on several things at once, life and death, truth and falsity, reality and imagination, held in opposition by itself. "You have another story to tell," I guess.

"No." He shakes his head emphatically.

"What is it? I give up."

He does a 360 degree turn before he answers. "I have another story. Not the story you're thinking of. A different one. This is about a movie I saw in which a monster eats you and then I pull you out of the monster's stomach and throw him in the ocean. When he falls in the ocean the monster melts."

I am only barely listening, which he is quick to notice, registering his displeasure by thrusting his thumb in his mouth and sitting on the floor with his back to me.

When his feelings are hurt it gets him furious when you humor him or say you're sorry. In fact, there is nothing to do when his feelings are hurt but wait for them to heal. After a while he gets up with a wearied sigh and patters out.

A few minutes later a piece of paper slides in from under my door. "I'm going to the movies with my grandma," it reads. "The baby-sitter is coming to stay with you."

I have barely gotten my thoughts together when he comes in and asks where the baby-sitter is.

"She's probably at her own house," I say.

"No, she's not." He shakes his head. "Do you know where she is? She's in the refrigerator, baby-sitting for the food." He waits for a laugh and when he doesn't get it he repeats his remark, laughing himself at the appropriate time as an example for his listener. "I was just joking," he says. "Is a joke a story?"

In the progress of my explanation, in which I draw it seems to me some telling distinctions, he puts his thumb in his mouth and takes a short nap.

When he wakes up he asks, "Is it today or tomorrow?" He doesn't wait for an answer. "I had a dream about Pagina Man," he says. "If you don't look at me, if you don't talk to me, if you don't say I want to hear a story, I'll tell you the story of my dream which is a secret."

His stories tend to present themselves in the disguise of something else for which I have no explanation. The present one, as you can see, comes doubly disguised. He insists that I promise not to tell his mother the secret, because the secret he has for me is different from the one he has for her. Besides, he says, she already knows the secret from her own dream. A somewhat abbreviated and restructured version of his effusions follows.

THE BABY'S SECRET STORY

During the day when it is light and everyone is playing or not playing, dependent on a variety of factors, the baby is a charmingly ordinary small person of unspectacular capacities. At night, however, and on cloudy or rainy days, or when distant cries for help are heard in the land, the baby changes his clothes, disposes of his diaper, and becomes the super-hero, which is his secret identity, Pagina Man. Pagina Man is not afraid of anything or, which is almost the same thing, acts as if he's not. He can also see behind him without turning around and when he wants to—this skill subject to his feelings about himself and variables of weather—can leap into the air and fly. He is stronger, mostly through secret tricks, than the general impression his stature conveys. He is a force for good, although like everyone else he sometimes wakes in a bad mood.

One day the whole city is crying its heart out and the baby hears the crying in his room and it sounds a little like the baby-sitter's toilet which is broken. Something bad, something very bad, is going on. Pagina Man flies down to police headquarters to offer his services, where he discovers, which is one of the saddest things he's ever seen, that even the police are crying.

"Help us, Pagina Man," they blubber.

"I can't help you," says the diminutive super-hero, a formalist in such matters, "until you stop crying."

The policemen blow their noses, one after another, in diminishing order of importance, but the crying, once it is started, is very difficult to stop.

"Is it a robot?" Pagina Man asks.

They shake their heads, indicating it is not, noses sprinkling like fountains, the station like a rain forest. "It is worse than a robot," the police chief says.

Pagina Man sits down on the chief's desk, preparing himself to receive the chief's worse than bad news. "If you were larger," the police chief says, "it would be easier to tell you."

"I'm larger," Pagina Man says, growing three inches in a minute, standing on his toes, which is one of his super tricks.

After a few minutes of suspense, the chief tells him that there is a terrible monster loose who is causing all the trouble.

Pagina Man, whose costume itches and so is impatient to get going, asks for a description and gets none.

"All we can tell you, baby or Pagina Man or whoever you call yourself, is the monster is so ugly that no one who has seen him has survived that terrible moment. It's the only evidence we have." The police chief rolls on the floor again and cries, banging his head in a way that looks worse than it is.

Pagina Man, who in real life is a baby, is a little afraid for a moment, though he doesn't tell anyone and it passes. He puts on his orange sunglasses and jumping through the window— with his glasses on he doesn't notice that it isn't open—he goes out to search for the ugly monster that has been the cause of so much innocent grief.

It should be child's play to find a monster who is that ugly, thinks the super-hero. A monster like that can't just merge with the crowd.

"Oh Pagina Man," a lady with a Bloomingdale's shopping bag calls as he flies by. "You're my favorite super-hero. Will you come home with me and protect me from the monster."

"That's what I'm here for," says Pagina Man, landing as if by intention, the wind deceptive in warm weather, with one foot in the lady's bag. "Have you seen the monster?" he asks.

The lady says no, but that she has had a letter from him.

The information is surprising. Pagina Man has never known of a monster to write a letter before and since it may be a clue to the monster's other identity asks to see the letter.

The lady says the letter is at her home, but that it is a very nasty letter and uses words that she wouldn't want him to see. When she sees him standing she says, "Oh but you're such a small super-hero. I didn't realize you were so small."

"Well, I'm big for my size," says Pagina Man, who gets angry and blows fire from his nose when anyone refers to his diminutive stature. "Last week, if you want to know, I saved this man from a monster by pulling the man out of the monster's stomach."

The lady says that she can see already that Pagina Man is bigger than the compelling deception of first sight, and though he doesn't completely forgive her unkind remark, he makes an unscheduled flight to her house to evaluate the monster's letter.

She finds the letter after a long search at the bottom of a large black purse. Before she will give it to him to read, the lady crosses out any and all words which might give offense.

THE MONSTER'S LETTER

Dear Sir or Madam:

If you have already made payment on your XXXXX bill of last winter, which according to the computer punch-out on your character is improbable to say the least, please ignore this XXXXX message. If, as we suspect, you have not settled your XXXXXX XXXXX account with us and have been XXXXXX yourself off to friend and neighbor as pitiably impecunious, you are in for big XXXXXX trouble. XXX XXXX XXXXX XXXXXX especially large teeth and ears. If your checque is not at our offices by noon of Friday next or by the third Tuesday of this month, whichever comes first, it is my unpleasant duty to inform XXX that I shall be obliged to make a XXXXXXX visit and collect said XXXXX by XXXXXX XXXX XXXX XXXXXXX.

Yours truly,
M. Smith, Monster

"Hmmm," Pagina Man says, studying the text of the letter for clues, "the typing looks familiar. Have you ever had a letter from M. Smith, Monster before?"

"Never," she says three or four times. "Never. Never. I always pay my bills at least twice. I'm plenty frightened and scared out of my wits, Pagina Man, as anyone would be who'd gotten a letter like that." She folds the letter lovingly and returns it to her purse. "I think he wants to marry me."

In a single bound, the diminutive super-hero leaps onto the nearest chair. "This may be a job for Pagina Man," he says characteristically.

The lady applauds, which he enjoys though finds embarrassing, his face turning the color of his crimson cape.

Two days and a night pass without sight or sound of the monster. Then at the moment the super-hero closes his eyes— he does hardly more than blink—the monster sneaks in and out. The lady's scream wakes Pagina Man who, out of old habit, sleeps in a diaper to avoid accidents. By the time the baby gets into his costume, the monster and the lady are both gone.

The next day he reads in the paper that the lady and the monster have gotten married, which is very bad news. It is so bad, this news, it is like a dream he can't remember dreaming. It is so bad it is not even funny. It is so bad he flies out into the rain and gets his hair wet. After a meal and a short nap, Pagina Man goes to see a movie about a super-hero who slips on a banana and has a lemon meringue pie thrown in his face.

The next day, in a bad mood, he melts three minor monsters and a witch by pouring pea soup on their heads. The main monster, the one who has run off with the lady, continues to elude his pursuit.

Perhaps he has chosen to be the wrong super-hero. The one-time Pagina Man throws away the costume that was once his pride, and redisguises himself as a baby. He is so sad he walks backwards so that no one will see him coming.

To anyone who will listen he says, "Pagina Man is no longer my favorite super-hero. I think he died."

"No-o," they say. "We *need* Pagina Man. Pagina Man is the weirdest, the noisiest, the smallest and smelliest monster-beater of them all. And he eats well too."

"It's not funny," says the embittered former super-hero.

The baby's friends try to make him laugh, but he refuses, saying, "Fart isn't funny. I used to think fart was funny, but it's not funny."

"What's funny?" they ask him.

The baby is disgusted with the question and leaves the room with a serious expression on his face.

Wherever he goes in the city, the former Pagina Man sees signs that the monster has preceded him. The windows of department stores, for example, are filled with people who have been turned into plastic.

"This is a job for Pagina Man," he says, though he has difficulty working up interest.

Through secret channels the baby learns that the monster and the lady, recently married, are in the market for a well-behaved baby to be taken care of by their live-in baby-sitter. Pagina Man, in the disguise of such a baby, sends a telegram refusing the job. An offer that cannot be refused follows.

The first thing Pagina Man discovers in his new position is that the monster is away on inexplicable business almost all of the time. The second is that the baby-sitter is either invisible or imaginary.

"How are you and the baby-sitter getting along?" the lady asks.

Pagina Man, in his well-behaved disguise, pretends that he doesn't know how to talk, says, "Da da" or words to that effect.

"Wow, you kids talk a whole different language," the lady says. "I've never had a baby in my family before, so you'll have to excuse me if I don't understand you right away."

The super-hero is sent out to play with the imaginary or invisible baby-sitter with special instructions not to get dirty. "What happens if I get dirty?" he asks in baby talk.

"Doodoo. Ca ca," the lady says. "I hope I have it right. I'm not used to speaking that way. When I grew up I left my childhood behind me."

When she says that Pagina Man looks behind her and sees nothing but a blue wall. He spends the rest of the day keeping clean and looking for the baby-sitter with whom it's his job to play.

Later, a man with hairy ears in a business suit, carrying a green attaché case, comes to the house. The lady meets him at the door, takes his case, and pretends to kiss him, her mouth winking like a picture on the television set as it goes off.

"Did he get dirty?" the monster asks.

"He won't look at the baby-sitter and he won't talk to her," the lady says. "I don't know what to do. How was your day, hon?"

"Killing," he says, taking a bite out of her ear.

It looks to Pagina Man as if the man in the suit is the main monster or a close associate, his monstrous nature hidden behind a human mask.

When the lady turns her head the monster, who is always hungry, eats the table cloth with everything on it including a giant candle. Then he eats a dog and a cat and what looks like someone's missing child. The baby has seen enough. Undisguising himself, Pagina Man flies through the door to pull an arm and a leg out of the monster's mouth.

"You told me there wasn't any more Pagina Man," says the frustrated monster, putting yesterday's newspaper over his face so as not to show he is crying.

"That was a different Pagina Man," says the super-hero.

The monster's mask and newspaper are melted by his tears. When he sees his real face in the mirror it is too much of the same thing and he disappears. With the monster out of the way, which is a little sad (monsters nicer in person than by reputation), Pagina Man takes off his costume and reveals his secret identity to the lady who claps her hands in surprise. "It's a secret," he says, finger on lips.

"I must kiss you, you beautiful thing," she says.

Pagina Man doesn't stay for the kiss, but flies out a window which is the wrong window, and falls into a bathtub full of water. When there are no more monsters to be subdued Pagina Man loses his super powers. After the lady dries him off, they have supper together and discuss the nature of reality and future plans.

The baby climbs off my lap as an indication that the story is over. "Any questions?" he asks.

I admit to some curiosity as to the whereabouts of the baby-sitter.

He considers the question, plugging his thumb in his mouth as if it were a source of current. "The monster may have eaten her and the monster may not have eaten her. The baby-sitter may be from another story."

"It's your saddest story so far," I say.

He leaves briefly, then comes back with an apple with small teeth marks on one side, looking around as if the reason for his return is somewhere on the floor. "Remember you promised not to tell anyone?" I nod. "Well, you don't have to promise. Well, you can tell it to me if I forget it or, if I'm in bed and someone asks you, you can say you never heard of that secret story." He picks up a book from my desk and asks the title of it.

"Presences," I say.

"That's the title of my story too," he says. "It's the same story. It's a dream and a secret and the same story. Do you want me to tell it to you? In this story, Pagina Man flies to the moon and gets lost. In this story, Pagina Man falls into the toilet and is flushed into a tunnel of monsters. Don't laugh. In this story, there is no more Pagina Man."

"No more Pagina Man?"

"In this story, Pagina Man is shot by his best friend who doesn't know it's Pagina Man. The friend thought it was a bad guy or a big bird he was shooting. It may be that in the next story Pagina Man is a girl."

I find such news surprising, I say.

He patters out mysteriously without further explanation and after awhile I hear the story being told in another room, the sound of it but not the words. This one, I surmise, is not meant for me, a secret he shares with another.

MICHAEL BROWNSTEIN

is a poet and prose writer who currently makes his home in New York. He has published a book of poems called *Highway to the Sky*; a collection of short stories, *Brainstorms*; and a novel, *Country Cousins*.

Three Stories

FRAGMENT

"Just a fragment!" Harmon sobbed bitterly as he stirred the ashes in the grate and then bent down and transferred a shovelful of the sizzling embers into my lap. As my mouth dropped open he threw down the tiny wrought-iron fireplace shovel and shouted at me, "And you knew—all the time you knew! That's what I just can't understand . . . My God! At least you could have told me! The least you could have done was warn me—Jesus Christ, do you hate me? Do you really want to see me destroyed?" He began shivering uncontrollably again, his body twitching and shaking with fear . . .

"Harmon," I said as steadily as I could, "I'm sorry . . . Really I am. I don't think I understood the situation at all . . . I certainly never *dreamed* it could result in anything like this, for God's sake, so I just never bothered to mention it to you. Believe me, if I'd even *suspected* people could ever devote themselves to such aberrant, spiteful, destructive acts I would've warned you immediately. The last thing I ever wanted was for you to get hurt like this—because now I see they really *are* out to destroy you!"

"But Mike—" Harmon began imploring, when abruptly he was cut off. A gloved white hand streaked out of the shadows from behind him, clapped itself over Harmon's mouth and in an instant he was gone. Gone forever! I'll never forget the look in his eyes . . . Harmon literally was gone forever!

FURNITURE MUSIC

Throughout the Golden Age, throughout all of this—this—prancing, the tables and chairs in our bright clean apartment remain still. They remain solid. A confident, cool silver to offset our raucous gold. Such quiet, infinitely generous vibrations rise from the furniture and work their way across our faces.

Do you remember? Was it in San Francisco? That weekday that seems so long ago? A powdery, brushed-aluminum '40s feeling to the light? Because of the windows? The frosted glass parallelograms framed by handsome sleek strips of aluminum? The flat brass railings that ran like ribbons up the concrete steps outside? Was it too early in the morning to be going to the store? Were we waiting for the store to open?

But the door was open, wasn't it; children were playing in the yard below. In fact a thousand children ran screaming up and down the yard. So much noise they made! We wondered why, exactly. But an ancient person was in the backyard too, a teacher, quietly and sagely feeding instructions and structuring the squishy energy of the breathless children. Did the children all suddenly understand we were watching them? Did they look up and see us?

The tables and chairs lean forward: they act as if they want to know the answer, as if they have a right to know. Proudly they take their places amid waves of rich, hushed expectancy and whipped cream. The rugs and lamps and pillows expect an answer, too. They lean forward infinitely, together with the chairs. Time passes so outstandingly. The sun strikes out across the floor with a high yellow hand.

"People are the only sun! " the tables and chairs seem to say. They love us so.

. . . And now a story about Ned, a guy who used to live over here by 10th St., until one day there was a problem. He ain't around any more, but I hear that his memory is being perpetuated in an unusual way: Neddy was grabbed off the street and ground up into little pieces (don't tell anyone I told ya) and now there's a little bit of Ned in every jar of Skippy peanut butter. Hey, a living memorial! . . . But let's return to our story, which was written before he disappeared.

NED

Ned was a light brown guy with wavy green hair. He had a pillowcase for a face, a chest for a chest, and three testicles instead of one brain. The most important thing he had was his exhaust pipe, though. It ran from his asshole across the floor, out the door, and all the way down the stairs to the street.

Ned lived next to the dry cleaner's on 10th St. for a while, then he moved up behind Dogface Kelly's place into a little old place they had back in there behind a little courtyard. Dogface loaned him towels and sheets and gave him two piggies filled with pennies. Ned took the pennies to the cleaners and they came out clean. He traded his pennies in for food stamps and his food stamps in for food. That's how he lived.

Ned used to clean out his nose with kerosene, he said he liked the burned-out feeling it gave him. He joined up with a quick boxing match operation in the warehouse district for a while: he used to provide the weight for the weighted gloves Sammy Wisenstein used to provide his boxers with. Sammy's boxers usually won the fights they were in, unless money dictated the opposite.

Ned broke up with his wife Susie over a can of whiteface beans. Susie claimed Ned bought the cans for their "look" rather than for their beans, but then forced her to eat them all whenever a can was opened. Susie threw an unopened can in Ned's face and ever since then his face was a pillowcase, but that didn't bother Ned any. He just took the can of beans and crammed it up against Susie's brain, and walked out the very next day. He threw all his belongings into another pillowcase and just rolled out the door.

Ned held his head up high, no matter what. Not too many people could push him around, although plenty people managed to shit on him—shit all over him, in fact, if he didn't watch out—and it was this discrepancy of the one from the other that spun him around. He just couldn't realize that there was a system out there he was part of, that the system was controlled by actual people—big powerful guys he didn't see— and that the system was out to strip him clean, work him over, and let him have it. The system made sure he got just a piggie full of pennies and nothing more, while the big money went to the big guys. What could be more natural? A piggie full of pennies was enough for a guy like Ned, that was the reasoning. The system could do this, moreover, without resorting to any direct physical intimidation whatsoever. No sweat. Especially for guys like Ned. And so correct they were. Because as long as Ned felt tough, felt that nobody was pushing him around— that nobody *could* push him around—he was satisfied. He'd grumble, maybe, but he was satisfied. Nobody was gonna push *Ned* around.

JERRY BUMPUS

was born in Mt. Vernon, Illinois, in 1937 and lives in California where he races, dives, and teaches fiction at San Diego State. He is married and has two daughters. He has published stories in numerous literary magazines and *Esquire*; a *Tri-Quarterly* story was included in Martha Foley's *Best American Short Stories* 1974. His novel, *Anaconda*, is available from *December* magazine.

A Northern Memoir

They would arrive at dusk so the large rental truck could pass unnoticed down our main street and through the campus. Professor Czoc would be driving; her husband would ride in back with the books and things. She would soon find the road out to the old Wervel place, and when they topped the hill overlooking us all, Professor Czoc would masterfully back the truck through the stone gate, up the winding drive and across the lawn, weaving deftly through the bushes and trees without crunching a shrub or snapping a branch, to butt the truck just short of the same French doors which I see from my office. I just might have been standing at my window that night observing in a sense the Czoc's arrival, though I would have seen only my own dark reflection. In the following weeks how often I gazed up at that large house, where shadows roamed like mournful clouds behind the windows and French doors.

We met our new colleague at a party welcoming her and commemorating, at least for some, the retirement of Chuff Freyme. Poor Chuff had let himself be lured into a labyrinth from which there was no hope of ever finding his way—not that he wanted out after he came eye to eye with the great sleek thing which lurks in the center of labyrinths.

Lothar and I had just arrived at the party and were taking off our coats when Chuff, purple-pale, rushed up and with the mawkish earnestness of drunks, said, "I should have worn disguises. I should never have been where I was believed to be."

Lothar put his hand on Chuff's shoulder, his thumb in the divot of his collar bone, and moved him. For he was blocking Lothar's view of Professor Czoc across the room, tall and elegant in a metallic green gown.

I led Chuff aside and heard him out, and, poor soul, though his realizations and insights were rather late, he was right: long ago he ought to have planned on always being elsewhere, and as often as humanly possible he should have been someone else. Instead, he had held his breath, crossed his fingers, and prayed he wouldn't get caught so long as he didn't let loose in wide extravaganzas but limited himself to brisk, spontaneous stunts. But the accumulation of peccadillos eventually went rumbling out from under Chuff like a thousand lumpy little potato heads, trophies of his gnome-hunts in the labyrinth. So predictable was his downfall that his "retirement" fluttered gossips for only a week.

"There, there," I said and patted his arm. He smiled wanly, enjoying this.

Tonight's party would console him. And tomorrow, hung over, Chuff would load his things off to Moon Lake. He would read, reflect, and perhaps some afternoon take up again his brushes and palette, and thus plunge into the lonely dawdling that waits a lifetime for us. When he let himself, he would stare off, recollecting Dipsweth's dim, narrow-windowed classrooms, the chalk dust, the aroma of students, while out the cabin window Fall's abject beauty would slip forgetfully to duller, formidable hues, and further, with the customary inevitability of things, to the burials of winter.

Professor Czoc turned without expression when Lothar spoke to her. She went into another room, stood outside a group, and soon became its center, though she seldom spoke and obviously wasn't listening to the prattle. (Perhaps she listened for a far-off sound: Was Czoc, alone tonight on Wervel Hill, calling to her?)

Lothar stood back as others offered themselves to Professor Czoc in that dauntless, puppetlike way men do. They flashed their teeth and laughed for her. Standing on tiptoes they took a good look right into her, and—my! —they liked what they saw. One could distinctly hear the idea plink in each of them, and in their wives, too, whose hearts in creamy breasts surged up with hatred and adoration: "Why, she's . . . beautiful!"

The phonograph blared. We hopped and frisked, the floor flexing under us, and because Professor Czoc would not dance, it appeared we were dancing for her. Later there was scuffling and hilarity, and in the Game Room we threw darts at each other. Then food was spread and we feasted, braying in each others' faces; the steaming meat and our breath clouded our spectacles.

Afterwards I found poor Chuff, riddled with darts, crumpled in a corner. I nudged him with my toe and as he rolled over he mumbled, "Farewell." (He is already out at Moon Lake, wobbling through a fantasy with Professor Czoc: they stroll through the woods and Chuff explains himself, the pique and joy. We're amused, gazing across the lake into his dream: Professor Czoc is much taller than our anemic Chuff, and several times we see her grinning exaggeratedly over his head and laughing silently. And we're further amused when, widening focus, we see others watching: behind every tree and bush someone hides—a friend here, an enemy there.)

Lothar reached down and jerked Chuff upright. With his hands under Chuff's armpits and with Chuff's feet on top his, Lothar marched him into the bathroom. As I pushed the door shut after them, Lothar was bending Chuff over the sink.

I crossed the room to where Professor Czoc listened icily to a young instructor in the art department named D. H. Lawrence, who had grown a beard and dyed it red. Discoursing at length, putting on quite a show for Professor Czoc, he sliced and boxed the air with both hands. He ached to paint her: a reclining nude which he would shatter into a thousand shards and then, flinging aside his paints and pants, lunge onto her . . .

Coming from the bathroom, Lothar crept up behind Professor Czoc. He stared over her shoulder at D. H. Lawrence, who tried to continue but faltered. "All right. What do you want?" Lawrence said.

Professor Czoc thought this was meant for her, and her eyes tightened.

Lothar put his face in Professor Czoc's hair and whispered in her ear.

She spun about, backing from him as he opened his mouth wide.

"I have nothing to say to you," Professor Czoc said.

"You've answered my question." He motioned for D. H. Lawrence to be off. Frowning, the young man obeyed.

Lothar quickly stepped in front of Professor Czoc and backed her to the wall. He unbuttoned his jacket and revealed a blood red vest with gold buttons.

Professor Czoc glanced at the vest, down the row of buttons, then up to his eyes. She stared flatly at him. And then she smiled—archly, boldly. In her eyes there was defiance and expectancy. Was she aware this was the same smile she would give across a bed as she lifted her arms to unclasp her hair? Lothar made a great business of licking his lips, his tongue lolling far out.

"Disgusting!" Professor Czoc said. She looked at me as if I were to blame. "This man has tormented me all evening."

I smiled. "He follows his course with the precision and security of a sleepwalker."

"What?" she said. "What's that?...."

But Lothar leaned forward and said, "Wanda, I've got you now. And I know about Czoc, too."

I whispered, "A secret?" She glanced at me. "You and your husband will find tremendous seclusion. The endless snows, the impassable roads, the great woods and winding paths."

"Simply because my husband couldn't come ..."

"There's Moon Lake, famous for its steep banks and leaden depths."

Lothar said, "You've made a mistake with Czoc. He's not for you."

"How exasperating," she said. But her eyes were fading to vacant pathos as if right there before us she had begun dreaming. She leaned against the wall and spoke barely above a whisper, "Who are you?"

I stepped nearer. "This Northern land is Lothar's ancestral home, to which he returned last month for old time's sake. He previously held tenure at a renowned institution not unlike Dipsweth." I ran my hand up her smooth arm. "And could it be your Czoc, too, is returning to the land of his ancestors, bringing his bride to the breeding grounds?"

At that moment Chuff Freyme came up and said in Lothar's face, "Treacherous jerk!"

Lothar spun Chuff about and gripping his shoulders held him straight. "Look. How do you like it, Wanda?"

Lothar turned him around and said, "All right, Freyme, play dead."

Professor Czoc slid to the side and out the door.

Lothar would have followed, but Chuff grabbed his lapels and with his face in Lothar's, his purple lips puckering, said, "You're killing me. You know that, don't you? Don't you?"

"Ha!" Lothar shot his hands between Chuff's, breaking his grip. He shoved Chuff and bounding from the room reached the door at the same time Chuff crashed into a china closet.

Lothar ran from room to room but it wasn't until he looked out a small round window on the staircase that he saw a car pulling off—the same car I would often see from my office window descending Wervel Hill.

Lothar returned, his eyes big, amazed. We stepped into a dark room and he bucked in my arms as he sobbed.

On one of those crisp Saturday mornings when men in our town don old duds and rake leaves, or saw wood and smiling, cap in hand, surprise widows on their back porches, I drove up Wervel Hill.

The old two-story house, inhabited for years by the Wervels, who had enjoyed success in several enterprises, would now have the icy brightness of Professor Czoc's touch: green and white would slide smoothly into each other, the rooms aprance with wee gazelles, blue glass griffins, wings spread and rearing into flight through ivy. Professor Czoc, the mysterious Czoc, and I would sit in a sunny room. Professor Czoc would wear a flowing peignoir, mauve, or darker, her hair loose, allowing sensitive nostrils to catch the cheesy complacency of sleep. Our conversation would be beautifully tedious, an elaborate exercise in restraint, interminable. By and by, Czoc would step from the room to fetch his pipe or look out the study window at the feeder, where he feared a huge white cat was molesting the birds. I would then, speaking low, come to the point. Professor Czoc would lean forward, touching the table with the tips of her fingers. She would rise and rather wistfully leave me sitting in the sun-bright room amid zinnias and white curtains . . . Czoc, dottering fool, blind in one eye and milky in the other, would return, apologizing befuddledly, at which he would be a master, having recently retired from a career of fatuity. He wed his wife by grand fluke; she stays with him because she is, alas, easily controlled; he caned her once, or at the beginning he subdued her with a Great Dane . . .

I reached the end of the winding driveway. When I knocked at the door, the echo sank into the house. I walked around the side. Brown curtains dense as earth covered the windows. As I stepped onto the terrace above the garden, the curtains there weren't shut, and I caught a glimpse not of a sunroom with droll ivy and boisterous zinnias.

I looked into nothing. A room so enormous the far wall was

hidden by the day's reflection on the glass. No furniture or new-painted walls with pictures, no glass tables with bowls of fruit. No flurry of peignoir with a surprised, trilling, "Eek! "

The entire first floor was a cavern, the walls knocked out, the huge house beams exposed. Framing my face to the window, I saw laboratory apparatus sprouting on work benches, an arbor of copper and glass tubes hiding small black boxes. Beyond the benches lay a great shadow like a pile of broken sofas.

Then the brown curtain crushed my view, the pulley beyond the pane screaming derisively, yet forlornly.

Several days later I stood before the science building, a monstrosity of three old buildings interconnected: an ancient, crooked dormitory; Dipsweth's original administration building; and what had once been a railway roundhouse.

When I entered, the building at first seemed deserted. But deep within, where the odors of gases, old fruit, and wet fur hung in the air, specialists scurried along, staying close to the walls and darting into offices niched in the corners of the twisting corridors. These runty, yellowish individuals were involved in the research for which Dipsweth was well known; they were Asiatics, Lapps, and Pygmy scholars who from years in the lab were bleached a pasty ocher.

I found Professor Czoc's office hidden on the fourth floor. The door was ajar and the tiny room was filled with a jumble of crates, books, and filing cabinets. At the end of a trail through all this, a white telescope stood before a window no wider than a slit but providing a view of the house on Wervel Hill and the woods beyond.

The hulking shadows stirred in the office and I heard whispering. I pushed the door open wider and saw a desk where Professor Czoc sat with none other than Dipsweth's star athlete, Buck O'Brian, a neckless, huge-shouldered lad who, a veteran of perhaps too many seasons, had been so thoroughly socked about that his features had solidified to perpetual bovine woe. (Returning from a walk in the woods early one morning, I passed a field at the edge of town where a crowd of men were fighting. I watched from behind a tree and realized they were ruggers playing by Dipsweth's rules. Before a row of wooden chairs they beat and stomped each other in silence. At the far end of the field the ball was being trundled off into the woods by a squat, dark creature, perhaps a badger.)

Apparently Buck O'Brian had excellent hearing, though his ears resembled snails nailed to his head; he looked over his shoulder at me. His brows were thickly plastered and beneath them his face was a suave blend of black and purple.

"Professor Czoc is expecting me," I said from the doorway.

"I was not expecting you," said Professor Czoc, pushing her swivel chair from the desk and slowly crossing her legs. "What do you want?"

"My business is of a highly personal nature," I said.

She touched Buck O'Brian's forearm with two fingertips and the young man rose. I hurried right up and sat in his chair. He stepped out of the office, turned, and lifting his arms, leaned against the doorframe as if he might push the door apart and bring the building down on us.

I began. "Coming from the world at large to Dipsweth and our shrouded village, you will have several difficulties grasping situations. There has been early shame, and, all in all, no little travail. But surprising coups have set things straight, and we live it down, somehow, deriving solace from the quietude so oppressive to newcomers and outsiders." I sighed. "You've no idea what we're really doing here."

"Oh, I think I have a notion," Professor Czoc said, her eyes bright as dimes.

"I suppose you mean that, as a lady of science, you're up on Dipsweth's recent history—the experiments of the 1940s, the great Biblical beast scandal, and that laughable conference on angels where Jung made a fool of himself.

"I congratulate you on your scientific accomplishments, on your astonishing beauty, and your popularity with one and all . . ." The doorframe cracked loudly. "However, there is more to Dipsweth than science. Perhaps you have two or three facts, which you've stuffed up a pants leg and made a scarecrow. You've read dreams and even dreamed on your own. You've kept your ears open for every deranged rumor, and you've no doubt spun a legend or two yourself during summer vacations and published them in the Fall as contributions to the field. . ."

Professor Czoc interrupted. "Come to the point. You're afraid of losing that . . . person of yours, aren't you? That great buffoon what's-his-name."

"No, there's plenty of Lothar for everyone. But Lothar *is* the reason you've come here, though you don't truly grasp it yet.

"Lothar knew the moment he saw you. And it was a great anthropologic moment—historic, though ultimately in that category of anthropology reserved for feats of horror. But how could you connect Lothar with legends and vague rumor?"

"Please," Professor Czoc said, holding up a hand. "I have no idea what this is all about, but rest assured I'm not here for your Lothar. Science has brought me to Dipsweth, not your legends or your breeding grounds."

I looked away and after a moment said in my calmest manner, "Though you have no idea, bless your pretty skin, what the breeding grounds are and what transpires, you have indeed come to them. And now you must leave. This instant!"

She leaned back and said, "Leave? Why, I'm exactly where I want to be, and I know exactly what I want."

"Listen." I lifted my hands and spread my fingers. "You know what you want, but you have no idea how you'll get it." I stared into her intently. She could understand if she would only try. But she wanted more. "Listen."

A triumphant laugh exploded in the corridor. Shoving Buck O'Brian out of the way, Lothar strode into the office. I rose and went to the white telescope as Lothar grinned down at Professor Czoc and said richly,

Ding dong bell;
Pussy's in the well.
Who put her there?—
Little Dewey Dare.
Who'll get her out?—
Big Dick Stout.

He dragged up a crate and sat on it with his knees touching Professor Czoc's. He said low, "I want to tell you how much I liked our chitchat at the party. I've come to pursue it with my best."

"You again," she said.

He scooted still closer, ramming a knee between hers. He whispered, "Remember what we were saying?"

"As a matter of fact, no."

He unbuttoned his jacket, letting it tent their knees and thighs. Putting his face almost in hers, he said, "I have brought a great treasure."

"I would rather," Professor Czoc said, "hear the legend."

"Which one?"

"There are more than one?"

"Twenty, thirty. There's Happy Joseph. He became a frog. Eight feet long from head to toe when he stretched out on the bank to sun. You want the rest?"

"Yes."

"Ha! Happy Joseph got itchy. Interfered with the girls' gym class at their swimming lessons. So he got hauled away."

"Is he dead, then?"

"Dead?" Lothar laughed with all his might. "Did you say *dead*?"

I looked into the telescope: it was focused on the woods—on Moon Lake. There was Chuff Freyme's cabin, and as I looked, the door flew open and out came Chuff, running like mad. "It looks bad for Chuff Freyme," I said.

"Freyme," Professor Czoc said to Lothar. "Tell me about him."

Grinning, Lother opened his jaws wide and banged them shut. As he spoke he wagged his leg between her knees, swiveling her slowly back and forth. "He was searching for his big dream ideal. And when he got it, they fired him. Ha!"

She closed her eyes, leaning back as if dizzy from the swaying.

"Something's after Chuff!" I said.

Lothar got up and, pushing me aside, looked into the telescope. "Hm. Freyme's in for it good this time."

Lothar walked back to the desk and tilting back Professor Czoc's chair, wedged open her knees. Buck O'Brian slowly came and stood beside him.

Tiptoeing up the path between the crates, I glanced back. Shoulder to shoulder, they leaned over her. Buck O'Brian reached down; either he lifted one of her legs, or she lifted it at his touch. As I shut the door, Lothar turned the telescope to perhaps give Professor Czoc a wrong-way look at Chuff

Freyme and his tormentor or perhaps Lothar, his face serene in concentration, his arms extended from his sides as he leaned over the instrument, was expressing a sudden interest in science and would peer down the telescope into Professor Czoc.

At dawn I go to Moon Lake: a bumblebee in hardening paraffin, I move with incredible slowness. As if wandering off as people sometimes do, I pass through the high-hedged lane, and finding by dull magic my car I drive under the low sky through the woods and take the Moon Lake turn-off. Clumps of snow hide bushes, shroud evergreens, pack the crotches of trees. The road lobs off where stuck cars in struggling to free themselves dug great holes. I round a curve and see Moon Lake, a flat lead face staring at the sky. Above it the cabin leans back on itself. On the porch I call, "Chuff? Oh Chuff!" I open the door, call again. I go to the end of the porch, then behind the cabin. Up the hill I see a man, dark as leather, shirtless and barefoot, upside-down in the trees, his stick-man arms straight down, one leg straight up and the other gone at the knee. My heart thrums in my ears. Through the black branches I stare at the rope tied to the ankle. The leg points accusingly at the rope and at the tree limb. I run slowly up the hill and stop, my breath steaming, eye to tiny eye with the face ballooned with the whole body's blood which gravity called to earth, the blood answering as far as it could come. I go down to my car and carefully turn it around. I drive slowly and stopping several times I have only to stare into the woods a few moments before hanging men, some stretched in X's between trees, emerge through the dense branches. In town they hang along telephone lines. One dangles by his wrist from a flagpole. Driving through the campus, I see a fringe of them along the eaves of the science building. I proceed up Wervel Hill, and of course no one answers when I knock. But this time when I turn the corner of the house I find Professor Czoc standing in the garden with a giant.

Mr. Czoc wore a coat of gray tarpaulins sewn together; the one covering most of his back said *Wervel Oldsmobile—Rocket 88*. On his head he wore a flesh-colored shower cap.

Professor Czoc was speaking intently, though the giant appeared not to listen, his heavy-lidded eyes downcast, his mouth sagging on a chin big as a shoe. Then his face flashed with a smile which vanished immediately—a tic that yanked up, then dropped, half his face. Professor Czoc leaned back and said up to him: "And fire." Or perhaps it was "Unfair." The giant shook his head and moaned.

They heard me on the gravel path and turned. "At last I have the pleasure," I said, going forward. Professor Czoc looked away, and Czoc closed his eyes as I seized his hand. "Allow me to welcome you home."

Czoc pulled his hand free and started toward the house. Professor Czoc followed, and walking close to her I said low, "I see Lothar was right about your husband. He remembered the large Czocs who lived here a hundred years ago. But tell me, has it done any good, bringing Czoc back?"

On hands and knees Czoc crawled through the French doors. We walked through behind him, and as he crawled to the far end of the room, I went to a telescope standing before a window and through it looked down at the village. "I have rather important news."

Did I detect a certain urgency in her voice when she said, "I frankly do not . . ."

"It pertains to a certain individual you were involved with the other day."

"I was involved with a number of individuals. Which do you mean?"

"My. I was referring to a rather athletic consultation . . ."

She stepped nearer. "Buck O'Brian?" she said low.

I chuckled. "Hardly. I meant the real thing." Through the telescope I spotted Lothar running down a street. He cut through a yard and burst into a house. Men, women, and children flew from the house, some leaping from windows. Lothar, his mouth wide, came running out, chasing first this one, then another. He stood in the yard, his breath making a cloud. Then he spun about, dived into some shrubberies, and dragged out a man by the leg.

I turned from the telescope. "Now that I've met Czoc I see just how really interested you are in the real thing. I suppose you brought him here hoping he would . . . revive. But he hasn't, has he?" She very slowly closed her eyes as if she would dream away from my words.

"No, of course not," I said, "for Czoc is only a giant, a big dud."

I swung the telescope around and looking at her through the big end, saw her miles away, tiny but distinct, "Now for the important news. You came to Dipsweth on a quest. I am pleased to announce the goal of that quest is at hand. You'll soon be getting it. Lift your arms. To unclasp your hair. Now —that smile . . ."

"Ha!" Lothar trotted through the French doors. He heaved a work bench out of his way, smashing the machines and glass tubing; through the telescope the shattering glass flew like a slow cascade of stars.

He grabbed her hair and jerked back her head. While he licked her face, he ripped off her skirt and slip. He bowed her backwards and with his free hand grabbed her. "Pudding!" He released her, gave her a whack, and sent her running for the stairs. He squinted at her as she ran upstairs, and turning to Czoc and me, said, "That's one sweet slice of gick." He charged up the stairs. "Slick gick! Tapioca pudding!"

Czoc grumbled at the far end of the room. I walked down to him. "Quite right, old fellow," I said. "But try to bear up. It's nearly finished. Listen." In the distance dogs were howling. Czoc cried, and as he did his tic lurched his face into its great grin, which immediately slumped. "There, there," I said and patted his hand.

The first of the hounds came bounding around the corner, their claws clattering, their ears pricked as they stared at Czoc and me for an uncertain moment. "You're warm, lads," I called and waved them toward the stairs. They tore across the room and up the stairs.

We heard cars and trucks coming up the drive. There was a commotion, then thunder crashed through the house as the front door was attacked by axes. Firemen, policemen, and fellows with pitchforks and big sticks, marched through, pale and resolute as they followed the dogs upstairs.

I whispered good-bye to Czoc and slipped out. Following a path into the woods, I went to the top of Wervel Hill and sat on a stump. The banging around in the house was muffled and hollow. Then a profound crash shook the house and all was silent.

They somehow got chains on Lothar, and with one end hooked to the bumper of a flat-bed truck, dragged him out. They chained him onto the truck, and as they started off, Lothar saw me on the hill. He called my name again and again.

I send Czoc off each morning and watch from afar as he moves along the hedge-lined lane through the campus, and much later I see his great shadow gliding across the windows in the laboratory in that part of the science building which was once a roundhouse: he works into the night, while the rest of us lie in bed or slump by our dark lamps.

The former Professor Czoc now and then writes us, but her interests have shifted; she is making headway in artistic areas with the acclaimed painter of shards, D. H. Lawrence.

Last week's letter from Lothar complained of the food and begged me for cigarette money. He claims he is much improved, and this seems true. But the officials assure us he will remain in chains until that institution crumbles—and that the day before that occurs he will be transferred to another and from there to another . . . By then the rest of us will be gone, never to return, and also by then, inevitably, Lothar's records will have turned to dust or will have gotten misplaced. The new officials, unable to explain why Lothar is being held, will in embarrassment and shame give him a parole, or whatever such releases will be called in that distant era. Lothar will have long forgotten us—even, sadly, myself. His thoughts will be on the future.

In a new suit of clothes, rather too small for him, and carrying a cardboard suitcase with a change of socks and shorts, he will head North, not knowing why, yet drawn to a distant village, which by then might well be no more than a clearing in the forest.

GEORGE CHAMBERS

Grandson₄ of Sir William Chambers, the eighteenth-century English architect of the Roman Ruins at Kew Gardens, George Chambers was born in Cambridge, Mass., and now lives on the riverbarge *Patricia* which he pilots for the Chillicothe Salvage Co. at the port of Peoria. Capt. Chambers came to literature late in life when his father sent him the family copy of Woolett's engravings which depict Sir William's ruins at Kew. This experience inspired his first novel, *The Artist Moved by the Magnitude of Antique Fragments.*

This unpublished ms. and most of George's other work announces his heavy and singular indebtedness to the artists who invented the eighteenth century. His novel, *The Bonny-clabber,* is available from December Press. Work also in the current issues of: *Tri-Quarterly, Fiction International,* and in Lucien Stryk's edition of midwest poetry, *Heartland II.*

From   *TH/ING*

(I will not have her agreeing to be my victim

Calphurnia awoke with this thing beside her face on the pillow. Touching it, she felt it growing out of her head . . . a thick floppy cock, a penis like a ponytail. What a classic, I thought, what a classic. I was delighted and jealous too. I mean I want to see a row of shark's teeth dripping blood, set in a cunt, one of those rare straight-haired jobs. Nevertheless, hope springs eternal in the human scalp . . . heh.

Well, to get it over with, I fell into the trap those two tiny noodle-cutters were preparing for me. Now when I was alone up there I was complete in my fantasy, they were my victims and I passed the time imagining how I would trap them and how they would do my didding, he he, and how I would work my will on their luscious bodies. I'd wake up, practice a bit, read a few scores, then I'd whip them with my belt before going off to teach. That's the kind of thing I did up there in Dr. Holes' apartment, that creep, that cockroach. Then I'd come home and have them rub me down with baby oil, then I'd fuck them until they screamed then we'd eat a fat bloody roast and they would lick me for dessert, right? Am I right? I mean I was intact, almost happy you could say . . . in the expectations I saw so clearly before me, or specifically, *underneath* me. Oh so lo mio, oh do re mi fa so la. Ah but I was a young man and therefore at the mercy of a force I didn't recognize. Gypsy and Maria, eh? You bet, but I ended up where I am now, a poor battered man, laid out on a slab at the county morgue. Love oh love oh deadly lu-uve.

(Peter Clothier's notion: *flack, flac*   Flying through this flac, weaving about, maintaining altitude, zipping along over "enemy territory" on a bomb-run.

Making agreements with myself.

That Donna, that dumb Donna, just sitting there and *knowing* like that, me peeking at her bags, I mean she *knows what I'm doing,* I mean she knows I'm gonna walk outta here with her right in LaVerne's face, she knows that and I'm gonna stab that Donna an she knows it, knows that too.

TH/ING 42–2–7–3

(or the Baron as villain-in white . . . the pure, driven man . . . humiliated by perfection)

202 allied chemicals

pork ribs, barbeque, red wine, a hard fuck "I blacked out/ I saw stars" morning moon in mist over messalonski, (mama!)

Beyond Necessity

It's morning again in Sawdust City, Chipsville, also known locally as "Chicago" folks. The winter sun is shining in the chips, what's left of the birds that inhabit this place is singing off the top of her collective head, ka ka, there's no moon tonight the forest and rivers are bright cold, oh darling, slip me the seed of love. The lucky citizens also hark! awaketh! Another day hath come to Chipsville, another day over the footbridge at Big Titty, another day for the river carry the dead away. Senior Chicagoess 707 is already down in the bilges of Pussy, the river barge. Pussy leaks a lot, needs regular pumping out . . . otherwise. 707 is manning the bilge pump, in a manner of speaking. She keeps the rhythm the old way like choppin cotton and pullin corn in the ol southwest 'ho bam catch-ratchit" style. She's doin the "suck-a/fucka." However, 707 also hath a mind and heart, as do most folks, no matter how much they ignore that pump. 707 is thinking about the show, she's brought to town the famous kabuki story teller Bozo George to perform "Hamlet" in the glue factory shipping room. That's what she's thinking about, she's seen a lot of posters of that Bozo, that George, screamin his fuckin head off as Hamlet, gettin dead n all, and she's, well, inspiring herself down there suck-a/fucka in the barge bilge.

(The bus is ripping along, whipping north on the Interstate, it's the same morning as above only nobody aboard d'bus knows it's day yet, since they got the curtains down, no one that is except the driver Peter The Great up front, he always is, and in the back the troupe leader Bozo Geo himself who has awoken restless and is laying the troupe Virgin on the back seat to calm himself down. While he pumps away he's got his mouth tight on hers, blowing into her lungs, so she won't scream and wake up the other virgins in the troupe who might also want a piece of the action. The seat they is fucking on is over the diesel engine so it's warm and thumpy, an inspiring spot. Feeling better after having done his damage for the day, he says to Virgin 44, "You'll get a car and a boat and a freezer and a quickoven and twenty-four cases of cat food and a dozen menstrual belts, and a boat with twin outboards and a pocket telescope and a mercury mirror . . ." And so on, the girls love it, love to hear about something specific like that they have won for being Layer of the Day. They could listen to Bozo forever, he talk so sweet. ". . . and forty range-fed steer, and a gallon of gas, and some Covercunt eye shadow and a dozen fertile eggs, and ten pounds of

TH/ING 42-2-8-2

be ma li'tle good luck charm

I remind myself there is a moon
besame! besame mucho!   semper   idem   walked
                                     down town to buy what
                                     had been on his mind
                                     since noon and his wife's
                                     denial of him. oh shit
                                     were they lonely, I mean

James Mechem

have you ever seen that painting of the two naked bodies, his and hers, in that room? Oh suck my stomach it was a lonely picture, I mean it said we have fed ourselves and fucked ourselves, we've gone to see the moon, we've fished all the waters, and we've just ended here sitting on the bed's edge, I mean they look so *reduced,* y'know? that's the way semper was with his wife now, so her denying him his scoop of chocolate whip after their soup and crackers just hung it in his mind. he could have served himself after lunch, but that was what she did, serve, after all, and to intrude on her operation would incite another of those tender catastrophes they had both learned to eschew in favor of domestic tranquility, and do I ever mean it was tranquil, oh it was placid, the quality of their life, I mean it *hummed.* and so idem was walking downtown toward the Ice Creame Shoppe with a scoop of chocolate fixed in his head firmly when he heard one man say to another, "Well, thankya Henry, it was good working with and besides we made a little money too." somehow, that all but knocked idem into the gutter, those words made him feel wretched, I mean they were words of interest and friendship, work and pleasure. and measured by the experience of those men he was humiliated to be walking out to buy a scoop of chocolate, the little treat that doris had so carelessly denied him. when he reached the Shoppe there was a line at the counter, a group of school kids, and it was slow moving because the ice cream was very hard that day and the girl's scoop was dull. tapping the shoulder of the girl in front of him, idem smiled secretively and said, "I've got an autograph from Mr. Elvis Presley in my wallet." oh shit you know what that kid did, I mean she made idem feel like he had drooled on his tie, pissed on his foot, just plain *exposed* himself, y'know. Then he said, "I think I'll get vanilla." Which doesn't seem to change the course of world events much, eh citizens, but for idem it was the beginning of what

he was later to call THE
TROUBLE.

TH/ing 42-2-9

something in the way she moves
the one-a-day girl, she's sure she
gets hers every day
                          "according to mighty workings"
Calphurnia reading from the TV GUIDE

Senior Chicagoess 707 is walking over the footbridge to in-
spect progress on her latest project. She's thinking she'd like it
to be ready by tonight, for Bozo George's appearance as kabuki "Hamlet" at the factory shipping room. Imagine, she's
thinking, as she watches the heavy waters swirling and stinking under her, our own glue factory, imagine the walls re-
sounding to the noble words of the Prince! Looking down
through the boards on the footbridge she reacts to a squadron
of pigeons flying by underneath. It unbalances her, causes her
to hold the wire-rope railing for support. She has seen his
picture, wonders how a man so round, a fellow so fat, can play
the play, can create the Dane whose part she understands as
"thin," as "skeletal" even.

(frog legs and a dozen Italian sandals and a year's supply of
pie-filling for your freezer and 20 hit records and a date with
Roy Orbison who'll sing "Pretty Woman" to you all night on
his voice, and a weekend in Hawaii with the sex-object of your
choice, and a genuine Persian Marriage Mirror and . . ." The
troupe Virgin interrupted Bozo: "Hey, Bozo, what that Marriage Mirror, what that?" "My dear, little ball of grease, ten-
derfoot, that's the first way you'll see your new hubby,
reflected in that cute little hand-painted mirror, and since
you'll also be seeing yourself seeing him, your little birdheart
will be gratified, for a man is but a pale reflection of yourself, a
mortal man, a hubby, a cloudy illusion in your otherwise bright
dreams." She looked at him directly, decided she'd better pre-
tend to understand. "Yeah, yeah, well Bozo hon, go on with
the list, ah?" "OK I can I do . . . enough soap to bathe the

Italian Air Force for a year, a Gibson guitar with steel strings, a genuine imported French bidet, twenty-nine palms, thirty

707 makes it across the river. She enters the factory and heads into the cellar toward the mailing room where it is being assembled, where she hopes she will find it near completion.

Gretal/Glück

"I'm a (   ), that's why I've been picked
"I'm a (   ), that's why they picked me to talk to you."

snapping forkfuls of mashed potato at each other
                                   I'm ah well, human too y'know
                                   I mean I have a thought once
                                   in a while, like evry one does,
                                   and it usually gets me into
                                   the same kind of trouble as
                                   anyone who thinks, and if you

---

JEROME CHARYN

is an editor of *Fiction.* He has published eight novels, including *Eisenhower, My Eisenhower, The Tar Baby,* and *Blue Eyes.* He is currently teaching at Herbert Lehman College, C.U.N.Y.

A Child's History of the Bronx
(From The Dutch Beginnings To The Last Slave In New York)

1. PAPARINEMO

Progenitor of the van der Root line in America, Klaes van der Roetch (or Rut, Rott, Rootch) was a drudge for the West India Company when he arrived in *Nieuw Nederlandt* around 1645. Prior to this nothing is certain about his life. Considering the sturdiness of the palisade he built on Paparinemin Island, latterday van der Roots like to proclaim him at the least as a successful *timmerman* (carpenter) in Amsterdam; he may also have been a convict, a bankrupt, a murderer, or an ordinary pest out of Rotterdam who was dispatched from Holland and glued to the Dutch West India Company. Whatever, he washed floors and fed black slaves at West India's Hoogh Straet offices until 1651; then we discover him at the tip of "Manhates" (the Manhattans) carpentering a primitive fort along the neck of Spuyten Duyvil Kill and burning out Indians who were skulking in the marshes of Paparinemin Island. His successes flabbergasted the Dutch farmers in the area. In 1653 the Dutch authorities granted Klaes a patent to clear Paparinemin Island of mosquitoes and other vermin, and to establish a tobacco plantation, a *koek-huys* (tavern and cake-house), and a bouwerie thereon, and Klaes became the first and only patroon of Paparinemo. To the horror of the boers (farmers), Klaes prospered straightaway. He imported Indian slaves and black servants from the workhouses of the West India Company, he abandoned tobacco and raised apples, peaches, and corn, he fortified the entire island and renamed Paparinemo *Colenrootch* (Rootch's Colony) in honor of himself.

Heer Rootch was unmolested during the English occupation of *Nieuw Nederlandt*. The new English rulers soaked their chins in rum at the "Spiting Divell" cake-house and called him the Dutch Millionaire. He would fetch them from Manhattan Island without charge on a modest flatboat; soon he converted this boat into the amazing Paparinemo ferry that carried a hundred passengers per load to *Colenrootch*, where the ferry rested and passengers availed themselves of the cake-house, then crossed the treacherous spitting waters of Spuyten Duyvil Kill to the mainland (now the Bronx). Dominie Krol, farmer and powerful minister of the Dutch church, with a bouwerie on the Manhattan side of Spuyten Duyvil, was particularly jealous of Klaes; and so began our three-hundred-year feud with "Manhates." The Dominie attempted to ground the ferry by placing boulders in the creek. He had his musketeers fire hot lead at the roof of the cake-house. He inspired the Weckquaesgeek Indians of Westchester to raid Klaes' peach orchard (this would lead to the infamous Peach Wars). He closed his church to the inhabitants of *Colenrootch* and demanded that Klaes be pilloried. He accused Klaes of stealing goats and pigs from him and plotted with Hubert Winner, the mayor of New York, to lessen Klaes' "libertys and priviledges on the Island of Paparinem." In accordance, Mayor Hubert set about to annex Paparinemo, bind it to Manhattan. The Dominie's incaution cost him his life; he ignored the obscurities of Klaes' past and reckoned that a former drudge of the West India Company could do him little harm. Heer Rootch might have countenanced peach swipes and lead balls in his roof, but he was the despot of Paparinemo and would allow no one to pinch his territory. After greasing his legs and chest he swam to the Dominie's bouwerie, slaughtered the Dominie's pigs, set fire to the Dominie's barn, and punctured the Dominie's throat.

It was the enormity of Klaes' act that sobered the mayor of New York. Had Klaes settled for the pigs and the barn, Mayor Hubert would have beheaded him surely, stripped off his flesh, and rolled his bloody skull in the streets as an example to future hog butchers. A man who could destroy a bouwerie singlehanded and kill over the rights to an island in a creek was beyond his jurisdiction. In addition, Klaes' death would bring him little profit; he could no longer count on the Dominie's bribes. Perhaps Klaes understood all of this, perhaps not. His patience, his talent for enduring the simpler indignities, and the neatness of his revenge, makes one suspect that the progenitor of the van der Roots was no ordinary hotblood. Albeit Mayor Hubert would have lost the respect of his citizenry had he not enacted some form of punishment; so he seized Heer Rootch with gentle hands and stood him in the pillory on High Street for a period of three days.

I see our father with his neck and fingers collared in hard wood. One of the mayor's henchmen has come to shave his beard. Chickens scrabble under his boots; after an hour his buttocks are sore. Children laugh at the man in the "stretchneck." They climb the platform, shinny up and down the post to follow a murderer's eye. A constable will chase them away. Worshipers from the Dominie's church pelt Klaes' weathered face with flour balls and poppy seeds. They recite hymns to the dead Dominie and move on. The sun crispens our father's cheeks. His Indian slaves wipe him with rags soaked in peppermint leaves. Occasionally he spits. Mayor Hubert has denied him tobacco; there will be no amusements for him on the pillory. The tradesmen who happen to be near High Street at this hour are mortified by Klaes' smile. It is not the correct expression for a man doing penance on his feet. They have misinterpreted his grimace. Our father was only wrinkling his nose to prevent the poppy seeds from falling in.

2.   THE PEACH WARS 1681

Having acquired a taste for fancy peaches, the Weckquaes-geeks continued to raid Klaes' orchards after the death of Dominie Krol. Our father tolerated these sporadic losses to his crop until a surly Weckquaesgeek pulled out the tongue of his orchardkeeper (the orchardkeeper may have insulted the Indian). He reacted with a swiftness and a cunning that befits the master of an island. He ferried over the new Dominie to bless himself, his servants, his slaves, and his only son (in 1659 Heer Rootch married a rich, landed widow who bore him a manchild named Lucas and promptly died; she was fifty-one at childbirth, this *huysvrouw*). Then he proceeded to coat the peaches of his northwest orchard, the one most vulnerable to the Indians, with poisons, emetics, and bowel-splitters (rhubarb, ergot, foxglove, belladonna, green potato tubers, chopped nettle hairs, mustard seeds, parsnip flowers, water hemlock roots, corn cockle seeds, Jerusalem cherries, pokewood shoots, chopped toadstools). For two days Weckquaesgeeks writhed in the orchard. A goodly number vomited, shat, peed, and dropped. The rest of them dragged their swollen bodies off the island. The stench and great decay rendered the orchard useless; mosquitoes, maggots, and a variety of roaches thrived amid the corpses and the human debris. Heer Rootch had to burn his crop. The Indians nearly ruined him. They purged their stomachs with bitter roots, they washed themselves, they feasted their dead, and came back. They shot dungy arrows at the Paparinemo ferryboat. They hatcheted whole sections of Klaes' palisade. They murdered his goats. They wasted his apple and cherry crops.

Klaes grew infirm during the wars. In his seventies now, plagued with gout and a chronic dyspepsia, Heer Rootch sat on a log belching and nursing the tobacco in his nose while his island fell to pieces. Servants tramped behind young Lucas grumbling about the end of the van der Rootches. Born of a tired mother, Lucas proved to be an ineffectual boy; he awaited his father without the slightest urge to stop the Weckquaes-geeks on his own. Then Klaes startled Paparinemo. Shunning the ferry, he rolled his log into the creek and floated down to Bronksland (old patroonship of Jonas Bronck, the first white settler of our borough; in 1681 the Weckquaesgeeks still lived in the wilds of north Bronksland). Klaes' servants feared for him, naturally. Lucas smoked his pipe and continued to buy property adjacent to the estates of his dead mother, on the mainland side of Spuyten Duyvil (in the Bronx). For this bit of heartlessness, Klaes' Dutch household nicknamed him *Koopal* (or the Buy-All). An Indian slave found Klaes' log near the ferry landing, blood and dung on it. About a week after the Paparinemins fired a cannon ball into the creek to memorialize the passing of Klaes, Klaes returned; he wore rags and clutched a long strip of bark with scratchings on it, which his household interpreted as a peace treaty between Paparinemo and the sachems of the Weckquaesgeeks (names unknown). Whatever, these moody Indians left the island alone.

Nothing could be gleaned from the resurrected Klaes about his labors in Bronksland. He spoke no English; nor did he use the gestures of the Weckquaesgeeks. Our father had the gift of tongues. The islanders dodged the spit that flew from Klaes. They summoned a Manhattan fishboy, a halfbreed who claimed some magic, to examine the tonguespeak. All the fishboy got from Klaes was that the savages had cleaned his ears. The subsequent history of the van der Roots redeems Klaes from any thought of charlatanism; his was the first of many parapsychic conversions, moments of ecstatic lumination under duress, that run through our family line like a bloodsore and have been our singular curse. The Paparinemins soon tired of Klaes' babble. They kept him out of the wind, they cut his fingernails, they saw to it that he moved his bowels, but they no longer looked upon him as master of the island.

3.   THE SINKING OF PAPARINEMO

Koopal allowed his father to rot in the sun. No one in Paparinemo recorded Klaes' fits of speech. The old man fell into a coma and died with his tongue still wagging. Koopal was too busy managing his holdings in the Bronx to fix Klaes' burial. He left such matters in the hands of Indian slaves who built a mound for their old master and buried him in the Weckquaesgeek manner, with sticks, a cannon ball (they considered Klaes a warrior foremost), and sheeps' blood, to quiet the monsters of the dead. The physicality of Klaes, even as a sunstruck babbler, had calmed the island; without him his colony suffered. The sticks of the palisade loosened and land began to slide into the creek. The ferry service grew erratic (Koopal's Indian boatmen would leave Manhattan farmers stranded for days). Mysterious epidemics gripped the island (a fifth of the population, including a daughter of Koopal's, succumbed during an outbreak of black measles). Koopal seemed more interested in becoming an English lord than being the new master of Paparinem. He shortened his name to Root and grabbed parcels of land in the Bronx with the help of renegade Weckquaesgeeks.

Chagrined by Koopal's landgrabbings and rotting ferry, a column of Manhattan farmers, English and Dutch, pestered the provincial governor of New York into giving them the "single priviledge" to construct a bridge at the neck of Spuyten Duyvil Kill so that they might bypass Paparinemo and ruin Koopal for all time. Accordingly, the King's Toll Bridge was opened in 1693 with the farmers pocketing half the revenue; the other half went directly into the governor's purse. But they couldn't get Koopal. As the bridge killed the ferry trade and forced the closing of Spuyten Duyvil inn, Koopal moved his household to the mainland and leased Paparinemo to a handful of Weckquaesgeek farmers. The farther Koopal entrenched himself inside the Bronx, the more rapidly the island declined. Soon he owned the north end of our borough, including the mainland approaches to the bridge. Thus he compelled the Manhattan farmers to split their toll collections with him and wheedled a fake escutcheon from the governor, which granted him certain obscure half-royal prerogatives (his heirs had the right to entertain future English kings in their home for one hour, should these kings visit the Bronx).

Koopal's guests learned not to chat about Paparinemo in his presence. Whenever they mentioned the Indians who had inherited his father's island, Koopal scratched his jaw with a knife. The Weckquaesgeek farmers abandoned Klaes' stone house and lived in the peach orchard. Water crept through the holes in the palisade. A goat drowned. Two Indians were crushed in a rockslide. Paparinemo became a bogland again. The remaining Indians climbed peach trees to avoid the accumulations of mud; the ferry landing slipped. Indian urchins disappeared in the swamps. Dutch and English farmers on

both sides of Spuyten Duyvil belittled the seepage and spoke
with contempt of the "savages on board Rootch Island." One
cannon ball, the farmers said, would be enough to sink the
entire Paparinem. Albeit the Indians survived for eight years.
They gobbled swamp berries and kept their horses and pigs
swaddled in the few outhouses that had best withstood the
bog. During the flood of 1703 the Dutch and English farmers
were too preoccupied with the broken struts of their toll bridge
to notice that the shoreline of Paparinemo had been eaten
away and that the island itself had begun to drop. Only after
the bloated corpses of pigs and cows knocked under the bridge
did they turn their heads far enough to realize Paparinemo was
gone. Several ambitious farmers talked of raising the island
from the bottom of the creek with God's mercy and the aid of
stilts and a horsedrawn dredging ladder they planned to build.
Koopal discouraged them. The farmers returned all subscrip-
tions to the dredging ladder and used their wits to strengthen
the bridge.

4. ROOTBOROUGH

In Anno Domini 1712 Koopal van der Root had already
pushed the Cartwrights, the Frankenfields, the de Witts, the
Van Grinkels, and the Steens into the Riverdale marshes. Before he could obtain the Governor-General's seal for the man-
or of Rootborough, he had to execute a treaty with Muscoota,
sachem of the Pudding Rock Indians, whose lands chopped
into Koopal's borders and would have given Rootborough an
unkind (pudgy) shape. The treaty, written in Koopal's hand,
was imperfect, because in spite of his royal ways, Koopal
knew less of the King's English than Muscoota did; together
they came to the following terms (the van der Roots possess
the only clear copy of the treaty's scratches, seals, and pulp):
HENDEYFORTH BEIT KNOWN TO ALL HOME IT MAY
CONSARN, THAT I, LUKAS VAN ROOT, CALL KOO-
PAL, OBLIGE MYSALFE TO PAY MACOOTA SHOOD
HE PERFORMEN HIS PART ACCORDED TO THE BAR-
GEN FOR CONSARNED LAND MANCHENED UNDER-
NEATH, AS FOLLAS: 1 HORS, 1 SADAL, 1 BARREL OF
SIDAR, 6 BITS OF MONEY, 2 KETTLES, 15 GOATS AND
A HALF, 6 SHURTS, 1 SHEPE. AND THIS TO BE PAYD

AT OR BEFORE THE LAST DAY OF FEBRUARY. LU-
KAS; X

I, MACOOTA, HAFE THIS DAY SOLD UNTO LUKAS,
SANER (senior) A SARTEN TRACK OR PARSAL OF
LAND SETUATEN AND LYEN WITH THE PROFENCE
OF NU YORCKE, WHICH LAND BEGINNEN AT THE
PARSAL LASTLY PURCH'D BY LUKAS, AND ALL THE
LAND WASSWARD OR RAT (ROOT) NECK UNPURCH'D
AND SO TO RUN UPWARD TO MACOOTAS REUER (Mus-
coota's River; lately the Harlem) AND DEVILSPIT (Spuyten
Duyvil), AND I MACOOTA DO OBLIGE MYSALFE, MY
ARS (heirs) OR ASSINS (assigns) TO MARCK IT OUTE THE
SEXT, OR SAVENTH DAY OF THIS MUNTH OF FEBRE-
RY: 17012 FOR THE TRU PERFORMANCE I HAFE SAT
MY HAND AND SALE (seal). MUCOOTA; KING; PUD-
DING ROCK; WECKQUOOSGEEK

5. NEUTER BURGH

Only one of Koopal's fourteen children survived him. Gilbrecht van der Root, the child of Koopal's old age (Koopal was
sixty-eight when he married for the fourth and last time), inherited Rootborough and snatches of Morrisania, Fordham,
and Riverdale Ridge in 1739. Gilbrecht was no less of a loyalist
than his father. He whitened his name to Gilbert Root and
formulated the family crest: *Gules six rabbits guardant or.* (Six
goldy rabbits on a red field. The rabbits point sideways and
have blue accessories: tails, tongues, and claws). He wore
periwigs of the finest English horse-hair, he married the young-
est and most treasured daughter of the king's trusty exchequer
of the Americas, and he had Oxford pillions put on his saddles
so that his wife and her lady friends might ride with him.
Although he never once left the colonies and he loved his
pasturage, his barns, his horses, and his woods, the mother
country obsessed him sorely, and he gave over his days to
gossiping with tenant farmers, servants, and his horse doctor
about the seesaws of Parliament, royal mistresses, men's fash-
ions, the queen's politics, and the mood of life "at home."

Like other landed gentlemen of the Bronx, Gilbert served
his king during the French and Indian War. With Ferdinand de
Witt, the lord of Riverdale (Ferdinand's estates began near

Gilbert's western line; this led to constant border frictions with the Rootburghers, since Ferdinand's uncles, cousins, and brothers-in-law had formerly owned a third of Root's Neck), Gilbert joined Col. Sid Yardbole's Virginia & Carolina Phantoms, a band of shaggy colonials who operated out of the Pennsylvania woods. For six straight years Gilbert bushwhacked Indians and French regulars near the forks of the Ohio. He returned to Rootborough in the spring of 1762, a veteran Indian fighter and a morose manorlord; his wife had died of cholera in his absence, and his very best horses caught the mange. This and other circumstances pushed him into close company with Eveline, the horse doctor's girl, during his bereavement. He developed a singular passion for her, and tongues at Rootborough began to wag about "Master Gil" and "the farrier girl." Yet Gilbert shied away from possessing Eveline as his country mistress. He wanted nothing but a wife. Because he had obligations to Geoff, his lawful child (and grandson of an exchequer), and he was disturbed by Eveline's low station, he entered into a morganatic marriage, whereby neither his wife nor her future sons could make any claims on his properties. Eveline bore him three sons in a row, then a daughter who died in infancy. Hervey, her firstborn, was a rawboned, hairy boy; snubbed by Gilbert, who became an ardent Tory and organized a militia at Rootborough after his passion for Eveline dwindled somewhat, Hervey waited hand and foot on the delicate, surly, dripnosed Geoff. Expecting little of his natural father, Hervey learned the art of Farriery from his grandad. He bled Gilbert's mares, cured wind-galls, and diagnosed the yellows with a skill so profound, the gentlemen farmers of the Bronx began to request the services of "the little bastard." Gilbert was too busy exchanging truculent stares and an occasional musket ball with the militia of Ferdinand de Witt (Ferdinand headed the lower Westchester Whigs) to notice Hervey's farrierings.

With the Indians quiet and the French out of the New World for good, the natives no longer cherished the protection of the British crown, and the Whig party in America, like a distempered child, grew techy and full of spleen. After the irascible Americans revolted against the mother country, the isolated Riverdale-Rootborough skirmishes and stare-me-downs developed into mean sniper attacks. When the British regulars captured Manhattan, Gilbert was given command of Root's

Royalists (a small battalion of Westchester refugees loyal to the king), and Ferdinand became a guerrilla in White Plains. The north Bronx was declared a no-man's-land, or "neuter burgh," between the British and American lines. Albeit regulars from both sides roamed the territory and plundered whole manors and single farms. These varmints murdered Eveline and maimed Geoff; and Ferdinand lost two boys. Hervey looked askant at the slogans of the Tories and the Whigs, the cannons, the musketoons, and the frostbitten horses of the king's chasseurs. He quit being a farrier for the course of the war and earned his toabcco handling pigs. He raided military pigpens in Manhattan and other points along the Hudson and he sold British-fed pigs to the Americans, and American-fed pigs to the British.

Returning to Rootborough in 1781, Col. Gilbert found himself without horses, pigs, or cows. His pasturage was ruined, his manorhouse was dunged through with human and fox turds, he had blisters on his lawns. De Witt's Liberty Boys seized him up near his empty barns, fixed a label with the words "Tory Love" on his buttocks, beat him across the forehead with sticks, and drove him into the woods. In 1783 the Whig-packed New York Assembly impounded Rootborough, "on account of the pernicious treason of Gil Root," although the State granted Gilbert and his maimed boy the right to occupy "all outhouses and sheds" adjacent to the south pasture, for a period of eleven years. Ferdinand de Witt, who had been on the winners' side, fared a few stripes better than his neighbor; impoverished, his eyesight gone from too much musket smoke, his teeth rotting in his mouth, he had to sell off great hunks of Riverdale to keep alive. Meantime, Hervey returned to horse-doctoring. The new Whig landlords spited one another to get him near their horses. Whatever the stink of his dead unaristocratic mother and the disavowals of his outhoused father, Hervey had the psychic gifts and stubborn mania of the van der Roots. He could cure a horse of crib-bite by staring at him; he could tell which of a gentleman's colts had gonorrhea without waiting for drips or inspecting any "yards" (farrier term for a horse's prick); he could see bots and worms in a horse's belly. He treated the strangles, convulsions, deafness, pleurisy, the staggers, mange, hide-bound, ring-bone, and wolves-mouth with the same sweet purge (syrup of marshmallow, castile soap, cloves thirty drops, gum arabic, and rattle-snake-root), which he quickened by adding a dram of jalop and either worked into a stiff ball with the help of buckwheat or fed to sick mares through a horn. No horse ever died on Hervey, and thus his reputation as "master farrier & mediciner" roared over Manhattan and the mainland until his countrymen eyed him with envy, wonder, and fear.

As his father had mishandled his education, Hervey decided he would profit from a tour of the Old World. He sailed for Portsmouth in 1785, bypassed London, and settled in Amsterdam for a while. In midwinter he wore bands of wool around his ears and skated on the Y, under the Herring Packers' Tower; he taught Dutchmen at the North Market the virtues of a Bronx walking stick; he stopped a farmer with a balding drayhorse and made him rub butter into the nag's ribs and croup; he played draughts with inmates of *Oudemanhuis* (the dry toothy faces, the botched skin, the cracked eyelids he saw at this old men's house were wholly recognizable to him, and he sat mulling the likenesses of old horses and old men). He gave a sizeable donation to *Maagdenhuis*, a new orphanage for girls; he watched the "river rats" from Frog Leg Bridge ("city of moats, rock islands and moats," he scribbled in his travel book, thinking of the sunken Indian island his grandfather had told him about and of the strip of continent his father had lost). He got to wear buckled shoes and hankies in his coat; he calmed a pack of wild dogs who were nipping a man's heels on the *Schapenplein*; he had one dizzying rendezvous with a servant girl near *Schrierstoren* (Weeping Tower), during which he communicated chiefly with his fingers and his knees; he sought his father's Dutch line within reach of the canals but he found no rightful van der Rootches. On his last day in Amsterdam an embittered vestryman from the *Portugese Synagoge* ran off with his hat, his stick, and his gulden ("the Jew's welcome to them," he noted). Hervey came home to Westchester in the nick of time. He prevented a grubby army of land speculators from buying up all of Rootborough and had the Commissioners of Forfeiture save the manorhouse and the south pasture for himself.

The new lord of Root House brought his maimed ha-brother out of the pasture and imported a young black from Charleston to look after him. The rapprochement between Hervey and Geoff remains something of a curiosity; it seems Hervey forgot his brother's past spitefulness (Geoff would wipe his nose on Hervey's sleeve and tell servants that "bubba Herve" had gone to slobber) and was uncommonly gentle towards him. Hervey, Geoff, and their two "negro men," Yorp and Updike, could often be observed pitching horseshoes on the front lawn, Geoff with a shoe under his dead arm, Hervey using his own body to shield his brother from the sparks that came off the metal hob after a pitch. But Hervey stayed on poor terms with his dad. Col. Gilbert sulked in the outhouse and refused to meet his "pigbreeding boy" (a dig, of course, at Hervey's contributions to the war). So Hervey, who was more Dutch than English or American in his phlegmatic calms, left his father alone and went about ripping off London bricks from his manorhouse and replacing them with blue and yellow Amsterdam clinkers (he also lengthened our name again to *van der Root*). Although he never got the colonel away from the outhouse, he did return our family to its Dutch-American ways. Gilbert died in 1808, sleeping on the privy that he had converted into a captain's bed; he willed his privy, the outhouse, and the pasture wall to his grandson Josh. (The old man skipped a generation trying to catch some family love; Hervey's little boy was the only person the colonel would allow near his bed.) Gilbert exemplified the internecine feuding of the van der Roots, that special rancor our fathers have had for their sons, always coupled with an unchecked devotion to their grandsons. Hervey outdistanced his father, grabbing hold of the family lands without the benefit of an entail (before the colonel's disgrace, Rootborough would have fallen to Geoff); heeding his father's wish, Hervey gave the outhouse over to Josh and buried the colonel in the south pasture.

6.   SLAVEHOLDING IN NEW YORK

The last two slaves in Westchester County, men called Updike and Yorp, belonged to the van der Roots; Updike died in 1819, the holding of slaves having long since been frowned upon by the best families of the County. Hervey van der Root, in his seventies then, was advised to relinquish his other slave. Hervey refused, saying that his negro man was his own affair. In truth, Yorp had lived in Hervey's attic for several decades at least, he had nowhere else to go, and would have considered it the grossest of incivilities if he had been forced to accept a wage from his "mister." He shaved Hervey, he warmed Herv-

ey's bed, he plastered Hervey's ceilings during shortages of
labor, he gilded Hervey's weathercocks, he fished with Hervey's eldest boy Josh, he wired dolls for Hervey's unmarried
daughters, he redecorated the family perambulator for grandchild Ben, and he would have tolerated nothing less or nothing
more. According to the certificate of purchase in Hervey's
keep, Yorp was three years younger than his "mister," and
above all things he respected this seniority in age. For his part,
Hervey preferred the company of Yorp over his wife, his
daughters, his sons, and the other creatures of his estate, except for grandchild Ben. After his seventieth year he no longer
practiced the complicated art of farriery; as a result his wealth
sank bit by bit; while neighbors begged "doctor Herve" to
cure their sick horses of bots, mange, and rheumatisim, Hervey sat in the attic with Yorp and grandchild Ben, playing mum-
ble-peg, backgammon, and nine men's morris. Managing the
estate fell to the boy Josh who was an indifferent farrier and a
lousy farmer; Josh blamed "dad and his nigger" for squaliding
Root Farm.

In 1827 the State Assembly outlawed slaveholding entirely
in New York; frightened by the new decree, Yorp wouldn't
come out of the attic; in his own despair Hervey erupted with
the mange on his eyebrows and scalp, further demonstrating
his theory of correspondences between horses and men. Josh
sent State marshals after Yorp. Hervey, Yorp, and Ben took to
the south pasture for a fortnight, during which Hervey's
friends asked him to resettle in the Carolinas for the good of
lower Westchester. But Hervey allowed that no "whore of a
government" would interfere with him and his man. So he
divided his time between the attic and the fields, and passed
into his eighties. Yorp and Hervey grew incontinent together;
they dunged up the attic and pissed on the stairs. When forks
and spoons proved unreliable, they ate with their hands; when
their hands failed them, they groveled mostly and had their
vittles mashed by Ben. Although he loved them both, Ben
found it difficult to live in the vicinity of their stench. And
Josh, who had a jealous nature, smoldered over his son's at-
tachment to "the two dotards." Fishing around for places that
would keep Ben away from the attic, he decided on Yale, thus
beginning our family's century-and-a-quarter devotion to this
College. Since there were no slaveholders in Connecticut that

Hervey could remember, he didn't follow his grandchild there. Soon Hervey and Yorp had to fend for themselves. Walking they clutched each other's shirt; crawling they mutually watched for bumps. Still, they achieved a kind of fame. The brats of adjacent farms would hog the fences and wait for "Mr. Monkey and Physician Root." One day in 1841 Hervey and Yorp went out to die without announcing this fact to Josh; rewards were offered but nobody could find their deathsite. Westchester historians assume Yorp scratched a single grave for him and Hervey, then lay down with his "mister," and pulled the earth over them somehow, leaving no signs of disturbance; it's also possible that they were eaten by a hungry bear or a wolf in one of the great pits that used to be part of the van der Root estate.

ANDREI CODRESCU

Born: Dec. 1946 in Transylvania, Romania. Came to the U.S. in 1966. Books: *License to Carry a Gun* (Big Table/Follett, 1970), *Grammar & Money* (Arif Press, 1973), *A Serious Morning* (Capra Press, 1973), *The History of the Growth of Heaven* (George Braziller, Inc., 1973), *The Life & Times of an Involuntary Genius* (George Braziller, Inc., 1975—autobiography). Awards: Big Table Younger Poets Award for 1970, Fellowship of the National Endowment for the Arts 1973.

From *Monsieur Teste's 30-Day Sojourn in America*

April 24

I woke up in panic. I thought, for a moment, that Monsieur Teste had stood up his appointment with my destiny, packed his bags and left me, swiftly, in the middle of the night. I was happy to hear him say:

"Your genes are like layers on an onion. None of your ancestors had enough imagination to make himself God."

"Actually," I began, tentatively, "my grandmother . . ."

"Cut the crap," he said, "there's no purposefulness in you."

"You mean purpose?"

"No. I mean 'purposefulness' like stature, like attitude, you know. I have watched you get up in the morning. Every morning is different. Sometimes you wake up feet first, sometimes you lift your head up and, at times, you feel the air with your hands like a cheap viola in search of a Nazi."

"You mean—no consistency?"

"I mean well," he said.

"And yet," I replied pointing to the piles of manuscripts lining the tops of our heads on shelves high enough so the cat wouldn't piss on them, "there is consistency in those. I want to tell the world about the prejudices of my time and how my personality reacted to them."

"Ha Ha HA," said Teste, "you don't even claim resistance —or distance. You are a lost soul."

Looking like a bishop, Teste joined his hands and put the mitre of his tangled fingers on my face. They smelled, slightly, of garlic and asparagus.

*

I worked all afternoon on a *Dictionary of Received Ideas* to spring on Teste when he returned from the walk he had now gotten into the habit of taking by himself. These were some:

If you look at fire long enough you'll pee in bed.
The underground's been forced there by mean weights.
Boys take after their mothers, girls come out of nothing.
The excess of reason makes monsters of boredom.
White flowers are funereal.
Black flowers are exotic.
The academia is taxation without imagination.
Carfax Anthrax.
Perspective is the eminently human point of view.
Don't look back. They might be gaining on you.
Birds filled with lead.
A sense of humor is a sense of authority.
Closeups don't have any sense of humor.
Truth sits in an autobiography like a bird-dog in an
*   underground hospital.*
The Exterminator is after the facts.
A man's name is his cage.
A miracle is the shortest explanation.

Intuition is the daughter of miracles.
Baby irony is transcendental.
Geriatric irony is worldly.
Worlds meet at ironic junctions; the resulting clash
  is a miracle.
Jews wander.
Mommy means I want. Money means I don't need her.
Heraldry is a structural horniness.
The penis is a barricade.
Poetry is mistranslation.
Being a man saves you money.
A discovery is followed by silence not applause.

I wrote many more of these but when Teste came home I didn't dare show them to him for fear he would open the refrigerator door and say nothing. Teste is not rude, he is just superior. Without him, I wouldn't even know there are better things in the world.

*

Teste is a gourmet. I won't even mention all the things he brings home from his walks: fragments of old fire-escapes, snails, dirty socks.

*

There was a poem in the newspaper that evening. Monsieur Teste & I read it together:

It's tough to be doing what you don't
find easy
It's easy it's really easy
To do what you want
The body takes the lead
over the head
the heart swings the whip
the body is hip
the head is dead

I expected Teste to fly out in a rage. "Teste" means *head* and I thought the poem insulted this part of the body.

Instead, Teste was rather pleased. He said that "teste" does not mean *head* but *taste.*

*

I thought I noticed a spark of eroticism in Teste. But I was mistaken. He was merely sticking his tongue in and out of his mouth to see how far it would go.

FIELDING DAWSON

I was born in New York on August 2nd, 1930, but was raised
in Kirkwood, Missouri. I went to Black Mountain College
from 1949 until 1953 when I was drafted, and spent a year
and a half in Germany, was shipped home and separated in
1955 and after spending a year in Kirkwood, in 1956 I came
to New York for keeps. I am the author of eight published
books, including *An Emotional Memoir of Franz Kline, The
Black Mountain Book, The Mandalay Dream, A Great Day
for a Ballgame,* and most recently, *The Sun Rises Into The
Sky.* A book of essays, *Hard, Fast, and Beautiful,* is forthcoming as is a book of new stories, *The Man Who Changed
Overnight.* My wife and I live in a lovely loft on the east side
in the teens.

Lavender Blue Lady

The young woman sat at the end of the bar near the door.
She was drinking a straight up martini with a twist of lemon,
and it sparkled in the sunlight from the front window.
She was thin and very tall, dressed mostly in lavender and
she flowed like something smoky. Her slender fingers fiddled
with the stem of the glass. The big stone on her finger winked
in the sunlight.
Her hair was long and silky and the color of light coffee. Her
skull was narrow, her eyes were big, dark, and heavy lidded,
and she wore false eyelashes. Her long nose stuck out like a
puppet's. Her cheeks were shallow but her lips were full, and
painted white. Under her tan she had a pretty bad case of acne.
Dark glasses lay beside her white handbag on the bar.
The way she sat we saw her whole right leg: the flowing
dress she wore parted to show her white panties, and her leg
looked about ten feet long, long tan and terrific.
Ten after two in a blue afternoon. We had stopped in the
terminal bar for a couple of cool ones.
The big Pan American jets crouched on the tarmac beyond.
Four dumpy businessmen in gray and brown double breast-
ed suits stood behind us drinking Miller's, and the bartender,
the other person in the place, was a middleaged bald man in
gray slacks, a white shirt and pink-pattern tie sitting on the

edge of the sink by the beer taps, looking out the front window, and occasionally at the tall long-legged smoke-lady. I could see his left eye dart.

She raised the glass. It drifted to her lips, and she emptied it down her throat as Lady Jekyll, lowered her head as she swallowed, and slid the glass forward and looked down at the bartender. Their eyes met, and he rose to his feet as she smiled and nodded, another, please.

"We'll get that," I said. The bartender looked at me, and then at Flap, and then down to the young woman. She nodded again, shyly, and after looking at us, he made the drink, took it to her and when he came back we paid him. She turned, and raising the drink to us, she said thanks.

"Thanks," she repeated, outwardly.

We nodded and smiled. You're welcome. She sipped the drink and turned to look out the front window.

Flap said, Well Bugs. What do you think?

She doesn't look very happy, I said, and we looked at the clock on the wall, finished our drinks, tipped the bartender, and hefting our luggage as he said so long, we walked to the door, passing the lavender blue lady as we went, through an aura of her delicate perfume. Take care, we said.

You take care, too, she said. "Thanks!" she called, so as to make sure. We all laughed, and outside in the corridor as we walked, Flap said, Bugs, you saw she was crying.

I nodded, and said, I thought that's why we bought her the drink. Did you see her legs? Jesus. We stopped walking. I said,

Things happen fast. Do you think we should have stayed a minute?

Shall we go back? Flap asked, and as of one mind, we retraced our steps to the bar. But no one vanishes faster than women who want to vanish, and we stood there like a couple of actors in a brand new play. Noticing everything. Her glass was empty, and as if on the surface of the fragile water floor of her delicate scent, and long-legged lavender vision, we saw twenty-three cents on the bar. We looked around the place. The gray and brown Miller men had left too, and the bartender was fast asleep. As we walked out into the corridor, and toward the local security cops, Flap said,

Too bad. She reminds me of someone, or is she someone of one?

Yes, I said. That's it. Of us, perhaps. I hope she feels better.

Wonder where she's going?
  Home, Flap said. That's where.
  Jesus, I said.

M. D. ELEVITCH

M(orton). D. Elevitch hastens to add. Roundabout rockbound Palisades New York, now. From stern beginnings
Duluth 1925 to avant-garde raillery Tirolo (Pound's castle)
1958, avoiding definition. Then devised *First Person*, "the
literature of personality," and co-mingled ALMA, Association of Literary Magazines of Amerca. Has since spent time
with self but expects full and capricious amnesty. Contribu-
tor of fiction, criticism, cartoons to various/many incl. *Audience, Trace, Chelsea, Lillabulero; Tri-Quarterly, New
Voices, Granite,* Spring 1975; New Departures in Fiction,
anthology edited by Robert Bonazzi (Latitudes Press, early
1975). Novel Grips *Or, Efforts to Revive the Host* (Grossman, 1972).

The Whale's Equation

"STAND UP STRAIGHTER," Wadleigh commanded the
frail young man oddly belted and crisscrossed with canisters
and frayed bedding rolls. He'd sat beside him on the bus from
the airport into Anchorage. So much of a heap was he Wadleigh's own precise feet had protruded into the aisle upsetting a
shambling comatose woman whose words were spattering
shale. "Move those feet *in!*" It was a craggy, rockbound voice,
typical of craggy rockbound continental shores—he'd encoun-
tered one last in Nova Scotia though this had a special urgency
as though it was due to crumble. He poked his meter. "In
where?" was his gruff return, never looking above the skirts,
sending the woman crashing into another victim at the rear.
Bipeds had not developed retractability, the population crisis
at least was nowhere near that stage, certainly not in this climate; and the man crowding him, sensing with not a little
intimidation that he had precipitated the disturbance, began to

smirk and laugh in embarrassment and had even pushed up his
yellowed fur hat with the thick black goggles straddling the
visor. "Displacement," Wadleigh had explained. "Scrapped
for wings and wheels our feet lie fallow and bloated. They get
kicked." He rubbed the streaked leather with a reddish, liver-
spotted hand. His instrument ticked merrily sinking into its
wedge of corduroy crotch. He licked his lips to relieve his
bladder. Displacement. This journey was a long one to the
alluvial outlands of the north. This man must have fleas; the
dial showed red alert. It wasn't that at all: the bus was moving.

"Lofty thoughts, lofty head," declared Wadleigh, still un-
raveling the companion. The fresh exposure to the snapping
air started him sneezing. He withdrew his lengthy red bandana
handkerchief and drove it into his nostrils in the manner of
Allen Goatherd, the poet, who had participated in a sympo-
sium with him at Queen Elizabeth Hall. That man was extremely composed flailing his wad of cloth; the design was
paisley, in the best of taste. Wadleigh had himself fitted for a
set of blue overalls and suspenders but they never would stay
in place on the spindly shoulders, not even with clothespins
attached and weighted in due time by roosting fowl. He'd had
to discard the whole clustering contagion. Now he was reminded of it by the man leading him through the broad, empty
thoroughfares of the flat city toward a remarkable silver range
of mountains rising to the north. The man's accoutrements
flapped in time to his self-generated gusts like Tibetan prayer
flags. Wadleigh dodged them, his agate eyes rolling toward the
gleaming turquoise heaped row after row in every window. In
every doorway the substance was displayed on clipboards.
And before one was a coke bottle molded of turquoise, elon-
gated and slightly sloped. Wadleigh was instantly, totally refreshed. At last the unrelenting pace brought them beyond the
shops and buildings to the critical gravelly meat. Seabirds cir-
cled; they had found the shore.

"Invern." The man suddenly whirled. "Some call me
Lyle." He swayed, creaking and crunching, toward the shorter Wadleigh.

"You're used to this." Wadleigh admired stamina. He
dragged out his bandana, winding it about his device to warm it
until it was needed.

"Oh, yeah. I got a bellyful at Katmandu—that's where I

started out." He reached into a bag, popped a cork and spurted a gray stream through his scraggly beard. "I'd offer you a drink but it's Jap water. Had a yen for it."

Wadleigh felt his blood seething and gurgling; he was in circuit. "Good. That was amusing. You're kin to Basic. He was pun a minute. Now he's converted."

"Basic?"

"His tribal name. I am basic. Made it Basic Hyam, that was slippage, but he'll outgrow it. Mine's Hannibal. Give me the flask."

"You spat my water!"

"A benediction. Like to like. I'd give you the story, but you're young, you can wait. You live here?"

"New Mexico."

"Albuquerq, is it."

"No, over near Arizona. I squat there."

"That's right, you and Basic, he's in California. On the line. Uncommitted. It's spatial biology. I'd give you the story but first let me supply you the dimensions. Peterboy's in Mexico. She's a compulsive buyer. Hope she'll buy pots. Cracked ones. The more cracks the closer she'll be to epicenter. You look uncomfortable."

"Sir, something's in the air here."

"Lyle, you are face to face with a superb specimen of uplift. Look with me." His hand raked at the bay drably indenting the coast all the way back toward Anchorage and its harbor so steady and low it wavered out of sight beyond a bend. The sky everywhere was milk-gray, bulging to drizzle. Directly before them tremendous shafts of fractured granite stood at tortured angles and on each of them, shining eerily, were broad black bands of dead and dying matter from the old water line. "Your Jap water—it's either a new forewarning or the last of the old wave. A mini-*tsunami* . . . The crescendo was back in '64. Anchorage was no longer a safe harbor! Irony, I'm conveying, Lyle. Displacement."

"What's that?"

"What's which that?" Wadleigh-Hannibal was cross. "Gauge's seismicity, this does. You won't find another like it." It lolloped in his hand.

"No, the smell!" Invern began to caper and exclaim in the other direction. Gagging sounds came from his throat, as though the Jap water was getting in its knocks.

"What is that—nose-think? Let me adjust this and I'll tell you what you're saying. I'm getting a lot of interference." There was a low hum and a sprig of white tape began to unfold from a slot. Wadleigh-Hannibal raised it until it resembled a forkful of noodles. "Magnificent. I never would have judged you had it in you." Fascinated, he used his cloth to wipe away foreign matter and moisture from the slot, thereupon disrupting his concentration on the reading. A supplementary register would interpret in the event of distractions; its preliminary name—and he stooped to record it with bold swipes on his knee—would be MOBILE RELATIVITY FOOTNOTER. Now, then, where was the subject: how had it been misplaced? He pounded his mackinaw for his emergency moose whistle but somehow, in rushing from the bus terminal, he'd left it with his gear.

Invern meanwhile was astride a boulder, his goggles down, ferociously crooking one arm around his face and gesticulating wildly with the other. "It's coming . . . It's taking off . . .!"

"Contain your enthusiasm, Lyle." Wadleigh-Hannibal jogged his attention. "I'm giving this a rerun. We may be onto a true force field and if that is so, we dig."

"Yeah, dig plenty. We got us a dead whale."

Hannibal saw the looming spectacle and flexed his feisty brow. Why had this unsavory carcass preempted his destination? Clearly, it was an overload. Clearly, the occasion would burst its ecological seams and the gulf yawn. Or it was a gigantic, self-inflating trial balloon. What better proof for his theories: it had come to the exact spot where he would bore! But he had to be sure, the alternatives were crucial: WHAT WAS THE EQUATION OF THE WHALE?

The whale was properly awesome, bulbous and blunt, stretching with darkening luster to the inlet's unseen mouth. In that cramping cove it was strangely tranquil, already bloating the wrinkles from an extraordinary white forehead speckled with birds. They seemed to cluster at the dried slime of a futile sounding. Water boomed and frothed, rocking him voluminously off-center, moiling the birds, which screeched and fought the updrafts each time he dipped one clouded, austere eye.

Lyle suddenly pitched forward and scrambled along the slippery, white-stained slope approaching the creature, groaning and beseeching it with his litter of private bundles. "Oh, you mother . . ." he screamed in nauseous ecstasy. "Pull the plug! "

Hannibal at once mounted the abandoned boulder and swiveled toward the road where two men tumbled from a yellow Range Rover truck. The news had traveled with volcanic speed. They were laden with cameras, lights, gasmasks, bristling and complex, advancing on high flashing hunting boots in twin vectors of reportorial persistence. Hannibal positioned himself with his usual stern demeanor to receive these fortunate strangers. His testy tool twitched from fist to lap. He saw the leader was a burly Indian wrapped in a straggling fake fur and was not at all surprised, as his mouth triangulated an oracular greeting, to see the man fling away his equipment and fall quaking to his knees. A dreadful, diminishing cry echoed far away from Lyle. Hannibal promptly reared back and decanted a whale. His cranial ridges were aflame. High above them, in ghastly pallor, rose a vast, oblivious dome.

RAYMOND FEDERMAN

is the author of the novel *Double or Nothing.* He writes in both French and English. His most recent novel, *Amer Elderado*, was just published in France. In addition to fiction, Raymond Federman has published a critical work on Samuel Beckett. He teaches at the University of Buffalo. This present piece is from his new novel, *Take It or Leave It.*

setting & tripping

First, I'll tell the first trip the way he told it to me.

I'll tell the first time first—THE GREAT JOURNEY as he called it.

Just the way he told it to me (approximately of course or if you prefer as best I can)!

Not exactly the way it happened but the way he told it to me on several occasions.

But don't ask me WHERE and WHEN and HOW because it really doesn't matter much where and when and how he told me the whole story!

> Of necessity I must rearrange his tale,
> substitute my own voice for his voice,
> my person for his person,
> and even, at times, my self for his self!

> Fill in the gaps, in other words!

For there are many things which I have forgotten, many things which cannot be told, many things which are not tellable, many things of unspeakable nature!

Therefore I reconstruct
> I invent (a little)
> I distort
> I simulate
> I dissimulate
> I suggest
> I exaggerate

I DO MY BEST (if you know what I mean) after all I'm only here to report!

I'm only a second-hand teller!

And in those days I was only there to listen. I did not witness. I did not experience. I only heard!

Thereforepleasestopbuggingmewithallyourfuckingquestionsleavemealonewait!
Listen!

. . . ?

The first time?   Good!   The great discovery . . . The first trip?

That'swhat hecalled it!
That'swhat I'llcall it!

Make believe that it was me that it happened to me that I was
there that it is my story that it's me speaking that I'm appropri-
ating his words in other words
that that that . . . And so here we go!   Make believe!

The funniest (he began) is that I had no idea where I was going
(that's for damn sure!), no idea what America was all about
(who does?), geographically speaking (that is), no idea particularly of the size. Yes! Endless spaces and tremendous colors.
Wow! Unbelievable the colors and the spaces (isn't he something?) You've got to see that to believe it. At least once—
once in a lifetime (if not more!) And distances —— distances
that never end — ENORMOUS distances —— between
places!

                                             Ah what places!
We're getting there . . . Wait!   Between people too!
                                             Between words also!
And all these people (all these words) all of them Americans
who look (what a way to start!) at you, who scare you shitless
(sic)
                    who scare the hell out of you because they too are
scared
scared to move
scared to speak
scared to screw
scared to let themselves go (most of them, I added)
scared to be to be proud mad insolent delirious talkative
     (right on!)
scared to be to be   (or not to be)   to be . . . . . .

(What a two-bit philosopher!)

FIRST TRIP then (we're getting there . . .)

I didn't even know where to begin
In which direction to go
how I was supposed to get started
how to get going

to go from one end to the other—from the EAST COAST to
                                    the WEST COAST—
                                    from coast-to-coast man—
                                    and *prompto!*
BLAH BLAH BLAH . . . ?   [Soft shy voice]
Why?
That's a good one. Because . . . just because . . . he was really
dumb, really dumb in those days (no! not really dumb, naive
rather and enormously shy at that time, but that's not a
crime!) and quite inexperienced in our American way of life.
But that's not his fault. First trip, remember (I mention it again
not to confuse it with other trips). Was I timid in those days
(he'd say to me), but that's not a sin. Happens to a lot of guys.
And also ALSO I didn't know I DIDN'T KNOW a damn thing
at that time I was young (twenty I think he said at the most)
just twenty (not even) but AMERICA yes AMERICA I had
already three years of it behind me yes THREE YEARS [I tell
you] and UP to here FED UP above the head and plein le dos .
. .

GRRRRR GRRRRR . . . ? [In a kind of mumbling between the
teeth]
How he came?   But by boat . . . by BOAT of course.   You
guys are really something!

Yes but this time I was going to discover IT—America
                          to see IT close—America
                          to dive into IT—America   (once
and for all you might say) Because up to this point ME—
America! I hadn't seen much of it. Two years in Detroit (yes
DETROIT—you guys seem surprised!), and then approximately (more or less) one year in NEW YORK (city) What a
place!

SHID SHID SHID SHID . . . ?   [With a certain ironic smile]
Why did he stay?   Because . . . because AMERICA
(gentlemen) it's a bit like a drug: the more you're there the
more you want to stay, the more you touch it the more you
want it, the more you get used to it the more you dig it, the
more you dig it the more you want it to force you to dig it, it
grows on you, and so on, the more you want to take advantage

of it, and the more you dream about the great fabulous things
that are going to happen (to you). And at the same time the
more you feel like dropping the whole thing immediately, like
giving up, like screwing it all, like taking off, cutting out on the
spot, full speed, and tell America to shove it, to go, anywhere:
AFRICA (for instance), yes Dakar, Timbuktu, anywhere:
CHINA (even). Like a drug! For the birds (you might say!),
believe me, AMERICA pour les oiseaux (messieurs)! Yes, it's
just a matter of TAKE IT OR LEAVE IT (damn right) I tell
you! Takes a good ten years (and even more) to get used to it.
What! Twelve or fifteen or more, to get used to it (and even
then)! And even if you've taken it, even if you've hung on, for
a good ten years or twelve or fifteen or more (depending I
suppose on your temperament) you never really get used to it,
and even if you do, even when you think you are used to it and
it begins to be better (or worse, quite worse), even though it
appears to be better, it's only an illusion, a joke, an ENOR-
MOUS joke, a fake, and yet they think it's better, they think
it's okay, at least that's what the people imagine (those jerks
who have not taken off or killed themselves) I mean all the
lousy foreigners who came to America their heads full of shit
full of dreams!

Most guys who arrive in America suffer at least ten or twelve
years in the beginning (that is to say 99%), and since most
Americans (100% in fact) at one time or another (originally)
come from a foreign country that means in fact that 99% of
these people suffer at least for a good ten years or more before
getting used to America, therefore it means that only 1% (the
upper crust) doesn't suffer like the rest, and these are the guys
THE LUCKY ONES who arrive with lots of money, all kinds
of wealth, or who have rich families in America (American
uncles loaded with dough—millionaires) whereas the rest of
them (the 99% under crust) they have nothing, they just are
fucked from the beginning, and for them it's just a matter of
taking it or leaving it, like a bunch of IDIOTS, just like that,
without ever asking if it means anything, without ever asking
themselves what the fuck this whole shit is all about, what the
hell they're doing here working their asses to the bone a good
eight or ten hours a day in shit holes, for nothing, not a damn
thing, or else, eventually, for the birds!

But me, poor slob, I had it UP to here, three years already,
three years I had of America behind me, and I hadn't understood a damn thing yet NOTHING
Absolutely nothing!

> I arrived (just like that) by boat
> and there she was AMERICA (big and
> fat and beautiful like a cow) just
> standing there and I looked at her
> and I wondered (in the beginning a
> bit puzzled as I stood on the pier
> in my old outmoded double-breasted
> blue suit) without understanding a
> damn thing of what it meant (and I
> stood there like an ass a poor shy
> Jewish emigrant) to be here (alone
> on the platform) my head bent down
> towards my hands (not even crying)
> simply asking myself what the fuck
> am I doing here (in French of cour
> se) with my beat-up suitcase at my
> feet with my stuff spilling out of
> it like a pile of dirty laundry on
> the platform (and AMERICA in front
> of me nervous excited ready) and I
> suddenly feeling like jerking off!

> Absolutely nothing!

B. H. FRIEDMAN

is the author of four previously published novels, *Circles,
Yarborough, Whispers,* and *Museum.* He has also written
several art monographs and the biography *Jackson Pollock:
Energy Made Visible,* one of the year's Notable Books se-
lected by the American Library Association. The present
selection is from his forthcoming novel, *Almost a Life.*

From *Almost a Life*

I wanted to be exactly on time. Partly because punctuality would seem neutral. Partly because, on this story, I had preconceived ideas about a man who works within hundredths of a second. At 3:59, just before getting into the elevator of the loft building where Jeff MacMaster had his studio, I squinted at my wristwatch, a gift from my wife Jennifer. The numbers weren't large and clear enough for someone as nearsighted as I am; nevertheless I loved its subtle face and thin elegance—Jennifer's image of me and, I suppose, mine too.

It took a minute for the heavy doors to close and for the elevator to lift me to the fourth floor. Minutiae ran through my mind—the preliminary research that would contribute to a good interview. I carried a tape-recorder, confident that he would let me use it. How could a photographer object to another mechanical recording device? But just in case, a notebook was in my pocket.

The elevator doors opened directly into the studio. MacMaster was on a stool, with his enormous back to me, bent over a large table supported by filing cabinets. He straightened up and turned around. I expected the face I knew from photographs, but it was almost hidden by a full gray beard, which itself was partially hidden by the phone he held.

"C. E. Wilton," I announced.

"Just a minute," he said into the phone, then lifting his head: "Make yourself at home."

"All right if I look around?"

"Sure. That's what *I* do." He grinned and turned back to the table.

One end of the studio was set like a stage, a sectional platform with lighting above and a plain canvas backdrop behind. On either side and in front were several flood lamps and tripods, some with cameras on them, and against one wall a couple of mattresses, a table, some folding chairs, and what looked like a rolled-up gym mat. All this surprised me. I had never seen a picture by MacMaster that looked staged. Everything I knew was candid and immediate. I couldn't imagine him making official portraits or working with props and models.

In profile, MacMaster's head was a gray mass of hair from

which brow and nose protruded, eyes receded. He was talking to someone—his agent, I guessed—about a job in Los Angeles. Only once did he raise his voice: "Five thousand's not enough. . . . No, Abe, not even with expenses. . . . Fuck the expenses."

By then I had hurried to the other end of the studio. There three rooms were partitioned off: a bedroom (with an adjoining bath and an open kitchen/bar/counter on the wall just outside the bedroom door); across from it, a darkroom and a printing room. In the bedroom something else surprised me: the number of books. I had thought that photographers didn't read. This one did. It was a serious library, heavy, some topical stuff, some picture books including those of MacMaster's own photographs, but mostly beat-up standard editions of the great poets, philosophers, novelists—Oxford, Everyman, Viking Portable, Modern Library, quality paperbacks. . . . I took it in at a glance, the way writers do. Nothing of mine was there.

On the walls outside these rooms were pictures from every period of MacMaster's career, the early work done in New York and Hollywood, the Depression and war photographs, the self-portraits made throughout his life and later collected in his book with the punning title *I*. Many of the pictures I knew. Others were variations, a camera's click away. Still others I didn't know at all. Of these, two looked as if taken in the studio. One was a recent self-portrait, all gray hair with a life of its own, more life than appeared in MacMaster's tired sunken eyes or pitted nose. It suggested hair growing on the head of a corpse, but it also reminded me of a nearby early photograph of his first wife, Susan Atwell, resting between takes: the interest again in the hair itself, its vitality and protective quality.

The other studio-photograph was of a naked, teen-aged girl on her back on a mattress. The picture must have been shot from above, perhaps from a ladder, but it was still intimate, really naked, not nude. I could feel the texture, the warmth, the moist freshness of her flesh. I could smell its fragrance, taste its sweetness, hear its heartbeat. I could share what must have been MacMaster's own lust for her exquisite budding body, all gentle curves against the rigid striped ticking of the mattress. Yet I felt something too that was nowhere in the picture—a vague embarrassment like that which had made me hurry past MacMaster's table, knowing I was overhearing something.

"Sorry," MacMaster said, hanging up the phone. "The rest of the day's clear. How about a drink?"

Until he got up I had not noticed that there were several empty beer cans on the table, among prints, negatives, magazines, correspondence, scissors, rulers, cigars, cigarettes, matches, ashtrays, jars of paper clips and pens and pencils and marking crayons—all this, except for one full ashtray, pushed back. In the resulting crescent of clutter, the beer cans stood out.

But now I focused on him and could really see him, standing. The beard had been a small surprise. His size was a big one. I had expected two hundred pounds or so. He must have been closer to three hundred. I had expected the athletic build I knew from early photographs. He was mostly stomach, a great tub extending from chest to legs, in a curve constricted only by his belt. Even slightly stooped, he was six-four—only about two inches taller than I am—but twice my weight. He put his heavy hand on my shoulder and led, almost pushed, me toward the refrigerator. It contained mostly six-packs of beer, a piece of cheese, part of a loaf of bread and, on the upper shelf, bourbon, soft drinks, a milk bottle filled with water. He pointed at the beer and bourbon.

"Developer. Character developer."

He grinned as he had when saying, "That's what *I* do." I was memorizing these remarks, while waiting for an opportunity to ask about using the tape-recorder, when he said, "What'll you have?"

"Beer's fine."

"In moderation." Now he laughed. "Everything in moderation. Life in moderation. . . . What do you want to know?"

"Okay if I use this?" I held up the recorder.

"Sure. But you're making a mistake. I don't say much that's worth recording. You'll have to do a lot of editing. Wouldn't it be easier to do while we talk?"

"Yes, easier but less accurate. I could ask almost the same thing: Why do you take so many more pictures than you publish?"

I set up the recorder and turned on the switch. The spool was spinning when MacMaster, back on his stool, replied:

"Publication's a separate issue. I can't sell all the pictures I take. But mostly I know if a picture's right, when I take it. What you're doing is more like a motion picture—of words. In Hollywood they shoot ten, twelve, even twenty times what ultimately gets shown. The ratio of pictures I'm satisfied with is better than that; but not of pictures sold. I doubt if I've averaged one in a hundred."

"Have you ever thought about making a movie?"

"Sure. Hasn't everyone? Haven't you?"

"For me, writing a novel would be that kind of fantasy."

"Would it? A biography maybe. I've read you in *Manhattan*. I didn't guess you'd want to write a novel. If I had, I wouldn't be here talking to you. What I like about your work is the respect for facts, for what you see and hear."

I was pleased that he knew my work. Though as far back as college I'd dreamed of writing a novel, I thought it best not to say any more about that. Nor did I deliver the obvious lecture on the fact in fiction.

"So, if you'd made a movie, it would have been a documentary?"

"All movies are documentaries." I must have looked puzzled. "What I mean is all photographs are documents, and of course a movie is just a series of still photographs. The great movies, the masterpieces, are the ones in which every frame works, thousands of them. As against that, think of a little book like *I*. What is it, a hundred and ten photographs?"

"A hundred and twelve."

Maybe he was testing me. Anyway, he seemed to like my correction.

"A hundred and twelve," he repeated, almost whispering the number to make it sound small. "On the screen that would last what, five seconds?"

This time I didn't answer. I didn't know. Until now frames-per-second had not been part of my assignment.

He waited, then said, "*Say*, five seconds. One twelfth of a minute out of, *say*, ninety minutes." He was having fun, like a child who knows the answers in class. "Less than one thousandth of a masterpiece. A finger from the Venus de Milo. A finger *nail*. Van Gogh's ear. His ear *lobe*."

He got off the stool and trudged to the refrigerator, muttering something neither caught by me nor (I discovered later) by the tape recorder. The next word on tape, almost shouted, is "Another?" It was a word, a question which would come up often.

I shook my head—I hadn't finished my first—but he returned with two anyway.

"Just in case," he said, as you hear the cans go down on the table and the sizzling pop of one being opened. "It's frightening to imagine having to make one perfect shot after another for an hour and a half, which means *trying* for fifteen to thirty hours—not including hundreds of preparatory hours. God, to work at that rate, compared with one hundred and twelve good pictures taken over roughly thirty-five years!"

His teeth showed yellow in a grin: he was still proud of his arithmetic. And yet there was something self-denigrating about the performance, something specious about the reasoning. I said:

"That's just one book. What about the others, and the newspaper and magazine work?"

"Altogether maybe they total a thousand good photographs. That's still only a fraction of the total in one good movie. But my decision wasn't esthetic—there were other factors. I don't really believe in collaborative art. Nice theory, but I've never heard of a great movie, or novel, or play, or symphony made by more than one person. Movies may seem communal, but the great directors were all dictators, and I'm not. Same is true of architects—they always come up in these discussions—but even with the great cathedrals, there must have been some master builder in charge, someone to lay things out.

"Anyway, Hollywood didn't look right. For me. And something else. Movies were Susan's thing. My first wife," he explained. I nodded, knowingly. "That was her world: the clutter, the activity. Mine was stills. She could have gotten me a job, but I didn't want to move into her world. I wanted her to move into mine. Not that I ever asked her to give up her career. That was her idea, that and children and homes. . . . Other actresses have had kids and gone on acting, even some who started having kids late. When we met, she had everything but children."

"If you hadn't met, if it hadn't been like going into your wife's business, do you think you would have made a movie?"

"No, the other reasons were more important. But I suppose if I had been given an assignment to do anything on any subject that interested me—some novel, some theme—I would have done it."

"A novel? I thought you didn't like fiction."

"I wouldn't want it to be made out of *my* life. I don't want anyone guessing about what I did, or said, or thought, or felt. But I like fiction when it's made out of an author's own life."

"Still you would have preferred to make a documentary?"

"Not necessarily. And not as narrowly as the word is used. I said before that all films are documentaries. I meant bad ones as well as good. You can learn a lot from bad mvies. They rely more on the clichés of a given moment—not only in dialogue and plot but in staging, costuming, sets, everything. Of course one can learn still more from the good ones. *The Gold Rush* says a lot about the twenties just as *It's a Gift* says a lot about the thirties. But neither Chaplin nor Fields needed me. They wrote their material *and* visualized it. I would like to have visualized something that needed me. *The Man Who Was Thursday* would make a great film. So would 'Swann in Love.' All of Proust would be too much, the way all of The Twentieth Century would be too much."

"Well, what about *those* films? Do you regret not making them?"

He waited a long time before answering. He must, with a motion of his hand, have reoffered me the second can of beer and, when I again refused, opened it for himself. There is another small sizzling explosion on the tape.

"If I'd made a movie I wouldn't have done something else. No, I don't have any regrets, none about the past anyway. I have present regrets."

He closed his eyes—it was the first time I had seen him do it —squinting down deliberately and without any suggestion of weariness, as if seeking an answer in less and less light, somewhere deep inside.

"Yes, my regrets are in the present. I'm drinking more—in the present. I'm getting fatter—in the present. I'm working less—in the present. I'm fucking less—in the present. I'm dying—in the present. It's all in the present. That's the only tense there is. I've built my life on it. Like everyone, sometimes I need a change of tense. Historical romance. Science fiction. I like looking at old pictures of me and at things I've seen long ago. I like looking at history. But I also like looking at the future. I like looking at young bodies before they become fat. . . . I like looking at the present, even if it no longer belongs to me.''

. . . I said goodnight and got into a cab. I didn't feel I had to explain cutting the evening short. I knew there would be other nights. Jeff was already part of my life. His wife Edys was moving into it, emerging from his shadow.

On the cab's windshield deck a family picture was propped —the driver, a wife, a son, a daughter—a family like mine in a crowded living room like mine, all smiling and bright in the Polaroid flash.

I preferred continuing to watch the city nightscape pass, more and more quickly now, dizzyingly, as the driver swung into the park toward my apartment in the East Nineties. The cubistic composition of dark and bright masses seemed suddenly to have what all the kids these days were calling "mystical significance." The park was the heart of a mandala, a great mirror in which I could see both myself and beyond myself, interior and exterior landscape, a landscape with which I identified and from which I remained detached. Despite my drunkenness, or perhaps because of it, I realized— not really for the first time but never before more clearly—that a biographical subject, too, is a sort of mandala into which one looks, concentrating over long periods of time, for both the other person and himself. With effort, in the semidarkness of the moving cab, I wrote the single word *mandala* on my pad, where it remains really no more or less decipherable than those words about the *animal who has locked himself in a cage and one who has been locked there.*

What did I know about MacMaster? What would I ever know? That he had great vitality and that, at the same time, he had ceased being really productive. That he was open, seemingly without secrets, and that he hid behind his garrulousness. That he was a pro and a lush. That his life was "free" and that he'd made a mess of it. . . . Dozens of such contradictions— aspects, again, of identification and detachment; aspects of humanity, of our mutual humanity—went through my mind.

But then, as the cab left the park, I lost my "vision." I came down to earth, thinking about the fare and getting my wallet out. I left a state of something like transcendence and, for the last few blocks, returned to this world of mundane comparisons. I had always been proud of my professionalism and had clung to that in the face of artistic ambitions which, if grander and more human, had still at times seemed not to require the same degree of discipline I exercised in my work. But every time I had comforted myself with such thoughts, a Picasso or a Stravinsky or a Chaplin (the indefinite article is not literal, but self-protective)—and now a MacMaster—had come along to remind me that there is a life which includes professional discipline but goes as far beyond that as professionalism itself goes beyond talent—into reaches of heart, mind, will, and courage I had never thoroughly explored, even in others. I left the cab thinking that MacMaster even drank better than I did.

Jennifer was asleep. I was glad of that. I didn't want to talk, didn't want to expose my feelings of inadequacy and mediocrity. I wished only that I too could sleep—and perhaps dream a masterpiece about Jeff and Edys which would appear miraculously under my pillow in the morning. But for a long time I couldn't sleep. The two of them remained in my mind, "bigger than life," as they say—or if, by definition, that's impossible, bigger than *my* life. My life, floating like a twist of lemon peel in a sea of martinis. My life as mediocre writer, mediocre husband, mediocre father. . . . My life halfway up the mountain. A literary joke. Like me. But tomorrow, I kept telling myself, I would scale the highest peak. . . . I must have fallen asleep not realizing that tomorrow had arrived.

ISRAEL HOROVITZ

"is a young man, so nice, so charming, a tender American hoodlum. As soon as you meet him, you must like him.

"Like all the tender ones, like all the sweet ones, he writes the cruelest things there are. And these are real works. Israel Horovitz is at the same time sentimental and realistic. One can imagine to what point he can be ferocious.

"I'm not going to explain or present his play to you, rest assured. I will only say that it's loose, it has no action, nothing happens. Nothing except everything.

"Put two men together, then three, single file, then four, then five. Introduce a woman among them. After a few moments, the competition, the conflict, surfaces. The unknowns become known to each other, profoundly, and because they know each other, they hate each other, mistrust each other, and fight for first place [of course], they lose and retake it, and lose it again. Time after time. They're ready to kill each other, even ready to die, first, if it is the only way to be first.

"In *Line* [le 1ᵉʳ], Israel tells us all, which is nothing. I leave you to discover this. I can't tell you how very much I liked this play. But let me be the first to say it."—Eugene Ionesco

Nobody Loves Me

ONE

There seems little point in continuing. There was a time when it all seemed in order. No more. All gone now. I am holding my dog's leash and I cannot even recall how ugly he was. I named him for Murphy. His name was Murphy. I called *Murphy.* An old fisherman unclenched his eyes, scowled at me. I avoided his face neatly, turned straight around, walked on down the beach screaming *Murphy Murphy Murphy* as though I could see the bastard. No point to it at all. He was gone. I had his leash. That was something. I can't remember precisely how ugly he was, but I can report that he was ugly. In the past five years I've collected these cursory insults.

1. Ugly dog there.
2. A man and his dog grow to look alike.
3. What blend is he?
4. Your dog has character.
5. Is that a dog or what?

The really painful slur came from one of the whores who lived in the tenement next door.

Whore: I really like your dog.

I am truly amazed to be alone out here on the beach calling him as I do. It's night now, cold and lonely. The tide will be high soon. Not me. I'm just another fool calling a dog. *Murphy!* No. No reply. He's really gone.

I never should have trusted him.

Two

We continued to sail along although we were both quite anxious about the wind. Margaret had insisted she had sailed before. She lied. She has taught me nothing about the boat except to be frightened by it. The chances of my avoiding conscription through naval enlistment have just lessened. I am vomiting. I want to go home. Neither of us can steer the boat. Margaret has lied to me again.

I never should have trusted her.

Three

My work goes slowly. I have been hired by a great scholar who wishes to remain nameless. I am copying all of *Clarissa* by hand. My penmanship is weak for this kind of work, but even I must admit that a bulk of handwriting is really quite impressive. He is building a great library of hand-copied work and will no doubt turn a sizeable profit. I am told that my hand-copied editions of *Swift's Letters* brought him a handsome offer which he refused.

It's a pity I can't reveal his name, for it is certain that you know him.

Strange, but I am only pleased by the graphics of my work. The shape of the page. Perhaps that's why he employed me instead of any of the other applicants. He seemed pleased when I didn't know Defoe, Sterne, Richardson, Dryden, Pope, Swift, Addison, Johnson, Wycherly or Joyce. Of course there's one in the list I lied about—I had to, once I saw how pleased he was by my ignorance. A small lie told with discretion has never killed a golden goose. Of course I've had to cover the lie often. If he knew I knew *Tristram Shandy* he might go into a rage. I've seen his rage. Leather whips, chains, pincers. It's awful. I wish I hadn't had to lie. Nonetheless, I did. I've covered it well. The year I copied the fat Sterne book,

I pretended great confusion. I was delighted to see that he knew nothing—that is to say, he knew less than me. Still and all, I can only find passion in the graphics of my work. Small wonder I was struck by Sterne, for certainly he would have agreed. There is no other pleasure in that fat book.

Oh, Clarissa, you are so young yet so boring.

Ah, well. The pay is good; better than most I've had. He'll never know.

He never should have trusted me.

Four

The dog was a gift. There's an object lesson here: Never give life to strangers. Too late for me. Murphy was presented to me as though he were even likable. Normally, I loathe dogs. In this matter I am the consummate chauvinist. I think it is imperative that we support our own species first. Let people nurture people, dogs nurture dogs. My philosophy may be wrong but it is nonetheless my philosophy. Unfortunately, I was given just the dog to go with it. The first instant I saw Murphy, I wanted him dead—I thought he was a rat. There were two reasons for my error in this judgment. First, Murphy's fur was ratty in texture and coloring. Second, Murphy leapt at me, causing me to throw down my wheat thin and a chubby wedge of Caprice de Deux which was earlier on it. Murphy ate the entire wedge and cracker in one gluttonous munch, as soon as they were each on the floor. I put two and two together—small wonder that I made such an error in judgment. What is fact however is Murphy's present rattiness—he is a puffier version of what I first saw. Except for his size, nothing has changed. In this matter, dogs and people are not unsimilar.

Except in size, of course. One must never trust his judgment through size. It is to note nothing.

Five

Nobody Loves Me. Sixty-eight now and looking backwards. No. No hope. Nobody loves me. Close once. Yes, I was. Her name was . . . started with a J or K . . . No. Ah, well, not important. She was perhaps the best lay ever. Really. Oh, not

for everyone. A good lay is in the eyes of the beholder. For me
she was incredible. How I was for her? How would I know?
Really. How would I know? Too old now to give the easy
answer. Want it? Okay. Fine. I was a good lay for her. She
didn't say I was a great lay nor did she say I was a bad lay. It
seemed simple enough to divide and find the average: that I
was a good lay. There. That's settled.

How's your wine?

I'm out of the apartment now. Sitting here at the restaurant
with my closest friend. Telling him HOW IT WAS and am
delighted he appears to be listening. Delighted.

I was younger then. My back was never straight but I was so
slight, skinny. My slouch suited me. She told me so. Compared me to a fat sloucher and remarked upon the unpleasant-
ness of his slouch. I queried her upon mine. She said flatly and
clearly that my slouch was not just permissable but actually
attractive as I was skinny enough to carry the extra bend without seeming repulsive. How we came to fornicate—that's still
a matter of great confusion. I was never able to believe anything but the worst. Our first union was indeed just that: the
worst. Not that she was a bad lay. To the contrary. She was
the best I ever had. It's just that—I haven't any proof of this—
but—it's just that I am convinced she was falling the moment
when I met her. Not falling, for or because of me—she was
quite simply falling. If I had been so bent, I am convinced I
would have been her first paying customer. I just didn't figure
it out in time and I am convinced she simply lost her nerve and
never asked for the money. You see my dilemma? A whore
who forgets her fee is merely a weak businesswoman, nonetheless a whore. And there has never been an accurate report
of the relationship of business acumen to sexual deviance.
Interesting when you actually think about it. There isn't a drop
of proof to any of this, by the way. This is my own—what?—
detective, no SCIENTIFIC that's it—this is my very own scientific conclusion. Funny, but our relationship went along well
until I told her about my conclusion. Then? Oh oh oh. From
then on, she hated me. She went from the best lay I ever had to
no lay at all. And as I've said time and again, this was without
any proof at all. None. This conclusion was totally mine. My
own judgment.

I never should have trusted my own judgment. Nobody else
does. Why should I?

SIX

I first saw them together in late July. They were both hot, but so was the day. They made an odd pair: he twenty-eight and she eighty-seven. To each, his and her own, I thought. We greeted each other warmly and but for the utter discomfort of the temperature and humidity (Humature), we might have even lunched that day. We didn't. A week passed and I saw them together again. This time it struck me that they were even odder together than they were the time before. It was nothing they said or did—it was where we were. The nickel ferry past the statue then was for the workers and lovers. They were not by any stretch of the imagination—even mine—workers. I was. I was on the way past the statue to the island to hand-copy the new *Book Six of G. T.*, cutely constructed by an Englishman, Godhart. I was in an ill mood, annoyed to know I would spend a week with parody. When I saw them there on the ferry. I had great difficulty clearing my mind of the seven days ahead and walked straight past them. In my foggy side-vision I noticed that she not he pointed to me. I quickly knew them and smiled—perhaps oversmiled—a greeting. We sat together and chatted not uneasily. They were both quite easy with short words and so it went well if not far. Mostly they talked about a fine batch of cookies they had baked together and another he had baked alone, using her recipe—a surprise from him to her. I wasn't repulsed, but I wasn't delighted either. It was all well-constructed conversation in short simple ideas, sometimes rhymed. The ride did, I must admit, pass rather quickly with the news of their most recent bake-off. I said my goodby and noticed they walked together to the returning ferry. A lover's shuttle. I made a note not to forget that they were strange people.

The next two years passed slowly, but without incident.

It was two years and six months to the day, when I saw them again. Not them, actually—just him. They were—by his report—experimenting with certain fudges, and he was rushed to join her before the newest batch was complete.

I saw him—on the average—each third day thereafter and he was always in a great hurry to join her. Once, I should note, we did lunch together. He gave me these clues:

1. She owned a house.
2. He let his room from her.

3. He called her "My old lady."
4. He was losing weight.

It was during the following July I saw him next and he was a man who had seen horror. His words.

> She's dead. That's right, she's dead. Murdered. Last week —Thursday night. The place is still crawling with police. I went straight home after my lecture. She had been dabbling in fruit-tarts and I was anxious to see if our calculations had paid off. When I got there it was too quiet. She was on the kitchen floor. Naked, but no blood. Her clothing was all over the place. Upstairs, downstairs, all over the place. The tarts had turned out all right, but they were jammed into each and every orifice of her body. It was shocking, really shocking. I dressed her and ate the tarts before the police arrived. I wouldn't have called them, but I really didn't know what else to do. So I called them. They're still all over the place. Since last Thursday. They've eaten everything in my house. Who would murder an old lady?

She never should have trusted him.

SEVEN

I was younger then. Much younger. I would never visit such a place now. Then? Then I was much younger. I could drool then and not be humiliated. On the day that hurt most, I had Murphy by my side on the chain leash. He was a pup then and really, so was I. I just didn't know it. Murphy had repulsed most of the young girls, but some had stayed in spite of him. My reputation as a fine hand-copyist was growing—in some small circles—and I suppose the young girls who remained were not unimpressed by WHO I WAS then.

There was one girl in particular, the one who promised the most and gave the least. Her name was . . . I've forgotten. Not important. Her name was . . . DAMN IT ALL. Not important, I suppose. It's just that it seems so much faster with a name. Sometimes a name alone can actually replace all else. A clever man gives his name quickly. Only the cruel are purposefully nameless. The cruel and the dead. Her name was . . . no matter. She had a most impressive profile; more contemporary French than ancient anything. Her breasts were impressive,

her hips a near miracle. She was striking to me at once. Even
Murphy wagged when she first sat on our blanket. The intro-
ductions back and forth went smoothly. I talked about my
most recent copying and she sat rapt for the better part of an
hour, before she spoke. When she did, finally, it all crashed
down. Her words.

I I I love my hips. Do you love my hips? I I I I used to love
my stomach even more than my hips. It's so flat. I I I I I love
to rub my hands across my stomach and press the flat of my
hands against the flat hard surface of my stomach. I I I I I I
hold my hips now before sleeping. It's really quite a pleasure
to hold them. Really it is. They're soft but not in the slightest
bit flabby. That's the way the hips should be. My hips
weren't always perfect; it's just in the last two or three years
they've grown so terribly exciting. It's a lucky break for all
of us. I I I I I I I can remember liking my feet more than
anything else. I was incredibly young then. My feet are lovely, but hardly my best part—at least *not* the part that is truly
important to anyone—how shall I I I I I I I I say it?—Not
important to any truly *romantic* interest in my life just now.
My neck? Oh my neck is quite something. Long and thin and
with just the right slight bend forward. It's almost Victorian,
isn't it? I I I I I I I I I I've always admired that irony, that—
what?—contradiction—good—that contradiction in my
shape. My face? My face was burned when I I I I I I I I I I
was a baby. My mother was cooking pudding. Boiling but-
terscotch. Deep yellow. It fell onto my face—my screams—
I . . .

Suddenly she began to slap Murphy. It wasn't any love for the
dog that forced me to restrain her that way—it was the sudden-
ness of her moves. Also, Murphy's screams were childlike
then and he'd been so terribly involved in her story—poor
dumb cur—he was completely amazed by her first slap. I had
to restrain her, but I wish I hadn't slapped her face that way. I
held her arms, but she was actually too strong for me. Finally,
I had to slap her face.

She ran until the horizon devoured her. Murphy, the milder
beast, mistook my restraining her as an act of love, from me to
him. He spent the better part of an hour licking tears from my
face with his tongue.

From that day, Murphy, damned fool dog, fully, really, deeply trusted me.

EIGHT

The old painter had been color-blind for eight years now and his paintings hadn't changed at all. He was so used to dabbing his brush into specific paint-cups for so many years, there was little chance that anything as superficial as color-blindness would change his pattern of work. Indeed, his reds and greens were still his trademark, even though he'd not seen either color as it was for years upon years. Still his paintings were unchanged and his prices were as stable. His best customer was the old lady, the Unitarian widow . . . Mrs. . . . Mrs. . . . I've forgotten her name . . . Damnit . . . Mrs. . . . Mrs. . . . not important, I suppose. His best customer was an old Unitarian widow. She had also been color-blind for as many years as the old painter had been—nothing had changed for her either. Strange, it was as though color-blindness was an infectious virus that had passed lovingly between them.

He was involved in his most ambitious work, a painting of Middle-Eastern war survivors. He had to work without models, of course, so it went slowly and there now seemed a possibility that he would be forced to leave the work unfinished. The pains came to his chest daily and there was no joking them away.

On the Tuesday I visited his gallery, he spoke quite openly about his dilemma, admitting his fears and their logical source. We had first met each other through my former employer, who was a strong collector of the old man's canvases, until they had gone out of fashion among the urban homosexuals. I had been the carrier of messages and thus had known the old man enough years to be considered a friend, if not an intimate. I liked to visit his gallery now and especially enjoyed seeing him with the old Unitarian widow. He tended to speak romantically to her, though he had admitted to me years before that he had not slept with her and never would—that he intended to keep her on as his best customer and would not know how to adjust his prices were she to become one of his ladies. He was a reasonable man, always.

I was touched by his dilemma, partly because I believed he

would soon be dead, partly because I believed he might not soon be dead. The contradiction bothered me as well. Also, he needed money, which I considered an irony, simply because the completion of the painting would assure a great sum of money.

The truth was that the canvas was but half completed.

For a reason unknown to me at the time, he had called the old Unitarian widow and promised to sell her the completed painting that very evening at seven o'clock. It was an impossible promise, but the more I questioned it, the more confident he seemed to grow. At five in the afternoon, he announced that he could assure delivery, as planned.

He had done nothing to the canvas but spray turpentine on the painting, softening the oil dangerously. He had also removed the canvas from its stretcher and had tacked it to the wall. At six o'clock in the evening he took pliers and untacked the painting.

At a quarter past the hour of six, he laid the painting flat out on the floor.

At half past the hour of six, he folded the canvas in half, allowing the wet oil to touch the half of the canvas that was yet unpainted.

At a quarter to the hour of seven he unfolded the canvas and tacked it to its stretcher again.

At seven in the evening, the old Unitarian widow arrived, purchased the painting for a great deal of money and soon left, carrying the still-wet canvas carefully on a hand truck designed especially for their special relationship.

Rumor has it that she made triple the purchase price in profit when she sold the painting just six days after his death.

He never should have trusted her.

NINE

Losing my job was one of the twelve major low points. All those years for what? I have the distinction of having copied more in my period than any other living copyist—that's my reward. I should have thought he would have supported me through my late years, but it never quite works out that way, does it? Still and all, it came as a shock when he let me go. I wouldn't have minded quite so much if he hadn't made me interview my replacement. One should never have any view of one's replacement—not in this life. I interviewed him. He is young, bright, tall and blond. He does not drink nor does he use dope by smoking it, shooting it or shoving it up his ass. He is a pure and almost holy copyist and I am sick to think about it. The interview stays vivid. His words.

I was born tall. It wasn't easy for my mother, but live and learn. My height was an advantage—gave me an edge. I could reach shelves far above children my age. Thanks to the Dewey decimal system, my height allowed me a great deal of knowledge from Az to Apr. I was in fact an expert in that area. I grew to learn about the tops of heads and seemed destined to construct a valid phrenological study of famous heads between Aa and Apr. I was unable to find a suitable woman and when I did come close to it, I was shamefully cursed by my tiny penis and the enormous myth surrounding it. Thus, my celibacy was set and locked. No matter. I was still thinking then. My blondness and brightness caught the eye of several older scholars who counseled me and taught me to copy as I do now. Most of those fine old men loved me deeply and I shall be eternally grateful for their many gifts. Some of them are in fact still wearable, for my size hasn't changed in twenty years. I am grateful for all my good fortune, really. My blindness is barely a handicap now. I should have known better even though accidents are accidents— live and learn. There is nothing I regret. There is nothing. Really.

He continued, but I had to accept his application. There was little choice: he was quite the best man for my position and I knew it at once. I wished I had known him when he was thinking, but perhaps life is best as it is.

Years later, in fact not long ago, I heard that the tall bright blond young man had burned much of my work, by accident. He knocked against a kerosene lantern in the library and the flaming liquid spilled destroying twenty volumes of my hand-copying.

I do wonder why the tall bright blond but blind young man needed a lit lantern in the library. In his situation, there is little logic, but . . . accidents are accidents. I do wonder though. I really do.

TEN

So then, it finally adds up to less now than in the beginning.
Then there was the future. Now? Now I am childless, wife-
less, futureless. NO NO NO. There is no plan. Leave me be.
I'm an old man. It's all behind me now. No regrets. Forget
your troubles c'mon get happy. NO NO NO. No plan. Leave
me be. I'm an old man. I tried.

I did. As recently as last month with the old shoplady in the
town. She seemed interested, if not alert. NO NO NO. It was a
shambles finally as was everything else.

I met her the very first day here on the island farm. I wanted
to walk alone and the town seemed a reasonable size—small
enough to wander without being overwhelmed; large enough to
wander without being seen. I walked the beach path to the
town. The old fishermen were as hostile to me that day as they
are today. Small wonder. The farm must serve handily as the
purest reminder, the warning light, the unwanted messenger
who was created to carry and deliver nothing but the worst. As
I passed one, he cast his still virile line out into the water. The
baited hook and the bare lead sinker in a dangerous whiz
zipped past my nose and mouth. I halted my walk and smiled
to the fisherman, fully expecting an apology. Instead he stared
angrily at the sea that was taking his energy. He stared straight
past me and slowly wound his line clicking back onto its reel.
The hook and sinker dragged straight across my shoes and I
was really too amazed to either feel or express any anger Or in
fact anything at all. I just simply watched the hook and sinker
pull over my shoes, watching the line of water left there after
they passed.

My first farm day couldn't have been that different from
anybody else's. To be old and alone and cast suddenly into the
forest—that seems to be the WAY IT IS now. I wasn't surprised. I wasn't happily whistling show tunes, but I wasn't
surprised. No. Not at all. The farm was a reasonable enough
conclusion after all, the choices are few for a man of my
situation. NO NO NO—there is nothing, no regrets, no future,
nothing.

I wish the fishermen would have found me different enough
to consider me, but I'm not and they didn't. Not now, not
then. An old man's first farm day is the cruelest thing I know. I
found the town easily. Straight along the beach to the water

tower, turn right, up the wooden staircase, up the cement walkway—and there it is. My surprise was warranted. I had assumed there would be a mixture of shops and storerooms. Instead there was just the one linen shop, manned exclusively by her. She was younger then, but not young. I might have passed by, but the air was suddenly all rain and her shop was the only shelter. I excused myself. She was stern, but did allow me to wait out the storm. I told her I was from the farm. She asked how long. I answered, first day. She walked to me, hugged and kissed me. My tears surprised me and for the longest while I assumed it was rain still trickling from my thin silver hair. Finally the taste was the answer. I smiled at her. I didn't know what to say. When she saw me searching for words, she put a finger to her lips and relieved the burden of my searching. I smiled again and she returned the smile, easily. The rain stopped as suddenly as it had begun. I nodded an embarrassed goodby, as I realized in that instant that a heavy rain carries a strong muffling noise. That too was gone and I could hear my quick nerve breathing. Nervousness builds on nervousness. I left the store with a false smile on my face and hurried to the beach where I watched the moon replace the sun as it would and had forever.

The years passed quickly. Years have a way of doing that. Everybody's years, not just mine. I claim no copyright on floating. We are the floating animals. It is neither sad nor is it not sad. It is the way it is. There is little pleasant to sustain. We remain until it exceeds all logic. And then we remain until it exceeds all possibility. Finally, I'm told, we are released. That I cannot yet describe. The waiting, the floating, yes—easy to report. It all passed quickly. With some incident, but nothing really nothing out of the ordinary. That is the way it is. I walked to the town at least once each day and saw her just that often. Some days I stayed out of the shop because I could see the others within. The farm-people needed her. Each of us needed to know she remained as she did, independent, whole.

It was just last week that I realized I was finally different. All those who were at the farm before me—gone now. All of them. All gone now. All those who joined the farm in the year I did—gone now. All of them. All gone now.

My visit to her shop was full of this news. Finally, I was special, different, considerable. I told her what I had realized but she had already known. I was amazed to see her compulsively neat tallycard. Names crossed out with thin straight lines. Mine was there, yet to be crossed. I wanted to run a pen through it myself. We should never know such a tallycard exists, but once we know, we should be allowed to tamper with the score. At least in jest. We must maintain a humor, for that is finally the energy to continue. When it goes, we continue without energy, without control.

I asked her to marry me.

She didn't laugh when she refused. She was actually quite stern. No, it had never occurred to me that she owned the farm. Why should I have thought anything of the kind? The farm is free. Yes, now that I consider it I realize that of course there is an owner and there is a bill rendered to a higher account. Such is welfare. But I was, I do admit, amazed to discover that *she* wrote and mailed the bill. Small wonder her tallycard was neat. Small wonder she helped indeed stroked those who continued after the energy was gone. No, there is but one amazement. At my age, with all that is behind and so little ahead, how absolutely incredible that I can still feel humiliation. That I can be cheated. That there is any notion of trust.

From the beginning to the end, we are vulnerable if we believe it. It is God's will that we believe.

ELEVEN

I am a fool. I stand on the beach screaming for Murphy and every fisherman is offended by my appearance of senility. I cannot blame them: they have each seen the ugly beast and know there is no reason ever to think of fetching him back.

He is both ugly and dumb. Murphy has changed little since childhood. If anything at all, he has grown slightly uglier and slightly dumber.

I am the perfect master. I stand now on the cold beach screaming his name to the pounding surf, holding his chain leash as though it might have once restrained something of value.

I call and I call, but only my voice returns to me. It is finally clear that I am alone.

If there seemed anything certain to continue with me, it was the horrid cur Murphy. That he would leave me was ... was ... surprising.

I fastened the leash to my own neck and led myself slowly back to the farm.

As I feel myself respond to the tug of the lead, I know the energy is gone forever. But for whatever reason, it is so. I am alive.

TWELVE

Now I have gone past logic and possibility. I should have halted thirty years ago. But no, the joke continues now long after I've lost my humor. I've heard that the frontrunner for life's greatest hour is for a parent to watch the funeral of a child. Wrong. To continue, childless, past the century mark—that's the lowest joke of all. I have watched *trees* come and go. Don't talk to me of mere children. I have watched companies fail, buildings tumble, governments and whole countries dissolve. Don't weep for a child. Homicide, genocide, pesticide—all came, all gone, and I go on. Oh, not that I haven't tried to end it. First I tried gas. That only left me this cough. Then came the leap! That crippled this leg. The blade only severed the tendon to the thumb. I continue in blatant incompetency. No, there's no getting off until it stops. No getting off at all.

The farm is closed now and I go on as best I can on the beach. I tired of eating fish long ago but they are free and as easy to capture as anything ever was. My pole, my hook, my lead sinker, all old but good enough.

I have joined the other fishermen, but they remain as unfriendly as ever. Just as well. There is nothing to say. My days are spent catching and eating fish, my nights are spent sleeping. What's to discuss? The silence is more interesting. We can each imagine what the other knows. In silence there is no limitation. Once silence is broken, limits are set.

There is still no logic to my continuing, but the faces of the other fishermen show the same wear. Small wonder I was never recognized by them as someone different, someone considerable. I am exactly as they are. We are held separate by our pain. Mine is mine and his is his. But that's the true scheme, isn't it? No real surprise there. So old if I had had children they would be memories now. What of it? Surely there would be ugliness to remember—even in the past pluperfect. NO. No point in WOULD HAVE BEEN. No point at all. What is is me and my fishing, me and my ocean, me and my hours of sleep that break each morning into this hideous joke, this interminable riddle.

Wait. There's a fish on my line. Easy. Food for another day. The ocean plays well. Bluefish today. Once it was blowfish. Several of the other fishermen gathered around until it deflated. Then they returned to where they each wait. That was an excitement for all of us. It passed.

The sun is half down now. Where's the moon? Ah, both together. Two other places now.

Now and again there is a small ugly sound from the ocean and I never cease to follow it with my eyes. I cannot stop myself from believing he's still near me, somewhere.

It makes no sense to think that I would be allowed to continue, that I would be spared, yet a defenseless truly helpless beast would be taken. I cannot help but believe he's out there somewhere.

Strange, but I never thought he'd leave me alone this way. I never should have trusted him.

MAUREEN HOWARD

born in Bridgeport, Connecticut, is a novelist and teacher who lives in New York City. She has published two novels, *Not a Word About Nightingales* and *Bridgeport Bus*. About her third, about-to-be published novel, *Before My Time*, Frank Kermode said: "The book is so distinguished that only a utopia of masterpieces could afford not to accept it as such."

Sweet Memories

I

"Ah, did you once see Shelley plain," one of my mother's beloved lines, delivered on this occasion with some irony as we watched Jasper McLevy, the famed socialist mayor of Bridgeport, climb down from his ancient Model T. "Laugh where we must, be candid where we can," was another of her lines, a truncated couplet, one of the scraps of poems, stories, jingles that she pronounced throughout the day. Like station breaks, her quotations punctuated the hours. Vacuum off: "One thing done and that done well/is a very good thing as many can tell." Out on the back stoop to take in the thick chipped bottles of unhomogenized milk, she would study the sky over Parrott Avenue: "Tell me Clara Vere de Vere from yon blue heaven above us bent. . . ." George and mother and me, pressed against the sunparlor doors watching a September hurricane play itself out. Ash cans rattling down the drive, gutters clotted with leaves, shingles flying, the rambler rose torn from its trellis whipping the cellar door. Her gentle, inappropriate crooning: "Who has seen the wind/ Neither I nor you . . . But when the trees bow down their heads. . . ."

My mother was a lady, soft-spoken, refined: alas, she was fey, fragmented. I do not know if it was always so. But when we were growing up, broken off bits of art is what we got, a touch here and there. A Lehmbruck nude clipped out of *Art News* tacked in the pantry, a green pop-eyed Siennese Madonna folded in the *Fannie Farmer Cook Book*. She was sturdy when we were children, with high cheekbones and red hair, like a chunky Katherine Hepburn, so the fragility, the impression of fragility was all in her manner, her voice. Her attitude towards anything as specific as a pile of laundry was detached, bemused. It might not be dirty socks and underwear that she dealt with at all but one of our picture books or a plate of cinnamon toast. As she grew older her fine red hair faded to yellow, then to white, but it was still drawn back from her face and pinned at the neck as she wore it in college. Her clothes were old but very good. And my mother—the least independent of women—always used her maiden name, her married name tacked on as though she was listing herself in her Smith Alumnae Journal. Loretta Burns Kearns. Somewhat wistful. You do remember me? Loretta Burns.

I sensed that my mother was out of place from the first days when, dressed in a linen hat and pearls, she walked me out around the block. She was too fine for the working class neighborhood that surrounded us. "Flower in the crannied wall/ I pluck you from your cranny." Down Parrott Avenue around to French Street we marched, taking the air—"As I was going down the stair/ I met a man who wasn't there./ He wasn't there again today. . . ." I never knew when I was growing up wheth-

er my mother didn't have time to finish the poems what with
the constant cooking, cleaning, washing, or whether this was
all there was, these remnants left in her head.

To the crowded A & P we charged on a Saturday morning—
ours not to make reply, ours not to reason why, ours but to do
or die. If she gave us a ride back to school after lunch and the
scent of spring was heavy over the convent wall as the nuns
filed into the school yard, my mother would sing out to us,
triumphant behind the wheel of the old brown Auburn:
"Come down to Kew in lilac time . . . and there they say when
dawn is high and all the world's a blaze of sky. . . . Come down
to Kew in lilac time. It isn't far from London."

"There once was a policeman who met a stumble-bum. . . ."
A witless ditty about bubble-gum (it ended: "Please won't you
give me some?") was chanted to us at lunch or dinner to show
what a good sport she was. "There was a little girl/ Who had a
little curl/ Right in the middle of her forehead . . .": she liked a
laugh. But it wasn't mere nonsense or chestnuts from the lau-
reates she quoted. My mother had studied German and I believe been quite a serious student before life caught up with
her. "*So long man strebt, er ist erlöst,*" she said. As long as
man strives he is saved. "*Wer eitet so spaet/durch Nach un
wind?*" "*Freude, schoener Goetterfunken. . . .*" We were treated to disjointed lines, lots of *Faust,* some Schiller and Heine,
the final watery gurglings of the Rhine maidens.

It sounded beautiful gibberish to me as did the Latin verbs
she conjugated to the remote pluperfect tense, but for my
mother it was to prove that she could still do it, could reel it off
with ease—as naturally as an athlete doing push-ups before the
flab sets in. "*Morgenrot, morgenrot,/ Leuchtest mir zum frue-
hen Tod.*" That was the trick my mother could do and other
mothers couldn't—as well as smock my dresses by hand and
overcook the meat to please my father and not speak to
George when he was rotten but be wounded, disappointed in
her son, a grieving queen.

We were dressed in our Sunday best and taken to the concert series at Klein Memorial Hall. My father wouldn't go near
the stuff. Helen Traubel stomped onto the stage in a black tent
and something like gym shoes. The *Budapest,* all young and
debonair, stunned us with the knowledge of their own brilliance. The Connecticut Symphony ground out their Debussy
and Ravel, their sloppy Beethoven, their inevitable Gershwin

jolly-up. Me and my mother and George, proud and rather excited by the grandeur we could pull off in Bridgeport. The audience—a sprinkling of local music teachers, a solid core of middle-class Jewish shopkeepers and professionals who were more sophisticated than the Irish in town, and that set of rich old ladies who stumble into concert halls all over the world, canes and diamonds, hearing aids, rumpled velvet evening capes from long ago.

We never made it to London where all the world's a blaze of sky, but to the first little temple of civic culture, the Klein Memorial out near Bassick High School and the Cadillac showroom. On those special nights we were there. The price of the tickets was something awful, but my mother wanted this for us. I ran off pictures in my head of beautiful scenery, lakes and rills, mountains and fens. I called upon the great myth that one *must* be moved. I strained, while the violins soared, for deeper finer thoughts, but it was beyond my childish endurance. I tapped my patent leather pump into my brother's ankle till it drove him mad, found that I had to cough, begged to go to the water fountain and was kept in my seat by a Smith Brothers' cough drop from my mother's purse.

II

What did it mean to her? Was my mother full of a passionate yearning like those noble, thwarted lady artists out on the prairie that Willa Cather is so good at. God knows, Bridgeport was raw land in the thirties. Before he died, my mother sat in perfect harmony with my father in front of the Lawrence Welk show. She was lost in the old sappy songs, lost. Walled in by her vagueness, all the fragments of herself floating like the million orange, green and purple dots that formed the absurd image, the bobbing head of the lisping bandmaster. My parents took my anger as a joke. Disgust swelled from me: at the time I was not ready for compassion.

Or did Loretta Burns know that her chance was gone and only want those ineffable finer things for me and George? Well, we sure got them. We got the whole culture kit beyond her wildest dreams. There came a day when George knew who was dancing what role in which ballet that very evening up at City Center. For the pure clean line of a particular *Apollo* he would leave his gray bachelor basement on St. Mark's Place, burnt out pots, ravioli eaten cold from the can, grit in the typewriter keys. His coffee-stained translations from the Spanish and Greek littered the floor. No closets. No bathtub. Now, as an adult, my brother takes with him wherever he lives an intentional chaos that is impressive, a mock poverty. Orange crates and real Picassos. Thousands of records and books but no dishes, no curtains. Money handled like trash. Twenty dollar bills crumbled in ash trays, checks left to age, income tax ignored. He is quite successful really. Her boy has become a strange man, but not to himself and he is not unhappy. My brother, a middle-aged man, can come to visit (filthy jeans and Brooks Brothers blazer), take William Carlos Williams off the shelf and read a passage, rediscovered—then tell me why it is wonderful. "At our age the imagination across the sorry facts"—and it *is* wonderful. As we talk under the skylight of my Greenwich Village apartment, he threads his speech with lines—like our mother, of course.

While I'm split—split right down the middle—all sensibility one day, raging at the vulgarities that are packaged as art, the self-promotion everywhere, the inflated reputations. In such a mood I am unable to sit in a theater or pick up a recently written book. I am quite crazy as I begin to read in stupefying rotation—*Anna Karenina, Bleak House, Persuasion, Dubliners, St. Mawr, Tender is the Night, The Wings of the Dove.* I play the Chopin Mazurkas until the needle wears out. Drawings are the only works I can bear to look at. The atmosphere I demand is so rarified it is stale and I know it.

Then again, everything is acceptable to me. In an orgy I can ogle the slickest movie or love story on TV, suck in the transistor music and thrill to the glossy photographs of sumptuous salads and stews, the magnificent bedrooms and marble baths in *House and Garden.* Our great living junk art. The Golden Arches of MacDonald's rise, magnificent, across the landscape, contempo-monolithic, simple in concept as Stonehenge if we could but see it. Then the nausea overtakes me in Bloomingdale's "art gallery" or as I listen to all that Limey Drah-ma on Channel 13. Sick. I am often sick of art.

It would never have occurred to my mother that the finer things might be complicated for us, less than sheer delight. She simply stopped after her children left home. There were no more disembodied lines, not even the favorite "Little Orphan Annie's come to our house to stay," or "Where are you going young fellow my lad/ On this glittering morning in May?'' No. She settled into Lawrence Welk, Double Jeopardy, Dean Martin, no less, and she had all her life been such a lady. She read the *Bridgeport Post* and clipped the columns of some quack who had many an uplift remedy for arthritis and heart disease. She followed the news of the Kennedys in *McCall's* magazine, until the last terrible years when she was widowed, when the blood circulated fitfully to her cold fingers and her brain. Then, from a corner of her dwindling world, she resurrected Ibsen's *Rosmersholm* in a German translation and underlined in a new ballpoint pen the proclamations of Rebekka West, all that heroic bunkum about the future and her festering spiritual love.

Mother would sit on the brown velvet couch day after day, rejecting tapioca and Jell-O, smiling at the pictures in her art books like a child—such pretty flowers . . . all the colors . . . by some Dutchman . . . in a bouquet. The fat ladies she laughed at were Renoir's, bare bottoms by a hazy stream. Her mind skipped the shallow waters of her past like a stone. George and her father were one man. My father was ''that fellow'' and there was a picture she found of Loretta Burns with a whole band of robust Smith girls, each one warmly recalled, who'd gone hiking up Mt. Tom on a fine autumn day in her sophomore year. Sometimes she could not place me and so she entertained me graciously, gave me pieces of crust and cake. She was tiny now, nestled in the big couch. Her thoughts fluttered away from her. ''By the shores of Gitche Gumee/ By the shining Big-Sea-Water,'' she said. Gaily she'd recite her most cherished lines of Heine:

Ich weiss nicht was soll es bedeuten
Das ich so traurig bin?

What does it mean that I am so sad? She seemed happy to remember the words at all.

STEVE KATZ

These books published: *Saw; Cheyenne River Wild Track; Creamy and Delicious; Posh; The Exaggerations of Peter Prince; The Weight of Antony; The Lestriad.*

Several screenplays. Most recent based on the life of Toussaint Louverture, Haitian revolutionary.

Some reviews.

Years of teaching, waiting tables, construction, mining, forest service.

Four years practice of Tai Chi.

Jingle. Three sons.

New York City; Ithaca, N.Y.; Winnemucca, Nevada; Pierce, Idaho; Eugene, Oregon; Lecce, Italy; Verona, Italy; Istanbul, Turkey; Swiftbird, South Dakota; Dwaarkill, N.Y.

A tipi on the Cape Breton coast. Snorkeling for lobster. Snorkeling for lobster.

Death of the Band

for Philip Glass

He felt two small hits as he listened to the music from the bandshell, as if he had been struck by some pebbles; in fact, if he hadn't glanced at his shoulder and noticed the blood that was seeping through his t-shirt he would have paid no attention to it at all. Now he had two wounds.

Behind him one listener tapped on the back of a bench with his umbrella, one slept, the scantily dressed girl turned away when he caught her eye. There was no one else on the benches. Cradled in the lowest branch of a large maple, the composer held his gun. He gestured at Arnold to move aside. Arnold moved, embarrassed to be in the line of fire. A parabola of dusty light suddenly filled part of the hollow in back of the musicians, then clouds covered the sun again and the composer commenced firing rapidly into the bandshell.

The gun had a silencer, but Arnold could hear the shells ricocheting inside the music. The effect was thrilling. Then the musicians began to fall. It was in their contracts that each of them keep playing until he is hit in the head, which happened on the count of seven for some, three for others. When all the players were fallen the performance was over. It was then that Arnold, who had got out of the way, began uncontrollably to feel guilty for the death of the band.

Peter leaned back against the trunk of the tree and cradled the .22 in his lap. This was the first piece he had written following strictly his ideas of irreversible subtraction. It had been exquisite, as good as his music could be played. The instrumentation, the live performance, the composer as performer: everything was coming together. A nice surprise for him was the role the audience took on its own, a potential tragic chorus. And Peter himself had worn the maple tree as if it were a mask. It had all at once become a ritual, and he the shaman. How interesting. No way he could have prepared for it. It was worth all the psychic hernias that one got dealing with the art world in the seventies just to make these few discoveries about one's own music. He sat in the maple tree mask and enjoyed the applause. All of it was the music, even Rumi, his sound man, backing up to the stage to remove the equipment. They had to get out fast. The bandshell was to be used again for a free performance that evening of the Pro Musica Antiqua.

Arnold passed through the zoo to the South end of the park holding one of his wounds. The hit on his shoulder had just scored the flesh, but the one that had pierced his back was still bleeding. He could touch the little slug lodged between his ribs where the flesh had stopped it. He could take it to the hospital but that would involve the police and infinite explanations, and put his favorite young composer through a lot of paralyzing legal rigamarole. And he would have to explain about the band. He didn't know yet how to deal with his responsibility in that regard. Would the band still be alive if he hadn't moved out of the way? No answer to that question. He propped himself against the park wall and slowly slid to the West Side. Perhaps he hadn't been in the way at all. Perhaps he was part of the music, turned loose now in the city. He didn't regret now skipping work that afternoon, just so he could go to this performance of the music he preferred but so rarely got a chance to hear. This had been a premier performance, and it had moved him greatly, but as a result he had these two wounds to complicate his response, and a slug lodged in his ribs like some dangerous information, and he hadn't figured out yet just how he felt about the death of the band.

The Detective touched the bodies with the toe of his wing-tip shoe. Eight of them, each hit in the head by a small caliber bullet. It was neat, the work of a skilled marksman. A syndicate wipeout? No. Robbery? Maybe. It was so clean, very little blood spilled. He didn't want to flatter anybody, but this was good work. Most of the hitters he knew these days had long hair, so this might have been someone's mistake. He doubted it. He pulled out his pad to make a note and noticed that an enormous crowd had gathered. "Oh screw these turtles," he muttered. They started to applaud. "Bullshit." He turned his back on them. He hated public capers because he didn't like to be in the public eye. He felt ill at ease on a bandstand. He liked the idea, so old-fashioned in the seventies, of a murder in a boudoir.

They came from the boats, from Bethesda fountain, from the merry-go-round, from the zoo, and they were still coming, climbing down over the rocks, busting through the bushes. This was amusing. This was human interest. It was the biggest crowd the bandshell had seen in years. The Detective hated the whole idea. TV crews dispatched from every network. A tough cop on the job. Ice Cream Wagons. Hot-dogs. Pretzels. Six-foot balloons. Howling yo-yos. Sanitation was immediately a problem. Dope. Dozens of camera buffs joined the police photographer, calling out f-stops and shutter speeds.

"Everywhere is punks," said The Detective, scanning the audience. They applauded and cheered and whistled. It was time to leave. He scrutinized the bodies draped over the music stands. One thing he had learned for sure from the spiritual studies he was pursuing to help him ease his mind in this tough line of work was that none of these deaths meant anything at all. That was something of which he was convinced. They weren't a drop in the cosmic bucket. His studies had taken him beyond worries about individuals, which were nothing but a lot of flesh stuffed with punks as he understood it. That was why he was becoming a better detective.

Although they rarely saw each other any more Arnold still had the key to Betsy's apartment. He let himself in. Betsy was a pisces and a liberal, full of cloying displays of kindness that he found tiresome, but at this point the prospect of Betsy wiping his brow and loving him a little was the only good possibility he had. Her apartment was sloppy as usual, dishes piled in the sink, soiled clothes on top of everything. He put his finger on the lump between his ribs. The bleeding had almost stopped and the pain was down to a dull ache. He scrubbed out one of her pots and boiled up her French paring knives. He felt remarkably clear about what had to be done. He wished someone with a video would record his excellent moves as he ripped an old sheet into strips and boiled them, got gauze and Hydrogen Peroxide from the medicine cabinet, laid the strips of bandage over the bathtub and sat down on the toilet seat cover with a paring knife. Betsy's knives had a surgical edge. He thrust out his rib-cage, keeping a finger on the lump of lead, and then touched the point of the blade to his flesh, stuck it in, and drew it across between the ribs. The slug squirted out over the bath-mat as if it had only been waiting to complete its trajectory. He felt as if he had suddenly shed twenty-five pounds. The stinging of the peroxide was wonderful. He was rising as if from dream to dream. He didn't need a hospital. He didn't have to tell anyone about the death of the band. He could keep the wonderful feeling the concert had laid on him.

He took some bandages into the bedroom. It was Betsy's bedroom all right: bed messed up, tube of vaginal cream open on the night-table, applicator fallen into yesterday's underwear on the floor. He sat on the bed and contemplated telling her everything, because she would understand, because at one time the deepest bond between them was a mutual love for the new American music. He leaned back on the pillow, the pain struck him, and he passed out.

"Your people are as prejudiced about us as we are about you. You don't have to be so condescending," said The Detective to the girl who had joined him at the table in the museum cafeteria. Betsy blushed. He was probably right. She touched his sleeve. "Sometimes I don't think."

"I don't want to implicate you as a hippie, but you ought to know that hippies have their own prejudices." Since he had been occasionally snacking at these museums he had been getting a lot more ass, and that made him a better detective.

"I'm sure that's true," said Betsy. "The hardest thing to understand is yourself." She saw a surprising sensitivity in this man. He was alive, tuned in, unlike the anguished, frightened, bored friends she usually spent time with. He was refreshing.

"People like yourself find out I'm a detective and immediately have some ideas. 'Excitement,' they think. 'French Connection.' Like I found eight musicians shot dead through the head in the bandshell this morning and I bet immediately you think, 'Heavy. Adventure.' "

"Eight musicians?"

"I don't know musicians from toll collectors. Maybe they were joggers. But they were all shot through the head, and what that means for me is another long bore. A routine. A good detective has to appreciate a routine. I love boredom. Here." He takes Betsy's hand and presses it to the gun in his shoulder holster. "You think that means anything?"

"I think it's horrible to have to live all the time with a gun."

"It's a routine. It's like your tampax. I use it once a month. Most of my work is paper work."

"There were really eight musicians killed in the park this afternoon?"

"It's the new American hobby. Mass murders. You're lucky it isn't California. Eight is a drop in the bucket there. What's your name, honey?"

"I'm Hilda," said Betsy, thinking it wouldn't be too cool to give a detective her real name. She liked his thick, stubby hands on the table, the cleft jaw like two small boulders.

"You live around here, Hilda?"

"I live across the park."

"I don't like to beat around the bush, Hilda. I've got a tight schedule. Let's go over there now. You know what I mean."

Betsy looked away, as if she needed a moment to decide, but she had already made the decision, and it was thrilling. The Detective got up. "No offense meant. If you don't want it I'll understand. But let me pay for your Tab." She let him do it. It was the first time she had let a man pay her bill in two years. She slipped her arm through his as they left. This was probably the strangest thing she had done since she was a teenager. "I don't know if those guys were musicians or not, but they were on the stage. They could have been parkies . . . interns . . . foreigners . . ."

No one could see her. No one knew who was with her. She walked close to his big body. They left the museum through a display of South Sea artifacts.

"You can't hunt with a crossbow in most places," said the salesman.

"I'm not going to hunt," said Peter Glucks. The instrument was fiberglass, very fancy, fitted with a brass sight and trigger, and a small brass winch to draw the string back; but it wasn't what Peter had in mind.

"Where do you intend to use this weapon?"

"I'm not sure it's really what I want," said Peter. "Do you have anything made of wood, like polished cherry or birch?"

"They don't make them out of wood any more. It's not practical. Where will you use it?"

Peter realized he had something more medieval in mind, something carved and elegant. "It'll just be in a small hall," he said. "No more than three hundred people." The piece was scored for viola da gamba, harpsichord, recorders and hunting horn, all of them amplified. It needed a certain environment.

"I'm sorry," said the salesman. He took the crossbow away. He wasn't going to be the one who sold a weapon to a madman. "I don't think we have what you want."

Peter didn't protest. This was the kind of resistance to his art he faced wherever he turned. He was used to it. He knew that when time came to perform the piece he'd have an instrument. More troublesome were the problems he would face when he returned from his tour of Europe. He had a recording session then, and that was infinitely more problematic than a "live" performance. Videotape. If they ever perfected video cassettes, that's when his new music would be a star. He left the Sporting Goods store. The crossbow idea wasn't so touchy. It wasn't nearly so delicate a problem as his piece for koto, piccolo, and blow-gun.

"Shit," said Rumi, when Peter got back to the van.

"What's wrong?"

"We got another damned ticket."

"Well," said the composer, philosophically. "I suppose we'd better pay this one."

Betsy gasped when she saw Arnold there, adding to the mess in her bed. It was a little disappointing. He had grabbed the tube of vaginal cream as he was passing out and had squeezed it out all over the sheets. "I'm not the neatest person," she told The Detective, who was looking in every corner. She slapped Arnold's face. He was really out.

"I'm meticulous," said The Detective. She felt weird to have him snooping everywhere.

"Are you casing my joint, or something?"

The Detective stopped at the foot of the bed. "Is this the junkie you live with?"

"This is Arnold," she said. "He's a good friend."

"I deduced as much," said The Detective. "But does Arnold stay or do I go or what?"

Betsy lifted the bedsheet and saw the dried blood. "He's been hurt," she said.

"We've all been hurt," said The Detective.

"Get some cold water," she said, feeling Arnold's pulse. "We've got to find out what's behind all this." The Detective shrugged and went for some water.

"Your kitchen is for pigs," he said. She swabbed Arnold's forehead with the wet rag. "Look, Hilda honey, either he's out of here in ten minutes or I'm going."

"You're a cynic and you're absolutely heartless."

"Maybe it's heartless to you, sweetheart, but a little blood is no new thing from my point of view. He looks okay. He moves."

Arnold opened his eyes. "Betsy," he said, touching her face and leaving a print of contraceptive cream on her cheek.

"What are you doing in my apartment, Arnold?"

"Betsy, he shot me."

"Who shot you?" She glanced at The Detective.

"Not interested," he said. "I'm off duty. It's not my precinct." He returned to the kitchen.

"Peter Glucks."

"The composer?"

"It was part of the music, the way he ended the piece."

"He shot you?"

"It wasn't like it was me he shot. I mean I was in the way. I don't know if I was part of the music or part of the audience. But then I moved out of the line of fire and he shot the band. He shot it in the head. It was wonderful. I mean it was horrible, but it was some important music, and I was involved in it. I mean I was morally involved. That's a real innovation. It was my decision to move . . ."

"He shot the whole band?"

"What's all this Lipton's?" shouted The Detective from the kitchen. "Haven't you got any good tea?"

"Who is that?" asked Arnold.

"He's a detective. We came here to ball, but I didn't know . . ."

"Don't tell him anything. Nothing. Don't tell him I'm here."

"He knows you're here. What should I say to him?"

"Say I was bit by a dog. Say I was in a fight. This music was very important to me. It's turned me around, Betsy. I can't explain it yet, but my whole attitude to myself and music has been changed."

"Arnold, eight musicians were found dead in the bandshell today and this detective . . ."

"I know, Betsy. And I'm trying to understand if it was my fault."

"How your fault?"

"Betsy, I moved out of the way after Glucks hit me. If I hadn't moved that band might still be alive, I think. Maybe not. But I have to figure it out."

"O Arnold," said Betsy, wiping up the vaginal cream. "Anyone can tell you had a Jewish mother."

"What do you mean by that? I even took the bullet out by myself. Look." He exposed his wounds as Betsy headed for the kitchen.

"He's really been shot," she said to The Detective, who was opening and closing all her cupboard doors.

"I don't want to hear about it. All I know is that you don't have a decent cookie in the place. And you buy this gummy peanut butter."

"He says he was shot at the concert in the bandshell. By the composer. By Peter Glucks." She enunciated very carefully, with great solemnity. "Doesn't that ring a bell?"

"Honey, everything rings a bell in this city. Nobody's to blame. Nothing's wrong. Everything's wrong. Everyone's to blame. Everything happens here and we don't need an explanation. It's all criminal activity. Nothing causes anything. Everything causes everything. That's the rules. Now why would a girl like you fill her bread-box with Wonder Bread? That's murder. That's suicide. You're just lucky I'm off duty."

Arnold stood as straight as he could in the door of the kitchen. He was white as a slice of bread, but he didn't feel too bad. His wounds throbbed a little. "It's okay. I'm going to leave. You guys want to use the bed so go ahead. I'll go home. I feel pretty good. I just want to talk to Betsy for a minute." He took Betsy's hand and led her out of the kitchen. "I'm sorry, Betsy," he whispered, "that I've driven you into bed with detectives." Betsy was moved. She and Arnold once had a very intense thing going. Tears dampened the corners of her eyes. "I'll always love you, Arnold," she said. "It's so impossible," he said, and went out the door.

"Aren't you going to do anything?" she asked The Detective as he stepped out of the kitchen.

"Just shut that mouth," The Detective said, coming at her down the hallway. "Shut your woman's mouth." He twisted her arm and pushed her against the wall. He grabbed her head and dug his thumb in just under her jaw. No one had ever hurt her like this before. She could feel his fist in the small of her back. "Look. I know your name is Betsy, and not Hilda, but I'll let that go. You're lucky I'm not on duty. Just let me attend to my business myself, and stop trying to make this into a movie. Now you do your trick for me."

She hated him but there was nothing she could do. He released her. As she turned around her hand grazed his cock. It wasn't even hard. That made him more dangerous. She knew she'd better do it with him now, even though Arnold had wasted all her birth control. She'd learned something from this experience, at least, that her prejudices about such men as The Detective had some foundation. She'd never make such a foolish move again, but for now it was too great a risk not to fuck. One consolation was that if anything happened abortions were now cheap and easy.

After that day time passed at a certain pace for everyone: endless for Arnold who was going through enormous changes; frantic for Betsy who cursed her luck when she missed two periods; for Peter Glucks time seemed not to pass at all; and The Detective put time aside and monotonously assembled evidence like a machine.

Arnold rarely left his room. Once he had consumed every bit of food in his cupboard he started a long fast. He needed to be ready for something, something immense he had to do. That concert had changed his life, a great compliment to the young composer, an enormous inspiration to Arnold. His two wounds became two scars. He stayed alone, turning friends away at his door. When his office called he hung up. His longest phone conversation was with Betsy, who for three quarters of an hour described her abortion to him. "Is that all?" he asked as soon as she stopped talking. She said, "Yes, but I . . ." He hung up. After that Betsy changed the lock on her door. She decided that for her Arnold was a lost cause. He was getting thin, contracting around his two ripening scars. They were a petroglyph incised in his flesh. They were the axis of his new understanding. Something about music that they held he was beginning to get a grip on, something outside the mastery of an instrument or the knowledge of harmony and counterpoint. He was reaching for a new, ineffable reality where art and reality begin to mingle. He practiced the guitar every day. He hadn't played it for years because he didn't like to hear himself. He had always been less than mediocre and he couldn't sing; but now it pleased him to do it. And so what? He was still terrible and the hours of practice didn't help. But so what? He realized that the art wasn't in the guitar or the ordering of the sound or the invention; it was somewhere else, somewhere he was girding himself to go, somewhere he had first been given a glimpse of when he witnessed, even participated in, the death of the band.

The Detective continued to piece it all together. It wasn't happening too slow and it wasn't happening too fast; but the end was in sight. His mixture of indifference and devotion made him a better detective. Long hours got him home late and he fell asleep with his service revolver on. When he woke up his mind was full of thoughts. Were they true? Were they false? He was being led to several inevitable conclusions. Did they matter? He was glad to be alone. He took off the revolver and the clothes and put on some pale gold pajamas. He set a cushion on the floor in the center of his living room and lit a joss stick. "Fuck the lotus position," he said and crossed his legs. Almost as if he had flicked a switch he emptied his mind of thoughts, canceling a whole week's work. His lids drifted down. His pupils floated up. Men and women. Good and evil. What the fuck? Hot and cold. Colors sifted through and stabilized themselves as pure white light in his skull. It was all the same. He had a job to do. Work and play. Guilty and innocent. A clear pleasant bell began to tinkle in the void he was attending. It entered his position through the left ear.

With the new music Peter Gluck's life had become several times more complicated, and much of what he spent his time doing had little to do with making music. The onus of booking concerts, setting up tours, getting accommodations, all fell on him, since he wasn't popular enough to afford a manager. His was classified, unfortunately, as "serious" music. He didn't really mind it, even though it wasn't really about music. He even enjoyed shopping for the new, peculiar instruments. Now he had a wonderful old crossbow with quarrels made of ebony and brass. More complicated was that he had to continually rehearse new musicians. He never thought he would find players enough willing to perform his new music, considering the consequences; but that wasn't the case. Every week at least two or three would show up at his loft with a viola or a clarinet and ask to be in the band. They all knew what that meant, but they wanted to learn the music, and as one older man said, who showed up with a baritone saxophone, "It's safer than walking the streets these days." And if they volunteered to play the music, Peter noticed, they did so with enthusiasm and feeling. It was frightening. Peter had never prepared himself to wield such power. "No. No thank you," said a very talented flautist when Peter offered, as he always felt obliged to do, to buy the man dinner before his performance. "I'm fasting today, anyway."

He finally had his band together for the Chicago concert: two electric pianos, an amplified violin, a bass clarinet, a trumpet, and a singer. The voice was a new notion. He didn't have it totally worked out, but it sounded wonderful. This was a great group of musicians to work with. The singer was a woman who had been a model once, had studied voice for years, had sung lieder. She was really good. And there was something about her personally that really touched him, but Peter couldn't let himself get involved. He had too many plans. It wouldn't be professional.

The singer answered the doorbell. Arnold was there, dressed in fatigues. He hesitated a moment, squinting into the light, and then stepped inside. "Is this Peter Glucks?" His voice quavered slightly, as if too finely tuned. "Right," said someone at the piano. Arnold set his instrument case on the floor. That he was moving very slowly made everyone pay attention to him. There was something new about Arnold, fine and ascetic, a pure glow to him. He could be someone you almost feared, but someone you also aspired to be.

"I want to audition for the band," said Arnold.

"That's weird," Peter said, "You're the eighth musician today."

Arnold looked at the singer. "You're very beautiful. Do you sing with the band?"

The way he said it made her blush. "Yes I do," she said. "Thank you."

"I love you," said Arnold.

"This thing is growing so fast it's scary," said Peter Glucks. He pointed at Arnold's instrument case. "If that's a guitar, man, I'm sorry. I've never really written a piece for guitar. There's a pop- country- folk- music stigma keeps me away from it. I know it's in my own head, but I have to deal with it. I mean I really appreciate that you came here." The composer laid his arm somewhat patronizingly on Arnold's shoulder. "But I have no use for guitar. You leave your number, just in case I write something."

Arnold slipped the composer's arm off his shoulder and stepped back. He unbuttoned his shirt and slowly peeled it off to reveal the two gleaming scars. "Do you recognize these?"

The band closed in for a look. Peter Glucks ran his finger down the scars. "O how strange," said the composer. "I almost forgot that piece. In the bandshell. You were heavier. Weird. There was something in that first piece that I still . . . wow."

"It's lovely," said the singer, kissing both scars.

"Thank you for coming by, man. I'd almost forgot how that piece worked." He ran the backs of his fingers up the piano. "The music never ends. Ideas just grow out of one another." He tapped his forehead. "A fantastic idea."

"Do you want to hear me play my instrument?"

"Of course, man. I'd really dig to. I might do a piece for guitar. I feel like I'm opening up to everything. Go ahead."

In the fluorescent light everyone seemed made of enameled steel. Arnold unsnapped his case. "I don't sing very well," he said to the singer. "Can you come and sing with me?" She smiled and crossed to his side of the room to stand beside him. He lifted out his instrument. As soon as she saw it the singer sang. Arnold stepped in front of her and put the butt of the instrument to his shoulder. The singer burst into her own rendition of East Side/West Side. Arnold opened fire. "All around the town," sang the singer. There wasn't time for the composer even to sit in on crossbow. The whole ensemble fell in every direction as they were lunging for their instruments. It wasn't the greatest performance, but it was Arnold's first, and he played as well as he could. The responsibility for the death of the band could now unequivocally be laid on him. He embraced the singer and they backed out the door. She was still singing as he lightly patted the beat into her arm. Something special had happened between them. They were a new duo, a direction of their own in the new music. The elation of it made them laugh and they hit the street both thrilled with their own, their mutual discovery, and they skipped away towards Chinatown, singing and holding hands.

CLARENCE MAJOR

is the author of ten books. The most recent are *The Dark* and *Feeling* and *The Syncopated Cakewalk*. Other recent works have appeared in the following anthologies and periodicals: *The Modern Age* (Holt), *Starting with Poetry* (Harcourt), *Open Poetry* (Simon & Schuster), *From the Belly of the Shark* (Random House), *Ten Times Black* (Bantam), *19 Necromancers from Now* (Doubleday), *Fine Frenzy* (McGraw-Hill), *The Poetry of Black America* (Harper & Row), *Poems of War Resistance* (Grossman), *Dices or Black Bones* (Houghton Mifflin Co.), *Contemporary Literary Criticism* (Gale); *Fiction, Chelsea, Fiction International, New York Quarterly, Mundus Artium, Quadrant, Unmuzzled Ox, Poetry Review, Essence, Works, Tautara, American Review, The Painted Bride Quarterly, American Poetry Review*. Major has also recently read his work on many radio and television programs and in various colleges. In 1970 he won a National Council on the Arts Award and received a grant from the New York Cultural Foundation in 1971.

An Area in the Cerebral Hemisphere

She is not absolutely anything. She is something naked, skin and thought but so hot today. Because the walls are pressed. The release for the electric lock downstairs. Incidentally, a man in the building across the alley had watched. Her naked movements ate candy from a heart-shaped box. Finally it becomes clear: she is behind fieldglasses.

Smelling like yards of flesh red flowers. She entered and climbed her second stage of privacy. Wrapped a thick silk nightgown around. Much to the disappointment. An old high school friend who liked laughing. Came toward blue bell bottom pants and blouse to match. These little thoughts that slide back down narrow, worn paths. To match other thoughts.

Girl, her best friend once said, you need to get a elevator for this fucking building.

Come on in and close the.

It's just too hot—I got my fan going but.

The friend lit a cigarette and sat on the sounds of her own voice. Motion. And made a blowing sound.

Say. Who were those people out on the sidewalk?
Grown men and they never go anywhere.
They were arguing together like kids.
I'm scared of them.
I think I heard your name mentioned, the friend said.
Did they say anything worth anything.
They might have beyond me.
See that picture of flowers they gave it.
Really.
The friend went over read the card attached to it and said why didn't they give you real flowers.

Laughter caused the first young woman to hit her own chest with a small hand. Turned darker and eyes closed tears fumbled in the fieldglasses watching her.

She went to see her mother and said tell me about my father, I don't know said the mother I told you all I know. Were just standing there with their backs to each other.

I don't even know why you two divorced.
I told you he wanted to treat me like a kid.
You mean—what did he do.
Everything I nothing.
Mother, said the young woman with tears, this is the first time in many weeks, I ask you again, be honest. Tell me.
I'm telling you all I know.
She was in no mood for this and the radio gave them B.B. King and that little baby next door was teething screaming. And mother's couch was eaten by what might easily have been taxicabs with hooks on them. Anything can happen. (In any case, swift traffic was known to move through her living room.)
Who got the divorce you or him.
We separated then later he.
Never heard any more from.
Last I heard he moved to. Then somebody said he was in. And had come into a lot of money.
I wonder.
The mother left the lowrent room and stuck her hands into soapy water to try to dream and not hear. The daughter though took the conversation into the kitchen where the traffic noise was also loud. But it was really no good to go on like this mother would not open.

She jumped into a yellow cab and was shot away into the traffic with the sounds of screaming children in playgrounds on both sides. *Had come into a lot of money,* huh. All these details add up she'd ask her best friend's advice. A pack of Salem's fell on the motion floor. *I'm scared of them I think I heard your name.* The traffic, however, at the friend's place.

They smoked a joint while trying to understand the strangeness of it all. Natural processes informed by instances that snag the spirit and strangle the hope of many ways. Much in the way of the probable when no clue comes. A small child does it unconsciously but adults like these must try harder and then only rarely it works. So talking with the friend is nothing new and at best not even a careful way to go crazy for fun. To be quiet or face danger are two other matters. But did she want her father or his money or his. You know what I think?

She felt she must be crazy or the moment was a mistake and she was not really involved in it—perhaps not even live. Let us see. Then really she had no idea why she got up or felt scared. Let's see. She had wet the bed and was warm and cold. Her own pee. At first it might be painful but there were sounds in other parts of the building. The people fucking next door the woman screams and the old couple upstairs fighting again, gin heads. And who was the man in the hallway talking at this hour? Can't you see how all these tidbits add up to a mistake. But maybe not.

Maybe she was alive and not dreaming. A little girl sitting on side the bed somewhere in dark room listening carefully for sounds outside. Be quiet or face danger. Seeing herself through grownup eyes or face . . .

At first it might have been without sincere meaning and the pain of just being not knowing created. Knowing who was not present. The father was not. And half way woke up grown but surely that had to be something that really happened. Not simply in a child's possession, a dream being the sounds of sex in the moaning, I mean in the morning, liquid youth wetdreams all the stuff that goes with the senses and organs.

But once sound asleep again she plunged right into sound. Delightful questions such as what makes your lips so pretty mother, your words yet so ugly with cold cheese sauce.

She looked out the window and the strange brothers were still standing on the sidewalk whispering. Might be some sort of substance or spy ring, for a delightful government that believes only in candysticks or mouthwash. Who knows what might be the actual point—if there is one. Dipped in blue sauce her thoughts were cheerful this morning. How was mother or friend. The men down there were all trying to talk at the same. The first time she'd seen them she'd thought. Plump fried shrimps dipped in cheese sauce, that's what I want. Did they really possess one. Just one idea, or motive. And incidentally, now she knew she was dreaming. Dreaming while she dreamed. Adventure with the playful picture of flowers. In a fine pink outfit, imagine it!

Her father was up early Sunday morning ready for. Lying awake with her large dark eyes upon him. Quietly by her young mother, the father lovingly looks down at his four-year-old . . .

His his his his!

But why couldn't everything be that simple forever and the punishment be taken out of ups and downs. Lord had blessed them with her, the child. Enough to be. Ones own image and they understood the dances in the spirit the spirit of what happened—this new person. Or were they simply going through the motions.

Meanwhile the father dressed darkly in a suit of cold wool and punishment was in his eyes. But she knew he was kind. Could it have really been this way. Dreaming of his death she'd cried in her sleep and came. Soon to become herself again, in the morning cold kitchen trying, with stiff fingers, to make coffee. The big man was father and was good. But soon came the terror of being alone with mother. Growing up and Lord . . .

Awake with those large dark eyes. He, the father, told himself, she imagined, I understand that. Old enough to be her grandfather. Getting ready for church on Sunday morning, a preacher perhaps even God himself.

Clad in tough white suit she gyrated into restaurant and sat next to nobody. Had milk shake was teenage head filled with bubbles of pain and anxiety music and frenchfries. That was not such a warm feeling. One guy she'd gone with was now in

Kentucky for the cure. Wasn't such a good memory or was the routine of school books a pleasant light in the brain. Her eyes were light and her mouth dry. Thankful for her good looks she walked with a uniqueness and even turned to acknowledge whistles. Both human and mechanical. Even the score. Two studs zipped into her once and left her angry as hell.

But these tough white suits she did not wear often and studs did not zip into her everyday. She liked herself best naked anyway though it was not an absolute hangup. With the odor of fresh flowers the stems just cut.

But those years in high school where dudes in Stetsons and Sansabelts and new cars were the In. And later the college crowd and the little income from the poverty program that sent her. Used her for an example of how smart their money could stretch and look. See, all the poor children aren't dumb nor are all the dumb students pennyless. Those were the dark days. And the boys around in a midget race for manhood! Who'd want a husband from that crowd. Each trying to get something for keeps for nothing, tight asses. All the talk shit like hay baby and pardon me and ain't dug that cat lately how you doing yourself though oh yeah he got busted that's news and maybe the cat got strung out or being a waitress after school for show money on Saturday or selling tickets in a dump theater. Often such tough young men would be very vengeful if they felt—nothing. But she felt like playing with her self, alone under the cover nights. What the answer would be to her life might be there in the wet substance. . . . Until the boss of that hole would come; often such tough young (or old) men never came. They too play with themselves, alone under the cover of night—with guns or flesh or comic books. Until their own bosses come.

So she had all this to look back on before knowing the right moment to jump into the space left her for future activity. But she certainly knew she had a future. A position of awareness, not being a waitress nor a student, without or with father's bread, she'd burn her bridges. Softly.

Her girl friend came (tho she herself did not) when they slept together that first time. They both got nice people all fucked up in their minds. They were trying to catch up with each other and talking out of their heads. I just wondered, she said. The friend said, wondered what. If the heat got to you that's what.

Anything else you want to know. No, nothing else. The friend sipped something through a straw and looked crazy. Her hair was uncombed and her eyes closed for a moment. Motherfucker, she said. Who, the friend said. Anybody. And, I'd hate to see you try to get really angry you'd probably kill somebody or yourself or—No, she answered, not me. I'm too careful, I like living too much. Too much? Well, not too much but I'm learning to roll with the tide, you know. How about your mother how is she these days. Anyway she can be I guess. You wanna know anything else? And the friend could see she was dead serious.

MARK J. MIRSKY

is the author of three novels, *Thou Worm Jacob, Proceedings of the Rabble,* and *Blue Hill Avenue.* His short stories and articles have appeared in *Partisan Review, New Directions Annual, The New York Times Book Review, Book World, The Boston Sunday Globe, The Progressive, The B.U. Journal,* etc. He is the editor of *Fiction,* a newspaper of stories, and an Assistant Professor of English at The City College of New York. His book of novellas, *The Secret Table,* has just been published by the Fiction Collective. The present piece is from a novel-in-progress.

Swapping

It is dark. I stare out the window into darkness. No light.

So I could have stopped it here. Made an end. And begun again.

A voice, faint, calls to me.

I am far away, in night. Deep out there, frozen, burying myself under the crust of the front yard, naked, the hot wax frozen in my ears, up to my neck in the drift, lips, nose, rigid, stiff as a stone.

I can turn to ice, give myself to white, a clear, crystal annex. Only it is cold, so cold, this transparency, absence, dry

flame that holds me rigid as its chill through shoots into the
surrounding arteries, ice.

Oh . . .

The voice

The last drop out of my veins, caught

Reaches me slowly, sightless, I turn from the window.

Yes.

"Job?"

"Yes?"

I am not in my study but downstairs, in a chair by a window
of the dining room. It is open, a few inches, my fingers stiff on
the sill. I draw them back and touch their pale tips to the
radiator. They steam. And in a minute I begin to shiver, sensing the draft from in front of me.

I smile. Shudder. No use to close the window. The house is
full of drafts. Spaces open in the walls, between the sashes,
beams pull away from one another: pegs loosen in their holes;
the heat of the furnace seeps away through more escapes than
we can plug.

The cold comes through the cracks of the old house. We curl
up in bed, pile on blankets, hug each other, rub, rub.

We had begun to make love frantic the last weeks. Leah
rolled under me, distracted. I dreamed of the minister's wife,
her lean body, to make myself hard. She kept on after I had
come, touching herself.

"Do you mind?" she asked the first time.

"No," I answered. "Why not? Go ahead." I turned my face
away, burning, her boundless soft lust that swallowed my one,
two emissions, even three, a fillip. At first she was snuggling
up to me after, to apologize, but later went on without asking,
bringing herself to some distant peak and then rolling over into
sleep far across the bed. I tried! Stroking her, touching her,
until my finger ached, the muscles up my arm stiff and sore
from their effort. And through it all she lay like passive dough,
damp clay, hardly wet, protesting when in my fury I forgot my
tremor, a feather's, and jabbed.

"Ow! "

"I'm sorry." But I wasn't.

"Job! "

She is calling me from the pantry.

"What is it?" She hates to be called loudly. I wince. How
aware I have become in the last few months of her dislikes.

There was no answer.

I took a deep breath to ask again. The air caught in my throat, a thick painful burr. Taking a few steps towards the pantry, my knees shake.

Leah appeared in the pantry doorway. "Did you call?"

"No," I answered, hoarse. "I'll do it now."

"Have you caught cold?" She heard the rasp in my reply. "Look, you left the window open." She walked over and slammed it shut. "It's freezing. Why don't you go up and get under the covers. Take a nap."

"Will you call?"

"No, you call."

She had badgered me about this dinner for a month now, yet refused to give invitations herself, insisting that I arrange it.

"It's probably too rough out for them to come," she added.

The flakes coming down steadily for two days now on top of a heavy storm from the week before. Drifts of ten to twelve feet lay across the fields and roads of Canaan.

"It stopped about an hour ago."

Leah went to the window. Our gate posts were buried: the maples, pillars of ice: the street, unplowed, trackless, as deep under the mantle as the front yard. We were snowbound.

"There won't be any traffic on that road until tomorrow."

She nodded. Ordinarily it would be a fifteen minute walk but in the soft wet snow the Hunts could not reach our front door for an hour.

"Call," she instructed.

I went towards the pantry where a receiver hung on the wall. "It's snowing again. Tell them to forget it," she called.

Hunt answered. "Hi there! This is Job Schwartz, right?"

"Yes," I whispered, taken aback. We had never spoken. "Listen, it's rather . . ."

"Nonsense," he cut in. "It's wonderful. A real storm. Is the food on the table?"

"Look . . ."

"We're just itching for an excuse to get out and take a good tramp. We'll be there in an hour. O.K.?"

"O.K.," I echoed as I heard his receiver ring back into place. "They're coming anyway," I said, turning around from the telephone to find Leah beside me.

"Why don't you set the table?" she asked.

"I'm going to be. I'm dizzy." The cold was coming up
through my bones. The minister and his wife would arrive
soon. The thought did not start apprehension through me as
before. Something in her husband's voice. I was dull. The
plague, I thought and without looking back, I climbed the
stairs to our bedroom, stripped and clambered under the covers, too tired for fantasy.

The ringing of the door downstairs did not wake me. Nor the
sound of voices in the foyer. It was Leah, shaking me,
"They're here."

"Where?" I was drowsy, thick-headed with sleep.

"Downstairs. In the parlor. Please Job. It's not polite."

"Right. I'll be up . . . in a second."

But it was minutes before I could draw the covers aside and
push myself out. I needed sleep. I knew it. Stumbling into my
clothes, Leah had switched the light on, I wanted to fall back
on the bed. Slapping my face, I shambled into the bathroom
and threw cold water on my cheeks. A blizzard was howling
outside. Clouds of snow blew against the windows. What a
night for a party. I swallowed some aspirin and hurried down
to the parlor.

"Hi there!" William Hunt sprang up from his chair and fell
upon me, shaking my hand, a vigorous oarsman. "Leah tells
me you don't feel up to snuff. Have a fever?" He let go of my
hand and slapped his palm against my forehead. The first name
of my wife so familiar in his mouth, jarred. "Better watch it,
you've got a temperature."

His face was ruddy, the cold frosting red apples in his
cheeks. How healthy he must appear to Leah, stamping the
snow off his boots in our foyer, steaming. I turned to look for
his wife.

Yes, my breath stopped in my chest as I started to say hello,
pale, her skin like ice, the trace of blue and green veins that
throbbed below transparent milk. A dress of wine velvet cut
away from her shoulders to expose the breasts, high and full,
the hem just catching.

"I . . ."

"You know each other, I hear," he boomed, "from the
library."

"Yes . . ."

"Quite a shelf of books you donated." He winked at me.

"You'll have more business than the corner drug store."

I blushed. Still giddy from the sleep, fever, the flush of seeing her, I let myself be guided to a place on the couch beside his wife. It was his house of course. A wry grimace.

"What are you up to?" he asked, standing over me, a genial but firm expression on his face.

"Excuse me?"

"That shelf, a new Rabbi, your sudden interest in the town . . ." I looked up at this bluff football player.

"What do you think?"

"That's not important. It's what you think that I'm curious about."

"Fun," I countered. "Have you ever heard of it?"

"A child's game?"

"Do you believe in the Devil?" I asked, standing up.

"No."

"How can you be a minister?"

"We're not in the eighteenth century."

"What are you running there, a Community Center?"

"That's hardly the alternative."

A fire was crackling on the hearth. He had started one while I lay upstairs. The flames shot through me like liquor, glowed in me. I spun around, put my arm on his shoulder, "' . . . the wealth/of simple beauty and rustic health.'"

"We're ready for dinner," said Leah at the doorway.

"Saved by the bell," chimed the minister.

We all smiled. "Surely my wife has told you what I am up to," I said, as we processed into the dining room.

"Only the vague outlines."

"Ah, well perhaps your wife will fill in the details."

I saw the blood start into her cheeks. She bit her lip, but did not look at me. We sat down to our places; bottles of Chateauneuf du Pape uncorked, we toasted. I rose to carve the pink and tawny hulk of roast beef. Leah circulated bowls of steaming onion soup & croutons; on the sideboard candied sweet potatoes, slender strings of potato french fried, baby carrots, a winter squash whipped in with marshmallow, beans with shredded pecans. "I have a present for you, a family heirloom."

"Yes?" The minister looked up, his face suffused in the good fellowship of the table.

"A knife, a poignard. It has the crest of the Hunts at the hilt."

"Where did you find it?"

"I dug it up in the cellar, curious, let me show you." From a drawer in the sideboard I drew out a stained green velvet scabbard.

"You are a real antiquarian, Job," the minister whistled. "Digging, restoring, that old church . . ."

"Your great, great, great, great grandfather's."

"Something in my family must fascinate you."

"And you?"

"Oh, in a pleasant sort of way."

How I despised him at that moment, the *Reader's Digest* prose he had turned his ancestors into.

"We should adopt you!"

"Perhaps I'll be an unnatural son . . ." I let the pause season, "a bastard."

"Come, come," said Hunt, ice in his voice.

"Let me show you something," I said, holding out the knife and its sheath to his wife. "There is blood on the scabbard."

Indeed there were the dried brown spots, plainly spattered on the worn velvet cover.

"A grisly deed, " she raised her eyebrow.

"Probably a pig sticking," the minister cut in.

"Why do you resist?" I asked. "Perhaps you have a secret inheritance, the heirloom of a murder, a whisper you had passed on by an aunt, grandmother."

"Come, come," Hunt repeated.

"Have you ever heard anything about it, William?" His wife's eyes struck against mine with sudden interest.

"You are determined to bring the Devil to Canaan," he fronted me.

"Your ancestor was familiar with him."

"Which one?"

I let the question hang.

"Why a conventional Devil?" I asked. "Isn't a conscious act of self-destruction a kind of tangible evil?"

"For instance?"

"Wife swapping."

"Would you like to exchange wives?" The question came back in my teeth, so direct it caught me. I could feel the heat of the candelabra against my cheek. The stillness in which no knife, fork, moved.

"It might be fun," I whispered.

"Anytime," the answer rang back so it made the silver tingle on the table.

Mrs. Hunt laughed, high, hysterical, a crazy gaiety in it. "How delightful. We must try it." All broke into smiles. Even Leah. The gravy was passed from hand to hand with tenderness. We began to make small talk about the food, weather, improvements in the town.

"Let us take coffee in the parlor," I suggested. Pushing back our chairs we left the cluttered board, its rank of empty bottles, savaged plates, bone of the rib roast, pools of gravy, fat congealing on the knives and forks, a linen stained with the dregs of appetite, filthiest under my mat, the minister's napkin soaked with the light red of the glass I spilled.

As the coffee came I poured out snifters, brandy, creme de menthe, minted chocolate, pear liqueur, insisting that we sample everything, dusting off syrups of cherry, apricot, plum, their labels in a dozen tongues.

"O God, I'm drunk I think," Hunt exclaimed, shaking his head, rising from the cushions of the parlor couch. He strode over in wide steps to the window and drawing the curtains, lifted up the sash.

A cold fresh wind, smelling of damp pine, swept through the room. "Put out the lights," he cried. Someone snapped them off and we stared in the orange darkness of the fire out at the night, slowly lighting up for us as the moon and stars reflected on the crystal earth, our eyes opening up to sparks that shot back from every facet of the snow.

"Oh, let's go out."

It was Leah. She stretched her hand against the window glass.

"Borrow my snow shoes," the other female voice said.

"I can't." It was I who had spoken, the fever trembling through me.

"I'll take you," Hunt boomed, his face florid, beaming, the moonlight wild in his silver hair. "Come on." He took her by the hand and I heard their laughter in the foyer, I shivered as the draft of freezing air from the open door blew into the parlor. The latch slammed back as I heard my wife cry, "Stop."

I went to the window and tried to force the sash down.

"Are you cold?"

There was no strength in my arms. My legs were buckling.
"I'm afraid I'm sick."

"Oh," I heard the rush of wind in her voice and the rustling
of skirts. "Come away from the draft." Her cool hand slipped
into mine and led me to the couch.

She sat beside me and felt my forehead. Her finger traced a
line on my temples, scoring like a delicate compass, a caress.

"Rachel."

Her breasts were below me. The thickness of the cognac in
my throat, my wife, the minister, all that I had dreamed, I
caught her snowy finger.

"Job."

She let me hold it. A cord to draw in all the happiness of my
nightmares.

And somewhere on the main street I saw my wife and Hunt,
the white powder stinging their faces, reaching into each other's parkas: Leah's large friendly hands feeling the firm outline
of his chest, the minister's fingers slipping beyond the sweater
into the bodice of her dress, catching the twigs of her nipples;
falling back together in a silver bank, sinking as their hands
grasped for the heat of each other, under the ski pants, into her
underwear.

My eyes were wet as I pressed Rachel's cold finger to my
mouth, kissed it. Bent the knuckles to my lips, hearing the
wind against the panes as it would lash them, pink flesh for a
moment flashing in the moonlight, then buried in each other,
rumpled pants and parkas, sitting on him, yes, they could, and
drew her to me, aching, my heart, quick and firm bit in, the
apple, apples, rolling under me, now my mouthing over them,
lost, forever.

"Don't," I heard. "Don't," but in a voice so soft it sounded
like a whisper to herself.

It was her hand that drew me on. I would have been content
to kiss, to hold her, draw out preliminaries and dream the rest
but she removed her skirts, lace, swiftly and gripped me, easily coming, only that hushed stop, like a cork, effortlessly
drawn out, unstoppering the fountains that flowed out to me. I
let myself step into them, slipping, my seed come without
thinking: I did not even see her but went under, losing
everything.

Spent, it was her eyes I slowly became aware of, as I struggled up from slumber. "I'm sorry," I said, "I meant to . . ."

"What for?" She gave me a pleased smile. And I remembered in the drowsiness, a cry of pleasure. I felt with my hand on the couch. It was dry. My hand slid against her buttocks, small and muscular. She rolled onto her side and I put my finger against her cheek.

"You are an imp."

It made me smile. Some of the sadness abated in my mouth and I realized how sad and cheap I felt, a stranded fish on a barren shore. I pinched her cheek. "You're cute."

"Is this the Devil speaking?"

I shivered. "Would you like some coffee?"

"Yes," she said, drawing up her legs. We retrieved our clothes, began to dress, the opium of the coupling wearing off. I watched her back and indeed she was lovely. I, I was cheated. It was not horror but emptiness I had fallen into.

I wondered what time of month it was for her and felt the first flush of terror, fruit.

I entered the Garden.

The hollowness within myself. I had created and seeing her wind into her velvet sheath, the real world seemed an imposture, abstract, one I would gladly leave below, ascending to my study, books and thought.

The bell rang and going to answer the brass pipes in the hall, a flood of shame rose in my throat. I swam through brackish seas. Leah, I have committed the impurity and it is dead. Released it. Aware, now, tasting the salt of each moment of the evening, stinging on my palate. I stood white and naked at the door. Hearing laughter behind me, opened it.

Muffled in an overcoat, Krapotnick President of the synagogue stared at me, his heavy face beet red with cold, ice on his fingers. I slammed the slab shut in his face, turned and sank.

"Job . . . Job! " I put my hand out and found my wife's stroking my hot fingers, an instant of consciousness in the dull eddies of the fever, ". . . the guests . . ." but it was days later when I woke and the evening lay behind, dark and unspoken between us. The only fact, our house, buried in a mountain of snow.

URSULE MOLINARO

is the author of three published novels: *Green Lights Are Blue* (NAL), *Sounds of a Drunken Summer,* and *The Borrower* (both Harper & Row).

Her stories have appeared in numerous reviews, including *New American Review, Iowa Review, Tri-Quarterly, Chicago Review,* and *Evergreen.*

Tourists in Life

The sun was hanging directly above the island. Repeating the island's shape in the sky. Excluding all other possibilities of shape. As though only roundness existed. The flat roundness of 2 disks, mirroring each other. Exchanging heat vibrations. Playing the hot grainy air back & forth between them. Grinding it to sweat.

Noon on the island, grainy & weaving, like silent films in which it seems to rain on all situations. Even inside houses. Making the actors run out of the rain with the nervous eagerness of sandpipers after a wave dissolves on the shore.

Noon deafness, laced with insect crepitations.

A boat swam into the silence. Broke it with the howl of its arrival, & docked. A tall blonde woman in faded-blue cotton pants & matching jacket limped off the swaying gangplank. Sideways. Crablike. Wedged between 2 tall blond men in faded-blue cotton pants & matching jackets.

Who looked like twins the woman's twin brothers; maybe they were triplets, to be wearing the same faded-blue clothes to the island women on the boat. Who were coming back from the market on the mainland. & were getting off the boat behind them.

Behind 2 suitcases which the 2 tall blond men were carrying in their free hand. Holding their other hand under the woman's their sister's(?) elbow. Setting the suitcases down on the dock, for her to sit on.

The island looked yellow, from the dock. 3 shades of yellow: the sunbright-yellow blossoms of prickly pears, itchy with bees; or wasps on goose-shit yellow man-high prickly-pear hedges along reddish-yellow sandstone stair paths that ran through the island like veins across the back of an old hand . . .

The clutching hand of an only daughter's widowed old mother. Whose blood has turned sap yellow with sublimated relating.

Who relates only to plants. Because plants are pure. Because no one can see/hear plants manifest pleasure. Knows how to interpret plants' manifestations of pleasure, in the act of procreation.

Pure & poor, separated by the sound of "you" . . .

Because plants sponges/coral/prickly pears stay "together." The parent linked to the offshoots. Which stay linked to the parent. & rarely drop off. Rarely drop off before they've dried up & wrinkled, & begun to look like the parent.

. . . Only daughters, beginning to look like their mother's twin, after 40, under identical wide-rimmed beach hats. In identical blue-&-red-&-white-striped beach coats . . .

Living with her widowed old mother was like a monk sleeping in his coffin, for a daughter. With a one-track future in constant view. Her own pending impending old age in uninterrupted rehearsal. A daily lesson in growing old: As your mother taught you. (Pronounce: Your Mother Torture . . .)

& then again, a mother might be filled with a wisdom of plant life, unsuspected by the daughter. Or suspected, but unlearnable, by the daughter. Who has learned languages her mother never learned. & has become what is called: a philologist. A profession which needs to be qualified, in the case of a woman, in unisex English. In which intellectuals . . . historians/botanists . . . thinkers . . . artists . . . statesmen . . . are MEN. Unless qualified. A woman philologist . . . a lady philo . . . a filologa . . .

Who has crossed oceans all the way to a yellow island; whose inhabitants allegedly spoke a kind of 15th-century Spanish to sever herself from the clutching root. Roots . . . the antithesis of motion. Of progress?

In the company of a botanist. Who looked like a flabbergasted cherub much of the time. & a historian. Who envied dead men of action. Because they were dead. Because the historian's father had died an officer in action when his only son was not quite 5 years old. & nothing the only son did from then on could match his dead father's stature. No matter how tall he

grew. Or how learned. As long as he lived. & therefore he
envied C. Columbus. & Marco Polo. & I. de Loyola . . .

& one dead man of inertia: Augustus von Goethe. For dying
before his father. The average-size son of a giant, getting even
with the giant by dying. In the giant's favorite city: Rome.
Where the average-size son lay buried: the true definitive
"Goethe in Italien."

A botanist & a historian who looked like twin brothers. But
were the only sons of widowed old mothers. In whose company the only daughter felt safe, crossing oceans. Because they
were her friends.

Because they were intellectuals. Who attracted her mind,
but not her body. With whom there would be no danger of her
falling in love. With them. & spoil their friendship. Even if
they had been susceptible to her falling in love with them. Or
to their falling in love with her. Which they were not.

She had never fallen in love with a friend. Always with men
whom her friends did not respect. But whom her body respected. & reached out for. For their dark stocky figures. With dark
strong arms. & dark strong smells.

Her "basic" men: as her friends called them: Her "simple"
men . . .

Did her body derive its pleasures from denying her mind?
Pointing lavishly painted purple fingertips at the nail-biting
puritan residue in her. At the hypocrisies she thought she had
left behind . . . I'm intolerant only of intolerance . . . under
the precious crystal butterdish-cover sky of her girlhood.
—Which had perhaps not been a crystal butterdish cover. But
cut glass, crystalized with piety.— Under which sex looked
brutal. Vulgar. The leisure-time occupation of the lower
classes.

& therefore to outrage her mother? . . . still? . . . at her age
. . . with thousands of miles of water between them she would
never not even on a desert island feel the slightest tempta-
tion to fall in love with men whom her mother would have
considered her "own kind." Either of the 2 tall blond men.
Who looked like her twin brothers, to the island women who
were getting off the boat behind them.

Who looked like tobacco jars to the only daughter, the philologist, on the suitcase on the dock. An Indian file of one-

handled tobacco jars, swaying down the gangplank in their
wide black skirts, one arm crooked upward to steady the
  mostly empty; a few still half full   tomato baskets on the
black-braided crown on top of their heads.

Pale-red oblong tomatoes. One of which had rolled from one
of the baskets, on the boat. & made her slip. In her cothurn
sandals. Which she was holding in her hands; thinking that her
mother would have worn flats. Sneakers.

A semicircle of interchangeable women with baskets on
their heads, standing barefoot, in wordless indecision, around
the 3 travelers on the dock. Before the Indian file re-formed. &
set itself in slow motion. Soon the first woman had disappeared between the walls of prickly pears that lined the reddish-yellow sandstone step paths. Which made it impossible to
go anywhere on wheels. Not even a hand-drawn cart. Only
one's feet . . .

The 3 travelers watched the women disappear. One by one.
& wondered how the limping lady philologist was going to get
to the tavern that was mentioned in their travel guide. —The
larger whiter stone cube, probably. Slightly in retreat behind a
loose semicircle of smaller less-white stone cubes. (With tomato patches in the back. Which added green & pale red to the
island yellow. But could not be seen from the dock.)— If
she'd be able to hop there on one foot . . .

& wondered why the last woman turned. & came walking
back toward the dock. Toward them. If she was perhaps the
woman from whose basket the tomato had rolled, on the boat,
& who felt responsible for the injured foot, when she touched
one of the 2 tall blond men on the arm, motioning an offer to
carry one of the suitcases. To place the suitcase on top of her
head, & her   still half full   tomato basket on top of the
suitcase.

Which prompted the second last   now last   woman to turn
& come walking back. Perhaps because she was now last, &
felt a void behind her. Or perhaps because she had seen that
there were 2 suitcases. Motioning for the second suitcase to be
placed on top of her head & her   empty   tomato basket on top
of the suitcase.

Which left the 2 tall blond men free to fold their bony arms
into a kind of cradle seat for the limping philologist.

Who felt very regal   like a queen   on her seat of human flesh
& bones. Mainly bones. & tried to strike up gracious queenly

conversations with the suitcase-bearing women ahead of her.
To find out if it was true that the island language was a kind of
15th-century Spanish. . . . Because her reality lay in words. &
she derived a thrill from learning new ones. From hearing a
familiar reality expressed in unfamiliar sounds.

Which irritated the loudly panting historian who was walking half-sideways on her right. Whose reality did not lie in
words he couldn't understand. & whose thrills were sedentary.
Rarely derived from motion sports physical exertion. Since
he had been raised in the admiration of the motionless dead.

His arms began to sag with irritation. Which communicated
itself to the arms of the quietly sweating botanist who was
walking half-sideways on her left. No longer looking like a
flabbergasted cherub. & the philologist stubbed her injured
foot against one of the wide-spaced uneven yellow sandstone
steps.

*

To the tavern owner's wife who was peeking through the
cork-bead curtain that separated the kitchen from the main
room; a storage room for wine barrels more than a tavern the
3 travelers looked like soldiers, in much-washed faded-blue
summer uniforms. 3 officers perhaps, to be wearing their hair
down to their ears.

But when she took them their tomato soup, she realized that
one of the 3 the one who was sitting in the middle between the
other 2; across from her husband was a woman. With purple
paint on her fingernails. & on her toenails too. & the tavern
owner's wife thought: Lord have mercy! Here we go again
. . . ! , when she realized that her husband was telling the history of the island to the 3. Over glasses of sour island wine . . .

To the woman in the middle. Because she understood his
language. & spoke a language he could understand, even if it
was not exactly like his language.

Which the woman was translating to the other 2.

Which the historian denied she understood, when she translated that: The island had once been a colony of 14 men living
around a single woman.

To whom the 14 men would make love in rotation during
the nights between the new moon & the full moon. But never
after the full moon. When they'd observe 2 weeks of celibacy . . .

Not: the historian said: that he had the slighest objection to a
woman in an authority position. He agreed with Saint Simon
who had said that: the only time a country was truly ruled by
men was when it had a woman on the throne . . .

But the tavern owner was obviously putting her on. Because
he'd had no trouble spotting her queen-bee notions . . .

& she said: Bees were the only creatures in the world she
had no use for. —Except for their honey.— Bees & ants;
because they were bureaucrats. & she had no use for
bureaucrats.

& the historian grinned. & said: But many bureaucrats were
"simple" men . . .

& the botanist wondered why there seemed to be no apiaries
on the island. With its prickly-pear hedges in year-round
bloom . . . Only wild bees . . .

& she asked the tavern owner who was pouring them &
himself more sour wine: How come all the bees were wild on
the island?

& the tavern owner laughed & said: Everybody was a bit
wild, on the island.

Although those bees hadn't always been wild. The One-
Woman Colony had kept bees, supposedly. Of which those
wild bees were the descendants. Just as he, the tavern owner
not everybody on the island, mind you was a remote descen-
dant of the initial lady who . . . His blood was half amazon,
half pirate . . .

Navigators, actually; not pirates. Far-Eastern navigators . . .

Who had cut out a life-size female he begged her pardon:
sex for themselves. In cork from one of the cork oaks after
they wrecked ship on the island. Before his singular ancestress
arrived from the mainland. & founded her colony.

A female sex, cut out of cork. With grass glued around it. It
could be seen he had seen it in the courthouse basement on
the mainland. Where it was kept under glass.

He had gone to see it the last time he had gone to the mainland. With his son. To accompany his son when his son had to
go & join the navy. Because he had wanted his son to see what
navigators might do in an emergency, before he joined the
navy.

His shipwrecked Far-Eastern navigator ancestors used to

squat around the object in a semicircle. Taking turns: he begged her pardon. For several months. Until people on the mainland began noticing lights on the island. A semicircle of torches every night . . .

One dark new-moon night his singular ancestress had left the mainland on a raft. To find out what was going on on the up to then uninhabited island.

Which she had settled, with the 14 navigators. They began building houses one house per navigator in the semicircle in which she had found them squatting. & a somewhat larger house for herself. Slightly in retreat; in the center . . .

& the historian said: that the tavern owner's fairy tale proved only one thing, with its alleged "evidence" in the courthouse basement on the mainland ought to prove one thing to her: how *impersonal* a thing sex was, with her "simple" men.

Unless she hadn't understood a word of what the man had been saying. Because it was most unlikely that the island had ever been on or even off any (Far-Eastern: rubbish!) navigators' route.

& she said: Why rubbish! Hadn't navigators lost their way before. His C. Columbus. The legendary Ulysses whom he admired so much. (. . . Because Ulysses was a notorious philanderer? A true upholder of the double-standard, with a wife sitting at home doing therapy on her loom . . .)

& the historian pointed out that: Ancient Greek society had been matriarchal more than patriarchal . . .

& she said that: she wasn't interested in hierarchies. No matter who was sitting at the top. She was interested in EQUALITY!

& the historian asked the botanist who was gazing into his tomato soup if he had observed much equality in nature?

& continued to say that: Trying to *equalize* everything on the same plane was a flat fallacy. Pretending not to be superior to an ant which was pretty easy, since the ant was hardly going to claim its granted equality from her in order not to recognize anyone as superior to her . . . Wasn't that the reason why she kept turning on to "simple" men . . . & for running to this faraway island! To escape competition. & turn herself into a mysterious foreign lady . . .

& she said: Hadn't he come running with her? He knew very well she had come to this island to do linguistic research. & she wasn't afraid of competition in her field.

The tavern owner had been looking at them questioningly. She smiled at him. & he began telling them the legend of his remote ancestress's death.

Which had not been a natural death. Although she had lived to be quite an old woman . . .

. . . What was the use of growing old? If all one learned was new ways of fooling oneself . . . : interrupted the historian. Who had been cutting his cigarettes in half, to cut down on his smoking.

Well into her sixties . . . When she assembled her 14 husbands or as many of them as were still alive. & asked the favorite or perhaps the one whose turn it would have been, according to the moon, since she had no favorites, supposedly or one of her sons, according to some people; one of her by-now-adult sons who participated in the turn-taking to put her raft afloat. The raft on which she had initially come over from the mainland. To float her raft at sunset, on the longest day of the year. & she had come out of the house in which she lived alone, dressed in flowing white chiffon. & had stretched out on the raft. & had asked one of the husbands or sons to row her out to sea with long staffs. Along the blood-colored path the setting sun was slanting across the water like a luminous bridge from the shore to the horizon.

& a mile or perhaps only half a mile out to sea she had slowly rolled off the raft & let herself sink. Together with the sun. Letting herself sink at the precise moment at which the sun slipped behind the horizon. & the husband or son; who may also have been a husband had rowed himself back to the island . . .

& she said: She thought that was very moving. Very beautiful.

& the historian said: That she was raving. Because of the tavern owner's attentions? That it was pathetic to watch her play spider to the man's fly.

Which might conceal a disappointment, incidentally. Might reveal less ego-gratification than she'd like to expect, from a "simple" man . . .

Who was obviously not too simple to put her on.

When you touch mud with a white glove, it isn't the mud that gets glovey: he said.

& the botanist thought: His mother would like the climate on the island. It ought to be good for her arthritis.

*

She was sitting in her old yellow bathrobe on the windowsill in one of the 2 rooms the tavern owner had rented to them. After this lemon-faced wife refused to rent them a third room. Which was her son's room. & not for rent, even if her son was away. With the navy.

Why couldn't 2 men sleep in the same room? she'd heard the lemon-faced wife say to the tavern owner, going down the stairs: Or were they maybe both sleeping with the woman with the paint on her nails, & were trying to hide it from each other?

& she'd heard the tavern owner laugh.

Women were always sitting. On imitation leather, outside offices. Behind glass, in cafés. On wooden benches across from *pissotières*. On steps around statues. On the edge of beds: freshly sheeted beds damp messy beds. Immobile grounded women, waiting for mobile men to arrive: Late . . . breathless . . . laughing . . . loving . . . desiring . . . tired . . . apologetic . . . caustic. Later. Later . . . Who pulled the seated to her feet. Ending the waiting siege.

She was waiting for the tavern owner to knock at the door of her room. & bring her the oval cork basin with heated sea water in which to bathe her injured foot.

He had brought her such a basin the afternoon before.

& the afternoon before that. Which had been the afternoon of their arrival. Assuring her that heated sea water would soon absorb the swelling. Her instep was not broken: he had assured her: only sprained. He could tell a fracture from a sprain. From his goats. That were forever doing things to their feet on the crumbly island rock. Lukewarm seawater would soon absorb the swelling . . .

Which he had begun to massage, that first afternoon . . . with her soap. For a long time.

Until she laid her other good foot on his shoulder. Which she could feel heaving with the massaging movements of his hands.

The heaving movements had stopped, when he leaned his mouth on his shoulder & began licking her toes. Like a goat. & she had wondered: Was he getting a taste of her soap in his mouth?

& had sat motionless. Frozen inside his desire for her like a prehistoric queen bee inside a chunk of amber, watching his wine-red goat tongue. Avoiding his eyes. Her body urging, under the slightly open bathrobe. She didn't know how slightly open. Feeling him looking at her face. To catch her eyes, to ask permission of her eyes, before he . . .

Not yet. Not just yet!

Waiting for her eyes to tell his eyes to tell his tongue: More! Higher! Go on! Up! Further up . . . Don't stop at the toes. Between my toes . . .

Not yet.

Not because his lemon-faced wife might come up if he didn't come down. Soon . . .

Or because the historian might want to borrow her mirror. Knock at her door & find the tavern owner in her room. On his knees at her feet. Kneeling with condescension? . . . Unable to stand up, perhaps . . .

Or because the botanist might feel the need to tell her about his exploration of the island, before he went to his room for a short nap before dinner . . .

But because she didn't want to spoil the tavern owner's beautiful desire for her by fulfilling it. Just yet . . .

Nor just yet, the following afternoon. When she had put on a white chiffon robe. To surprise the tavern owner with a different robe. Not unlike the robe his remote ancestress had worn to let herself sink into the setting sun. She had wanted to look like a different woman to the tavern owner when he brought her another basin of lukewarm sea water . . .

When the historian had been in her room, shaving in her mirror. Because there was no mirror in the other room.

It had surprised the tavern owner. Who had looked at her questioningly. & had waited for her to nod. & smile a delighted smile, before he'd knelt down again & begun massaging her actually less swollen foot.

& she had pressed her other foot down on his massaging fingers. & touched his fingers with her toes. Lingeringly. While

saying to the historian's half-averted profile: To let it grow.
Why didn't the historian grow a beard, here on the island?

In English. Which the tavern owner did not understand.

& the historian had turned one lathered cheek toward them,
& wiped 2 very red laughing lips out of the white foam. & said:
That he could take a hint. But not before he had shaved the
other cheek. She didn't want him to grow a one-sided beard on
the island, did she. Or was she in that much of a hurry?

& she had laughed. & said: No, no. To the historian's again
averted profile.

& the tavern owner had let her injured foot sink gently to the
bottom of the basin. & had grabbed her other ankle. So hard,
she had asked him: Was he trying to break it?

& he had said: Enough was enough. & got up & walked out
of the room.

& the historian had asked: Well, & what was the matter
now? Had something . . . not his presence? . . . complicated
her simple man? Or was her foot cured? So fast?

& she had shrugged. Her body raging with loss. Out of tune.
Refusing to believe what had happened to it.

& she had promised it: Tomorrow. . . . Tomorrow afternoon . . .

When she was sitting in the windowsill. In her old yellow
bathrobe again. Not to remind the tavern owner of the afternoon before. Of her white-chiffon behavior. Since it never
seemed to work out when one dressed up for it.

She was sitting in the windowsill, looking down at the tomato bushes. Counting the pale-red oblong tomatoes among the
leaves. When the cork basin knocked at the door of her room
 a high sound of cork knocking on wood & the tavern owner's lemon-faced wife pressed the door handle down with her
elbow & carried it in.

ISHMAEL REED

is the author of the following novels: *The Free-Lance Pall-bearers, Yellow Back Radio Broke-Down, Mumbo Jumbo* (Doubleday & Bantam, 1967, 1969, 1972), and *The Last Days of Louisiana Red* (Random House, 1974); books of poetry: *Conjure* (University of Massachusetts Press, 1972), *Chattanooga* (Random House, 1973); and is co-founder of *The East Village Other,* 1965; *Advance,* Newark community newspaper, 1965; Yardbird Publishing Co., Inc., editorial director, 1971; Reed, Cannon & Johnson Communications Co., director, 1973. He was nominated for 1973 National Book Awards in fiction and poetry, and 1973 Pulitzer in poetry.

From   *Flight to Canada*

Catzman, so named for his knowledge of events taking place at long distances, stood in his robes, barefoot, rich mane of gray hair, on one of the beaches of Tadd, a planet located in the galaxy of Dameronia in a universe one reaches through a black hole at the bottom of earth's galaxy.

Catzman and another Elder, Zolar, are watching as a technician clinks away at an object dug into the sand. It resembles a huge silver horsefly.

"He should be here soon," Catzman says.

"Undoubtedly," replies Zolar, "but will he take the assignment? You know how awful it is on that planet. We can hardly penetrate its belts with our radio waves it's so saturated with junk."

"He will. He'll interrupt his vacation on the 10th moon for the assignment. Bloom Dido is a true citizen of this world and all of the other worlds of this solar system: Good Bait, Fontainebleau, Hot House, Lady Bird, Bulla-Babe, and Delirium."

Suddenly, the men shield their eyes at the flash of white light streaking across the heavens. It's Bloom Dido and his economy spaceship *The Yellow Wasp* whirring and humming toward them. Momentarily it comes to a smooth rest on the beach and out steps Bloom Dido. "I came as soon as I received your call. It must have been pretty important for you to call me in from the resort of the 10th Moon."

Bloom Dido stands, hands on hips, in his silver skin-tight suit and hood which reveals only his electric face and red-coal eyes.

"It's extremely important," Catzman says beginning to walk toward some mounds away from the technician still examining the object in the sand. Zolar walks with them; Bloom Dido in the middle of the threesome.

"Many years ago our scientists learned to see through the black holes of the Universes and came in contact with worlds similar to our own. We spotted a planet that so resembled ours that it could be our sister planet. It wasn't long after beaming them in that we were able to examine them close and we sent Cyborgs there and they were able to infiltrate the normal population and find out the planet's civilizations and how they functioned. Now we've discovered that one Rockland Porke has set up scientists in the caves of Maryland who are toying about with diabolical systems. He has sent a probe of our Universe and one of them has just landed. A very primitive probe but nevertheless one that has already gotten into our business. He's taken over his own world and now he wants to besmudge ours. He and his brother, David, a man so strange, he works, sleeps, and eats—the man lives in a Bank and has never left the Bank, the epicenter of the great Porke Fortune which rings the world like blobs of sausages each tied to the other. We thought that Lincoln would do it but the man can't make up his mind. He can never make up his mind. It took him two years to fire one of his insolent generals and now he's been dilly dallying around unable to make up his mind about freeing the slaves.

They are interrupted by the technician who walks toward them in his white jacket and black pants.

"It's a very crude device by our standards your excellency. Low-gain antenna, airglow ultraviolet spectrometer, magnetometers, tiltable solar panel, infrared radiometer, plasma science, rocket motor nozzle, sun shade, steerable high-gain antenna—a real knickknack but capable of doing the job. It was probably sent here to probe our resources, learn our temperature, do a soil test, find out all about our surface this time but next time they'll probably dig a little deeper. Little gadget probably took thousands upon thousands of pictures before it blinked out."

"That does it," Catzman said. "We must stop this Rockland

Porke. The man is a crocodile. We must get rid of his slaves who build these things for him. That's the one mystery we've not been able to decipher. The man holds sway over his slaves so that they don't seem to want to be free though a few run away from time to time."

"Sir, what do you want me to do."

"We want you to zig-zag on down to that planet and tell their President Mr. Linkland—"

"Lincoln," Zolar corrects Catzman.

"O, yes. Tell Mr. Lincoln that if he doesn't free those slaves of Porke's we will put that planet off-limits to every self-respecting tour of the Universe. We will put it under patrol by all of the intelligences of the Universes, who will harrass it's airplanes—

"Hundreds of UFOs will buzz its nights scaring its cows and startling couples necking in their jalopies, causing them to drop their beers in their laps. We will bombard their radio systems with static so that people won't be able to listen to their favorite radio shows. In other words, we will put earth under martial law until further notice. Here are your instructions and our message to Mr. Lincoln."

"Is that all, Sir."

"Yes, Bloom, have a good mission." Bloom Dido and the two elders shake hands. He climbs into his Yellow Wasp and zooms off. On the beach, the technician packs up his equipment and leaves. Zolar and Catzman stand for awhile looking at the red trail that Bloom Dido has left.

"Do you think he'll be successful?"

"There's always another one to take his place."

"And you, so much the democrat."

"Democracy. O yes. For us. How do you think this system would work without our council of twenty-two. Each man voting his conscience. Our villas and our landscaped gardens, our lunches at La Rochefoucauld. Our full-time maids and our summers at Le Clerc. We need all those things so that we'll have time to think good and noble thoughts. But for those people. Never. That one, he's a little brighter than the rest of the Chumponoids but nothing will ever come of it."

ROGER SKILLINGS

from Bath, Maine, born 1937. *Alternative Lives,* Ithaca House. Chairman pro tem of the writing staff of the Fine Arts Work Center, in Provincetown, a nonprofit community that gives grants, lodging and studios to young artists and writers and lets them work independently. Not a school, no mickey mouse. Also on the staff, Stanley Kunitz, Alan Dugan, Keither Althaus.

Four Very Short Stories

DADE CITY

You won't believe this fucking scene. I just went to the Police Station to get an application for a pistol permit because I think we should all be armed. The guy behind the desk says What d'you want a pistol for? I says Why can't I have a pistol, you got a pistol. He says I'm a policeman. It went on that way a while. Well I says I saw a nice pistol in the window up in Orleans, I want to buy it, I want to do some target shooting out in the woods, I already got a rifle permit.

He said if we gave everybody a permit who wanted one it'd be Dade City here, where you from? I told him Havana, Cuba. He hits his forehead with his palm like in the Polack jokes and says You want to hijack a plane? No I says I want to start a revolution. He says Why don't you get on your motor scooter and ride south? Four years in Korea I says and I can't have a pistol permit?

The rest of them're watching NYPD on TV, New York Police Department. We couldn't interrupt that, the other guys kept waving at us to keep quiet. He says You don't have any need for a pistol. I says I want to do some target shooting, all the while I'm going plink plink plink with my finger like I'm sighting just a little to the side of his head. He says Here's an application, good luck. I says If I don't get it I'm going to take it to the Supreme Court.

THE LIFE

That's the hardest work I ever done in my life. I was a steelpourer in Pittsburgh, that was nothin to this. You're down in the hold fillin baskets with fish, thirty tons a fish, you're up to your knees, I didn't even have no boots. You stickum in the basket with this gaff, then you handum up through the hatch. Some guy's up there eatin donuts. I filled one of um too full, big fuckin fish fell out and hit me on the head. Hey! First time in my life I ever got hit on the head with a fish. Those baskets must weigh fifty pounds, I thought I was gonna die down there. I was so stiff I couldn't get outa bed this mornin, but I'm gonna try it again oner these days, it can't get any harder, it's gotta get easier, I musta learned somethin huh? Some fuckers don't like to work, I do. You work your day, you get paid, noner this weekly shit, you go get drunk a couple days, you get broke, you go back to work again, that's the life.

North Cambridge

I hadn't been home in about three months so one day I got it together and called my mother. I said Get the turkey ready and the cake and ice cream. I was just joking you know. She said What time will you be home? Oh I said about noon. I was gonna hitch-hike, I left early enough. You know what she did? She got up at seven o'clock and cooked a turkey and baked a cake and bought some ice cream. You know what time I got there? One-thirty in the morning, and I was stinking drunk. I ate a little bit of turkey and some ice cream, I couldn't eat any cake, and then I passed out. My father wouldn't even talk to me, I couldn't talk anyway. My mother gave me a lot of shit about that next morning.

What happened was my ride went right by a bar I used to hang out in so I went in for a beer and all my old buddies were there. They were telling me about the kids in the neighborhood, 17-18-year-olds, they all run in gangs now. They're very hostile, they think it proves their masculinity. They just hang around on the corner all day hoping somebody'll come by with a joint, they've got nothing else to do.

The cop on the beat's a real ballbuster. They throw bottles in the street, and then they wonder why. He's just doin his duty, that's his job. So they rolled his son one night, they got three, four dollars. One of them had a blade, he's trying to make it into the gang so he slashes the kid a few times in the back, gave him 100 stitches in the hospital. So the kid mentions a few names, what's he supposed to do, keep his mouth shut when he gets carved up? Now they say they're going to kill him. Like it's all his fault, like he asked to have a cop for a father.

I get along with my parents all right. My father can't stand long hair though. If I was in the service he'd accept me. He manages an autobody shop. He can't see anyone working less than fifty hours a week. All his friends do it, then they go home and watch TV and wash the car on weekends. I went to a community college for a year. It was just like high school, there was no social atmosphere like a university or anything. After class you'd sit in a drugstore and sip a coke and then go home, so I quit.

I happen to have an uncle in the phone company. He's an executive, he's been there thirty years. My father told him I wanted a job there, he didn't even ask me. It's good pay, they start you on your pension plan the first day, you're supposed to be there the rest of your life, but you have to have references. It's like being spoken for by a politician. My uncle would've had to do it, I didn't want him to have to lie, so I split. That's how I got down here. My father still can't understand why I don't want to spend the next forty years in North Cambridge.

IMAGE

Sometimes I think I'm going to die without ever escaping that room. It had a couch that pulled out where they slept. There was a crib where my brother and I slept, there was a yellow light, a window and a kind of stuffed chair. My father used to sit me on his knee and tell me about the Mexican Revolution. He fought, he shot people, they tied the rich to the railroad tracks, then he moved to America because he was tired of fighting. My mother was a waitress and drank herself to death at 37.

A memory I shall never escape, a memory I have every day of my life, is of my mother screaming and my father bending her back with one hand in her hair until she was like an acrobat while he held the iron she had been ironing his shirts with an inch from her face. That image is there every time I go to bed with a man.

PETER SPIELBERG,

who was born in Vienna, has for a long time lived in America (by grace of naturalization) where he writes and translates his own fiction from low German to high English. Stories and poems, fragments and shards of his longer works have been included in many literary magazines. *BEDROCK: A Work of Fiction Composed of Fifteen Scenes from My Life* (The Crossing Press) can be and was described, by one critic, as "a terrifyingly comic and seriously absurdist tour de force." His novel, *Twiddledum Twaddledum,* published by the Fiction Collective, is a "darkly postmodern and murderous" picaresque Bildungsroman with a twist. "Laissez Faire," printed below, is a segment from a work-in-progress, *Play Dead,* a jocoserious palindromic novel dealing with modern family life—sexual games and domestic murder.

Laissez Faire

dramatis personae:
    Richard, the husband
    Honey, the wife
    Dick, her bearded lover

It was a Sunday afternoon. Late, almost dark. Richard had not shaven in more than two days, not since before going to work Friday morning. The pricking of the stubble was keeping him from dozing off as he liked to do on Sundays after the heavy midday dinner.

He could not find a comfortable position. The couch's mohair upholstery rubbed against his nose. It smelled stale, forcing him to swallow a mouthful of dust with each breath. He turned on his back, but then his throat began to bother him, a tickling as if a hair had gotten lodged in his windpipe. He cleared his throat to try to expel the irritant and turned on his side, cradling his head between his arms, elbows bent, hands over ears.

Now the stubble of his beard rubbed against the inner sides

of his wrists. The wirelike hairs pierced the cloth of his shirt sleeves. Like horsehairs through a mattress cover. When he pushed his hands under the pillow, his pulsebeat throbbed in his ear. The ticking of a clock. He turned on his stomach. It was worse. He could feel a rash developing on his neck where stubble chafed exposed skin.

It was no use. There was no chance of falling asleep. Infuriating, since he had come to count on the traditional Sunday afternoon naps. They helped fortify him for the work days ahead when there was never enough time for sleep.

Reluctantly, he opened his eyes and swung his legs off the couch. The sitting-room lay in semidarkness with only a wan haze seeping through the blinds. The apartment was silent.

Everything was asleep. He had taken the phone off the hook. His wife was in the bedroom, far enough away, two closed doors between them, and between the two rooms a long corridor running the full length of the apartment.

It should have been the best part of the week, a peaceful, dead time. It wasn't. The beard itched worse than ever. He could not understand why he had postponed shaving for so long, especially since he was usually meticulous about his personal hygiene. The slovenliness was uncharacteristic. Perhaps he was coming down with a cold. A couple of precautionary aspirins might help. Even better if he shook off this lethargy. If he shaved quickly and quietly he might make it back to his sanctuary with time enough for a little nap.

But when he opened the bathroom cabinet he discovered that he was fresh out of razor blades. Of course. It came back to him clearly. It was on Friday morning that he had pushed the last blade into the used blade slot of the medicine cabinet, pausing, as he always did, to listen to the silvery sound of its fall as it tumbled down the hollow between the walls. A bottomless shaft. The thin metal slivers speeding back to the earth's magnetic core.

He automatically rinsed the empty, useless safety razor, shook it dry, and slammed the cabinet shut. So after all, there was nothing to be done. Then he remembered that his wife kept a straight razor hidden in the bottom drawer of her dressing table. He would go and get it—palm it while she was asleep, since she would no more lend it to him than he would allow her to use his. It was sure to be jagged from the strenuous use to which she put it on her legs and armpits. Still it would be better than nothing.

Cautiously, on tiptoes, so as not to awaken her, he crept along the dark corridor toward the bedroom. (He had never before violated their agreement for Sunday afternoon privacy, and neither, to her credit and to his surprise, had she.) When he reached the door he stopped. It stood ajar. And from the room: sounds. The bedsprings jangled as if the sleeper were tossing about, kicking at the entangled sheets. Someone moaned as if in pain.

TROMPE-L'OEIL

He first thought that she was not alone. But when he pushed the door farther open he found that he had been mistaken. As far as he could see (although admittedly it was hard to see anything in the deepening winter gloom) there was no one else in the room. She was lying on top of the bed. He could just make out her shape, the white slip on the crimson silk bedspread. She was not asleep. She had heard the door open.

Raising herself up on her elbows she called to him, "Is that you, Dick?"

He did not answer. Letting the door slam shut behind him, he approached the bed.

"Lord, I thought you'd never come." She fell back on the bed and pulled her slip up above her thighs. The nature of the gesture was unmistakable.

Its effect on him was unexpected. Instead of turning the lights on and confronting his wife with her error, he played along with the deception, taking to the role of the lover without a moment's hesitation, falling into the part smoothly as if he had done it before.

The excitement he felt was so fierce that he did not pause to take his clothes off. He took her with his trousers on; not once, but twice.

He would have stayed for more, but after the second time became concerned that she might recognize him as an impostor. He slipped from the dark room without looking back, barely pausing to mumble an assent to her parting "Tomorrow afternoon?"

Later that evening at the supper table he scrutinized his wife closely to see if there were a sign of recognition. There was none. Everything during the meal proceeded according to well-established custom. She passed him the dishes without a sideward glance. They barely exchanged a word. The radio was tuned to a continuous news station. The newsreel rolled on without stop, covering their silence.

He studied her face, but could not detect a trace of the afternoon's activities. She showed no aftereffects, not a smile, not a telltale bite mark, not even a faint blush—while his whole body burned. His face felt hot and raw, not so much from the close shave he had given himself immediately before the meal (he had taken the precaution to shave off every last hair of the stubble, having made a hurried trip to the Jewish quarter of the city where after what had seemed to him a long and dangerous search he had finally found a stall that was open in defiance of the county's strict blue laws, its shutters half rolled down, whose sullen proprietor had sold him the necessary blades with groundless ill-humor, an unknown brand, at an exorbitant price) but from the recollection of what had transpired on their bed. His hands were unsteady as he cut the cold ham on his plate. He had to be asked twice to pass the bread before he heard.

To Turn the Other Cheek

When he showed up for his rendezvous the next afternoon he wore a hairpiece on his face, a dark red beard, cropped to follow the outline of the jaw and cheeks. It was the best he had been able to procure on such short notice. Although its color clashed with his hair, the barber had argued convincingly that genuine facial hair is often a different shade from the hair on one's head. He was right. It passed muster and what's more it stuck fast to his face as tightly as a second skin, withstanding the most strenuous abuse.

Honey played with it, stroking it like the fur of a dog, twisting her fingers in its tight curls. She clung to the beard as he boarded her. She used it as a handle to pull him into position when he hesitated in fulfilling a promise he had made the day before, forcing his head between her legs.

"Say you love it, say you love my thing. Tell me! "

And when he complied, she continued: "Oh yes, you're my best lap pet, my hungry cunt hound. Yes, that's good. There . . . there . . . Lovely."

"My cunt, my lovely cunt," he echoed.

"Yes. Tell me," she responded.

When it was over he felt angry. He pushed her away so violently that her skull hit the headboard.

He leaped from the bed and made a dash for the dresser, pulling the drawers open, flinging her lingerie in all directions, until he found the razor. He would show her once and for all what she was really like, he thought. This was the moment to end the masquerade.

"I have you where I want you now," he heard himself shout.

Yet when he saw his reflection in the mirror—a naked red-bearded middle-aged man brandishing a cut-throat razor in his fist—the futility of the gesture struck him so clearly that tears came to his eyes. What was he shouting about? And the blade —he did not need it to get rid of the beard. What nonsense! Whom was he trying to fool? Some rubbing alcohol would easily loosen the mask. And once the truth was out, would her humiliation be any greater than his? He started to put the razor down, when Honey's voice checked him.

"No," she cried. "Don't stop now! Shave it off. I want you to. I do."

She had misunderstood his intentions.

"Yes, do it like you said you would." She pointed to her belly and pushed a pillow under her buttocks to raise the mount, offering the golden triangle to his blade.

It didn't take a minute. The hair came off with ease, in strips like lambs' wool; the locks fell away as in a dream. The expanse of denuded skin was dazzling, whiter than the inside of her thighs and softer—like new skin over a wound—more sensitive than her inner flesh, more secret. He rubbed his hirsute face against it, luxuriated in its total, absolute nakedness.

Anger was banished; resentment gone, leaving him cool, refreshed. It was like a new knowledge, the discovery of a new-found land, a sweet metamorphosis.

MIDWINTER BAWDINESS

It was dusk when he left the bed. The streetlamps had already been turned on. Oncoming night streaked the sky with black soot.

He did not notice the falling ashes. Even the rush-hour crowds which he ordinarily despised could not disturb his contentment. He pushed his way through them with unaccustomed ease, sidestepping an army of homebound attaché-case carriers that stormed out of the subway, leapfrogging over escaping school children, exchanging pleasant bumps and smiles with well-dressed young women who dashed in and out of food shops, secretaries and receptionists shopping for their makeshift suppers. The crush, the noise, the impatience, the hurly-burly was not at all unpleasant. All seemed fresh as if washed by rain—fecund; trees bursting out of season cast their seed on the asphalt ground and dusted the cars so that the drivers had to turn their windshield wipers on. Birds flew up from the roofs where they had been warming themselves in the smoke of chimneys. They darted about madly as if the winter were over and they were chasing a swarm of succulent maybugs.

He was sorry that he did not have farther to walk. He was there already, just around the corner and into the nondescript red brick building which housed the local branch of the public library.

Here the excitement of the streets had not penetrated. Permanent calm and enforced silence prevailed, interrupted only by the occasional creaking of a chair, the rustling of a newspaper, or the sound of a reader apologetically swallowing the saliva that had accumulated in his mouth.

Eyes lifted at the intrusion, but were immediately lowered when they saw that his destination was the washroom.

He locked himself in a stall, put his eyeglasses on, took a bottle of rubbing alcohol from his briefcase and unglued the beard. Then he flushed the toilet in case anyone was listening. A couple of minutes later he emerged as his old self, eyes distorted by thick lenses, shiny clean-shaven face, tie tightly knotted, stoop-shouldered, head tilted to one side as if to balance the heavy book-filled briefcase which he clutched under his left armpit. No one gave him a second glance.

When he arrived home, dinner was waiting on the table. As on the previous evening he searched his wife's face for a sign of recognition, and, not finding that, for any indication that her afternoon's lovemaking had left its mark. As before, he found nothing. Only her unperturbed, self-satisfied calm. There was nothing remarkable about that. Perhaps she drank more coffee than ordinarily.

As soon as the meal was over he retreated to the shelter of his wing-backed armchair and pretended to have fallen asleep. He wasn't sleepy though, only winded, physically spent— which was not surprising considering his performance in bed where he had carried on like a young buck of eighteen, having completely ignored the fact that he was a sedentary man in his middle forties, a head of a family, a good citizen and taxpayer, a father of regular habits; out of training as a lover, flabby, rusty as a hinge. He had pressed muscles into service that he had not called into action for close to twenty years, that he had allowed to atrophy by disuse, and others to which he had never had cause to resort.

Although he was bushed it was a pleasant sensation, like the warm fatigue one feels after a day of sunbathing and wrestling with the breakers at the seashore. The soreness in the region of his groin was particularly pleasing since it bore witness to the rebirth of his virility. Even now the flesh was not dead. The memory pictures of parted lips, of the intricate windings and turnings of her body which flickered before his closed eyes like lantern slides on a screen were enough to cause a flutter and a stiffening. He was amazed by the transformation. He covered his lap with one hand and pressed the other to his thumping heart, then quickly looked around the room to make sure Honey had not observed his actions.

Lust in Action

He enters the bedroom. His mistress has been expecting him. The curtains are drawn. Bedside lamps lit. She lies sprawled on a chaise longue facing the door. Her blouse is unbuttoned, the slit revealing a French bra which is barely able to confine its imposing contents. Her skirt, hitched-up to her waist, displays the matching accessories, a black garter belt over lace step-ins, the taut straps, lying snugly like leather reins on the naked thighs, stretching to charcoal gray stocking tops.

Her pose is calculated. The production has been carefully rehearsed. The leading lady has played the part before.

"Unhook me, lover," she whispers hoarsely, inviting him by arching her back so that her breasts are pushed up and out, straining to escape the restraint of the straps. Freed, the twin cones of firm flesh stand erect, their pinkish-brown tips coming to sharp points as if they have been whittled by a pencil sharpener.

"That's better," she sighs with relief, cupping them in her hands, jiggling them so that they quiver like molded jelly. She offers them to her lover who has stepped back to admire the display. The position is copied from an album of glossy photographs, *Famous Art-Tits by Famous Artists,* a gift from her suitor, which lies open to the appropriate page on a claw-footed vanity table.

She turns the page. The model's arms are crossed over her breasts. The slender egg-shaped face is turned up, eyes wide, blond hair rich, clinging to head and cheeks, sleek as a helmet. Her lips are swollen, full like bolsters. She wets them, running her tongue between them in a caress which is also an invitation.

While he is busy at her breasts, she undoes her skirt and lets it slip to the floor. Stepping dexterously out of it (without pulling the nipple from his mouth) she gives the skirt a swift kick sending it flying across the room.

"That's marvelous, my love. How I'd like you to milk me all day long, all night long. Now do the other." She moves his head, tugging playfully at his hair. "You've been neglecting my favorite titty. Don't you love them both the same? . . . Hush, foolish boy. I know you do. I was only teasing . . . cock-teasing, my pet."

She makes herself comfortable, pushing him down on the edge of the bed, while she kneels before him on a plush has-sock—a move designed to give him a full view of her lushness. The change in posture pushes her high buttocks charmingly out. The ripe cheeks ripple temptingly.

"Do you want me with my stockings on? . . . But don't tear them, you bastard! Don't be so rough."

And later: "Be rough. Good. Fix me. Make me your slave, your slavey, your whore. Screw me from all sides. Shove it all the way in. Yes, like that! Make me do it. Force me. Give me what I deserve. Punish me. Fuck me up the ass. Make me lick it up. Tell me I'm the wildest lay in captivity. The best all-round cunt in the world. Do it. Say it. Never stop." She recites *moderato cantabile,* her gestures studied, mimicking the mannerisms of story-book courtesans, her words following the script.

ENTR'ACTE

To avoid all suspicion the husband continued to perform his conjugal duties on schedule as before. When the night of his next semimonthly commitment arrived he was ready. The front door was locked and bolted, the shutters closed, the main gas cock shut. He had taken his bath. Now it was his wife's turn, and as always on these nights she was taking particularly long, soaking herself in the hot water till her skin became wrinkled. He waited impatiently in bed. The sooner they got started the sooner it would be over and the sooner he could get some sleep. But she took her time.

He was at the point of dozing off when at last she came out of the bathroom.

"Wait," she grunted as if his reaching for her came as a surprise. "I'll have to go put in that silly diaphragm."

He was half amused by the subterfuge since he knew from his afternoon sessions that she used no such protection at other times. He suspected that she was on the pill (or perhaps the intra-uterine loop would be more her style). This rubber article business was another way of putting him off.

When she reappeared, she checked that the bedroom door was locked and that the curtains were properly drawn. She turned the lights off and then finally came to bed.

"Your bathrobe," he had to remind her.

She took it off grudgingly.

It was difficult to get started. He fingered her breasts. They hung slack. Without definite shape, slipping about under his hand, yielding as melted wax. He reached between her legs. She shied away, but his fingers stubbornly returned to explore the perineum.

When his eyes had accustomed themselves to the dark, he forced her legs farther apart and crouched over her to have a closer look. She offered no explanation for the absence of pubic hair.

His interest in the shorn area was genuine. He had totally

forgotten. Somehow not associating the two. Of course, it made no sense. Yet there it was. What was even more incredible was that he now found the sight of the naked cunt disagreeable. Even offensive.

"Why, you're as bald as an egg!" The reproach was on the tip of his tongue. He caught himself in time, swallowed his disgust and proceeded as if he had not noticed.

The hot bath and medicinal douche had done their worst. The vagina felt waterlogged, like the rubber webbing of a cold hot-water bottle, its ridges hard and smooth. And despite her elaborate sanitary precautions, a stale gamy smell rose from the orifice as he pumped (unenthusiastically, yet keeping to a steady rhythm) as if their joining were like the action of a pair of bellows that forced fetid gas out of her rectum.

The act was no more pleasing to her than it was to him. Although she did not complain, she did not try to hide her weariness with the business. Her head was turned to the side, her eyes closed, her mouth open, set in a hard grimace, the lips drawn in.

"Now?" she asked. "Now."

But he could not terminate, no matter how hard he worked. The rubbery flesh encircling his semi-erect organ irritated rather than stimulated. He slipped from one slick wall to the other without finding a soft spot, not even a foothold which would enable him to pull himself off by friction.

"Aren't you ready?"

It looked hopeless until he thought of concentrating on the last afternoon Dick had spent with Honey, the sport they had had on the same bed. The stains must still be on the sheets. He had left her soaked. "My great big dirty Dick," she had called him as he pressed his point home, responding to his thrusts like a skilled horsewoman to a cantering steed, her torso twisting smoothly, rocking to his gait, hips churning, raised thighs pivoting as if greased. In and out, to and fro, up and down, fitted together like a ball-and-socket joint lubricated with sweet butter, rich as cream, smooth as honey, soft as silk, and oh! the final quiver and then a breathless pause and then, then the pulsating deliverance, her flesh pouting to receive the full gush, drinking it in in great deep swallows, straining to suck up the last spurt.

With a final twist he brought it off. The discharge trickled out like drops from a leaky faucet. He hardly felt the emission, as if his penis were anesthetized, carved out of a piece of balsa wood.

He was so worn out by the exertion that he did not have the strength to withdraw. He just lay there spent and dejected while the blood slowly and painfully returned to the shrunken organ. Finally, she had to roll him off.

TURN TAIL

The door had hardly closed before Dick had unzipped his fly. Without further preliminaries he pressed against Honey walking her backwards till she bumped against the dining-room table.

"Suppose he comes back?" she protested weakly as he pulled her skirt up and shoved the cobweb-thin underpants to one side.

"He won't," he shrugged the idea off. "But if he does, he'll only have himself to blame if he doesn't like the view. Might do him good to get an eyeful." And he turned his full attention to keeping his partner delicately balanced on the table's edge, inching her further back, adjusting the angle of contact until he achieved the proper position, her weight evenly distributed, his legs firmly braced. "That's better," he thought.

Honey obligingly spread her thighs wider to facilitate his entrance. Yet once the mechanics of the joining were successfully concluded, her thoughts returned to the possibility of an untimely interruption.

"We'll have to train him to knock first," she suggested.

Her lover would not take her concern seriously. "Who'll be the first to cry 'come!'?" he parried.

"Oh, you're wicked!" she joined in the laughter. "But wait, love," she added seriously. "Not yet. Not yet."

"Knock first and come later—eh?"

"Yes, later. Much later. Mmmuch," she agreed, forgetting all about her original apprehensions.

EYEWITNESS

The scene is cropped by the frame of the keyhole. To the right, the bottom corner of the bed; to the left, a dressing table and a backless chair or stool (or it may be a large cushion; the legs, if any, are cut off by the foot of the bed). Almost the entire bed, though, is reflected in the triptych dressing table mirror.

A woman lies face up on the bed, nude except for a garter belt and figured black stockings. The disparity between the black legs and yellow-haired head is forced to one's attention partly because the angle of the mirror focuses on the anti-podes, thereby foreshortening the midriff and bringing the legs close to the head, also because the legs are shown from three sides, while the rest of her body is reflected only once. It appears as if the legs belong to another woman—a brunette. The illusion is reenforced when the figure on the bed raises her arms and clasps her hands behind her golden blond head, thus uncovering her armpits. A shadow falls across them. The tufts of axillary hair look like dark cobwebs. An examination of the woman's belly does not resolve the inconsistency since the pubis is plucked clean, and the skin between the stocking tops and the garter belt is achromatic, of neutral pigmentation.

ROUNDELAY

They came off together on cue like a clap of hands.

"Bravo!" he called.

"Great!" she sang.

"Encore!" they chimed in chorus. And she turned over to make herself ready for another round, her quilted buttocks forming two perfect rings where cheeks joined thighs, the rich upholstery vibrating gleefully, the skin tight as a drum.

"Let there be no shillyshallying," she hummed, fingering his instrument.

"Let there be no dillydallying," he harmonized. "But oh, the joy of dingle-dallying!" And he saluted her best part with a melodious lip-smacking buss as a playful prelude to more serious organ grinding.

TOUCH & GO

When the evening of his next fortnightly obligation drew near, the husband knew that he would not be able to bring himself to discharge his liability. And as if she sensed his predicament his wife hovered over him, suddenly all too solic-itous, all too friendly, fussing over his reading lamp, adjusting his footstool, lowering the volume of the record player, ostensibly so that he could read his evening paper in peace.

Yet the quiet she offered was charged with her presence. She kept him under close surveillance with the tenacious eye of a creditor ready to grab the collar of the debtor who looks as if he is about to make a dash for it. Whenever he lifted his head from the paper, he found her watching him.

"Did you want something else? A fresh drink?" And she was up, trotting over with mincing steps.

"No, nothing. I was resting my eyes." He tried to ward her off.

It didn't stop her. She danced in unwelcome attendance, diffusing a trail of heavy musk.

"Anything interesting in the news?" peering over his shoulder. "Do you think that she is all that sexy?" she lisped, pointing to a photograph of the latest Swedish starlet sliding out of a limousine.

His noncommittal answer failed to put her off. She crowded possessively against him and read along as he turned the pages. Even when he deliberately folded the paper to the financial section, she remained at his elbow.

"Can you really make heads or tails out of all those figures?" Now playing the role of the helpless female, all innocence and big eyes.

Perching on the armrest of his chair, she breathed in his ear, "Let's make it an early night. You look so tired. Go on—up to bed with you. I'll just pop into the tub. No more than five minutes, I promise. Go on."

Pushing him down the hallway, she urged him toward the bedroom.

Just as he feared, he was a total failure in bed. Not that he didn't try!

He kneaded the recalcitrant flesh, stroked it, pummeled it, tried to slap it into life. He let it rest and then wooed it with erotic fantasies, telling it spicy bedtime stories of top-heavy Texan beauties, French maids, nubile African slaves, and precocious coeds. He turned the newspaper to the picture of the Swedish starlet. He coaxed it and scolded it. His wife whistled to it. He had her buckle up her brassiere and put her girdle back on, then her slip and stockings, and the tightest skirt in her wardrobe. He ordered her to bend over, to sit on a table and cross her legs, to get partly undressed again and strut around the room swinging her purse in the fashion of street-walkers. He forced her to kneel between his legs. He drank a water glass full of whiskey, neat. He invited her to curse him, to jump on him, to really rip into him, to haul him over the coals. He asked her to shame him, to taunt him. He begged her to let her hair down, to tell him about her lovers (to invent them if they did not exist), all about them, the most intimate, the filthiest details of how they took her, what they did with her, what she had done to them and what she would do the next time. He pulled on it and wet it. They dipped it in cold-cream. They tried forcing it in, soft and shrunken though it was. She tied it to a splint. He ran to get a shoehorn from the hall closet.

No use. Not even a pulse beat.

TOUCHED ON THE RAW

Her legs are spread-eagle. The epidermis denuded of all hair is as smooth as a freshly plastered wall. But what is more noteworthy is the absence of all primary sexual characteristics. The perineal region is blank. One can find no notch, no cleft, not even the faintest sign of an indentation at the apex of the angle formed by the thighs. Looking closer at this junction of the limbs, one is faced with a plane, shaped somewhat like the top of a crutch, the width of three or four fingers.

One's interest is focused on this area primarily because it lies at the direct center of the limited field of vision offered by the small aperture of the keyhole. The parted thighs lead the eye inward toward the blunted point of the triangle as effectively as two converging lines (or an arrow).

Neither the woman's face nor any other portion of her upper body is visible. The view consists of a close-up of the lower half, the segment between the knees and hips. The foreground is white (though not as pale as the white on white region between her thighs), probably the sheet on which the body lies, the open bed or an operating table.

One has the impression that the woman is strapped down. She does not move—yet she is alive, as indicated by the almost imperceptible rise and fall of her abdomen which matches the rhythm of the observer's breathing.

A pointed, wedgelike object appears at the lower edge of the circle of vision. It is shaped like an ice pick, though much fatter, or a spike. Before an exact identification can be made, it is suddenly thrust forward. The instrument penetrates the tightly stretched skin with ease. It splits with a plopping sound.

Immediately, the action is repeated. The same scene. The hairless pubic area. The skin sealed, unbroken, unmarked. Then the weapon poised for the attack. The blow.

Again.

And again. The stark naked drum positioned for the stabbing. The momentary hesitation before the instrument pierces the hide.

And again. In slow-motion. This time the weapon can be identified as a horn, like the cuspate growth protruding from the forehead of a bull or a unicorn, a single tusk ground to a sharp point, gently curving upward toward its tip, blueish-gray. It punctures the casing, twists, probes, then breaks through the cervical bone with a crunching sound, plunging home.

The woman is in position, thighs apart, slightly raised. The blank pubis offers a ready target, twitching now and again, the taut skin moving in and out ever so slightly as if breathing.

THE QUAKER-OATS BOX

Richard thought he was going to be sick. But his eye remained at the peephole. He no longer had a clear notion of how long he had been kneeling at the door. It was longer than he usually dared. There was no reason to remain, but then it was just as senseless to return night after night. Once had been enough. The scenes were repeated with monotonous regularity. Even the variations were predictable. Yet he came back for more and knew that he would return for another look the next day, no matter how he felt now.

The spectacle was over, the combatants separated. The woman was dabbing spittle on a ladder in her stocking. The man had rolled over. Soon he would be snoring.

His attention was no longer fixed on the view before him. Although his face remained turned toward the door, it was himself that he was watching. Without turning his head, by opening both eyes and looking down, he could just see his hands on his knees, the two white kneecaps, his slippered feet, the worn carpet between his legs, and by straining, a small arc to each side. By moving his head a fraction in either direction, he could get a glimpse of a somewhat larger portion of the hallway. But the region directly behind him remained inaccessible, his back vulnerable. He would have to turn completely, once to the right and once to the left, to check on the blind area. To do so would be as good as announcing his suspicions.

Bracing himself, he turned around. The double sweep revealed nothing. The corridor was empty. No movement. No one there. Yet he was not reassured. Directly behind his back, directly opposite the door before which he crouched, there was another door, identical to this one, matching in every detail, same porcelain doorknob, same old-fashioned keyhole.

The keyholes were on the same level. The view was unobstructed. If someone were spying on him he would be kneeling at the improvised Judas window behind the closed door in the room opposite, looking directly at the bent back of the first observer at his keyhole. (Hypothetically, if the path were not blocked, he could look through both keyholes from one bedroom to the other. And if there were another room, a third observer would have a clear view of the others at their posts. And a fourth, and so on.)

The impact of the discovery was physically painful, as if he had been dealt a heavy blow on the exposed nape. His head automatically jerked back to the keyhole, but he saw nothing. His eyes turned inward. He could feel the breath of the concealed watcher. It tickled the back of his neck, he was so close.

BESTIARY

The focus shifts. The lense narrows, images crowd together, overlap. The pit of the bed, wrinkled sheets. Entangled bodies, limbs contorted, distended beyond recognition. Engorged organs the color of worms twist, jerk spasmodically. Pulpy knobs, lumps, hard knots. Mammiform blisters, tumorous lobes, areolae beaded with sweat, swollen labia, moist folds, pleated skin. Stubby legs topped by bulbous breasts scuttle about with crablike movements. Tentacles reach out. Upended, legs flail the air. A bearded head, testicles for ears. Between the turned-out lips, protruding from its mouth, an erect penis. A bright red appendage flicks in and out with the speed of a snake's tongue. Locked together, lopped off genitals feed. Mouths, snouts, beaks, jaws, gullets, talons. The sheet rips. A probing finger forces its way up through the slit, parts the folds of slack tissue. The grayish-brown meat glistens. Cobwebs. Trembling antennae. Undulating hair. A bed of frog eggs. A slug crawls around the rim, leaving a trail of mucus. Agglutinated flesh. A pool of slime. Limbs trapped in the hardening jelly, sucked under. Turning, spinning slowly, the dismembered parts float in an oval sack, a film of semitransparent membrane, an egg of purplish veins, strips of flayed skin hanging loose, the shell stove in. A naked eye presses against the fig-shaped fenestella.

MARK STRAND

was born in Summerside, Prince Edward Island in 1934, but has lived in the United States most of his life. After attending Antioch College and Yale University, he traveled to Italy on a Fulbright Scholarship and in 1965 was a Fulbright Lecturer at the University of Brazil at Rio de Janeiro. Mr. Strand has also received grants from the National Endowment for the Arts and the Rockefeller Foundation, and has taught at various American colleges and universities.

Published books of poetry by Mark Strand include DARKER (1970), REASONS FOR MOVING (1968), and SLEEPING WITH ONE EYE OPEN (1964). He has edited two anthologies: THE CONTEMPORARY AMERICAN POETS (1969) and NEW POETRY OF MEXICO (1970), and published a collection of translations, 18 POEMS FROM THE QUECHUA. Poems by Mark Strand appear frequently in such magazines as *The Atlantic, The New Yorker, Partisan Review* and *The New York Review of Books.*

From   *The Mill Point Notebook*

My solution for the cemetery strike which affected New York City in early June of 1973 is as follows and I offer it to the city as a plan for preventing any such occurrences in future and as a means whereby cemeteries can be financially self-sufficient and with luck (good or ill) profit-making.

I think at some point in one's life, probably when making a last will and testament, he should make a tape of his own voice reciting words that he deems immortal, they can be words he himself has written or, more likely, the words of his favorite poet or most admired President. They can be words of advice that a friendly boss once offered him or words of an esteemed colleague. If he chooses not to recite the wise or beautiful words himself, then he should consign the duty to an actor, if he knows one, or to a friend with a pleasing voice. Without intending a sexist attitude, I believe it would be appropriate for women to have their surrogates be women, and men's be men. If this were not adhered to, the results would prove, I fear, comically out of place and character. Part of the tape might be devoted to music or to the sounds of favorite animals (a certain dog barking, a cat purring). For lonely souls a recording could be had of high winds lashing to the bare tundras of Canada, or for lonely souls of another cast, recordings be had of loud parties full of laughter and the clinking of glasses. For the ugly, recordings (at a high price) might be had, testifying to their undying beauty—voices saying things like, "My Dan, you are handsome, you are the handsomest man I ever saw." The possibilities for posterity are innumerable, but for the purposes of a representative selection falling within the time allotted each person's tape (fifteen minutes should be enough), a sort of Chinese menu might be prepared for easy choosing. A typical tape might have, for instance, an opening poem— "They Flee From Me Who Sometime Did Me Seek"—followed by the telling of "an unforgettable experience," followed by the sound of waves crashing against the rocky coast of Nova Scotia, followed by "Here boy, here boy" and a few barks, then a song like "For He's A Jolly Good Fellow," then a bit of organ music, then a list of favorite personages of the day, then a list of favorite foods and maybe recipes, then a closing inspirational statement to the world. These tapes would then be placed inside the deceased's tombstone which need not necessarily be of stone, but of brightly colored, heavy-duty plastic or of stainless steel or, heaven be praised, gold. A player and speakers would also be inserted and could vary in power and durability depending on the money and immortal longings of the person to be buried. There would be a slot for depositing money in each of these gravemarkers. I suspect that a fair price for having the dead among us again would be a quarter. In this way our dreary and forbidding cemeteries would become gardens of jukeboxes, vast sanctuaries of precious remembrance, places of entertainment, where people would go picnicking on Sunday afternoons, tuning in here or there; lovers would go, children would go and hear their great grandfathers or great grandmothers whose voices and wishes would otherwise be forever lost, strangers would go for inspiration, perhaps, or out of mere curiosity, but graveyards would come alive and be central to the more philosophical, deeper, healthier, aspects of our person. Death would be no longer despised and placed out of bounds, but embraced by our good will and private yearnings for a richer life. The adoption of my proposed solution for what ails cemeteries would be a victory for life in death and death in life or, put another way, something for everybody, dead or alive.

*

I have special plans for my own death. I want to be encased in clear lucite and I want my daughter to use me as a coffee table. I would not make a tape of my poems or anyone else's, nor would I have music. I would merely list my favorite meals and attempt some brief description of how each tastes. This would both support and dignify my contention that the best coffee table discussion usually centers around food. I leave the question of my attire to my daughter who more than likely will have a clear sense of my wishes when the time comes. I propose, also, if the lucite can bear it, that I be moved out in front of my daughter's house at Xmas and flooded with red and green lights. In this way the neighbors will be apprised of my singular jollity.

*

In connection with the foregoing entries I have an idea for a game which might make somebody a fortune. I have not chosen a name for it, though several come to mind. "Disease, A Game Of Life" or "End of The Line" or "Terminal Case." The game would be played on a board like Monopoly and each of the players would select at random a card telling him what disease he will have for the remainder of the game. The object will be to avert death as long as possible and the winner is the one who outlives the other players. Since all the diseases are fatal, there are no permanent cures, only the usual desperation measures taken by hospitals; surgery, cobalt, a new drug, would be some of these. Each player will have a certain sum of money to play with so the game will test, among other things, the player's capacity to spend wisely. And not only will each player seek to prolong his life, but he will have opportunities for finding pleasure in his remaining days. There will be comfort cards or agony cards which will be added or subtracted from a player's total score, the total score being the number of days he has survived since contracting the disease.

*

Another money-making idea is that of producing a pill that could be given to a dog and which would make its shit luminous. This would be a ray of hope for the city-dweller who, more often than not, ambles at night more fearful of stepping on a dog turd than of being attacked by a mugger. The dogs, then, would leave their radiant piles and the walkers in the city would be warned. With the increase both in the number and in the size of dogs, the presence of crap is ubiquitous and some of the deposits, especially those of Great Danes and St. Bernards, are monumentally large. All of which suggests that the potential for illuminating whole cities can be considered to rest on the development of such a pill. There are surely enough piles of dogshit in New York City, say, which, if they emanated even a moderate light, would keep that city bright and gem-like through the longest nights. I foresee a day when streetlamps are obsolete and the electrical power resources of urban centers need not be drained, when man's best friend really is man's best friend.

*

My company will be called Night Games Inc. Think of Night Croquet! Luminous mallets and balls of matching colors, luminous wickets, luminous gloves and hat to identify each player with his particular ball and mallet! Think of Night Horseshoes! Pitching bright horseshoes in the dark! I think of the velvety suburban nights in summer when there's nothing on TV and Mom and Dad have been drinking and prolonging their boredom and suddenly see the need for Night Croquet. The neighbors would come over, leaving their drinks behind, and everybody would stagger brightly around and around. And for those who prefer the indoors I would produce jigsaw puzzles that are blank by day but at night glow with images under a black light.

*

The toilet flusher must be brought out from behind the toilet where it hides in porcelain secrecy. It should be brought out into the open and cased in transparent lucite. It is, after all, the most interesting gadget in the house and should be treated as such. The simple machine should be made of brightly colored plastics or metals of different sorts. It might be placed anywhere in the house where its beauty could be observed, even mused on, as someone in the bathroom pushes the flusher.

*

It has occurred to me that flowers are no compensation for the boredom of bone white sheets. Those prints will not do. I suggest sheets and pillow cases on which famous poems are printed.

RONALD SUKENICK

His new novel, *98.6,* has just been published by the Fiction Collective. Two of his most recently published novels are *Out* and *Up*. He has published a collection of short stories called *The Death of the Novel and Other Stories.*

The Endless Short Story: Verticals and Horizontals

stand
up
straight
or
you'll
grow

up
crooked.
Like the tree. That's what they told him. In the Kingdom. His
tree. In a dirt strip between the sidewalk and the curb next to
the gutter on the street around the corner before the manhole
cover across from the garage in front of the yard alongside the
alley behind the house. That was the Kingdom. Between the
curb and the alley. Beyond that Neckstore was. And further
Down-the-Block and further further Next-Block was. And two
ways to school up the Avenue and by the pickle factory. By
the pickle factory was the short cut it was actually longer but
you came at school by the back through the empty lots and
along the cemetery the Pecker boy told him how you could ask
the pickle men for pickles. Everything was very quiet. You ate
the pickles at eight in the morning on the way to school and
they didn't make you sick. The Pecker boy lived Neckstore
and he always knew much more. But that was later. When you
lived in the Kingdom there was no need for school. Crown
Prince von Mocassin was his name the Kingdom was his claim.
When he was older the Kingdom came. When he stood up
straight. The Kingdom came. And went and came.

                                                   The reason
that time seems to be passing more quickly is that the earth is
spinning faster. You have of course noticed how hard it's getting to jam all you have to do into the day the explanation is
simple the days are getting shorter due to gradual acceleration
in the earth's rotation. Last year one already suspected it but
this year there is no doubt. Everybody is nervous and cranky.
Too much to do too little time to do it every chance you get to
look up another week has snapped by. And not only that the
earth is revolving faster around the sun. That probably ac-
counts for the change in the light the light used to be softer
clearer now you notice it more am I right. As if the light has
been thickening quickening becoming more than a mere medi-
um a jell of time and presence something like that. Of course
everything stays in the same proportion there's no feedback
from the scientists because it's all relative the same thing is
happening throughout the cosmos. Except our psychological
clocks deep inside we know it's all wrong we're all suffering
from time lag we're never going to catch up not with the whole
universe scattering like scared minnows or so the astronomers
tell us. Dispersion. Maybe the answer is cosmic saving time a

hundred minutes to every hour it would fit right in with the metric system. Or maybe we can scan. Think faster feel more go from one thing to another take it all in at once. All right what's your answer.

The tree. The tree was planted by Queenmother. For Crown Prince von Mocassin. A branch sprouting in a cylinder of chickenwire. There were chickens there then. Not in the Kingdom but Neckstore Pickles Pecker would pull them out of their cages to stroke them and show them off. The light was still and transparent. Crown Prince von Mocassin and Pickles Pecker would go down to the cemetery and stare. White verticals over dark horizontals in the quiet air. Nobody was in a hurry then. Each evening was the end of an era. King and Queen had their faults but they saw to everything. They didn't care about a lot of the things people care about today. Only Queenmother was in a hurry. She cared about a lot of things people didn't care about any more. She was in a hurry about the tree. Crown Prince von Mocassin was the sprouting branch. The Kingdom was coming. Maybe that was why Queenmother was in a hurry about the tree but did you ever see a tree in a hurry? She had no patience when *le peuple* used the young tree for first base in their stickball games. She would break into a demented fury when she saw them pulling and shaking the tree loosening its roots warping the trunk she would spit strings of Yiddish at them out the second-floor window shaking her fist. That of course was when it was still possible for old people to yell at kids now they would simply stone her to death on her way to the grocery store. Her arch enemy was Pickles Pecker Crown Prince von Mocassin's best friend. Naturally Crown Prince sided with Pickles even though he and the kids would yell back making fun of the family name von Mocassin what kind of a name was that you couldn't even pronounce it. The fact that Crown Prince von Mocassin's tree in a way was Crown Prince made no difference at all.

I. Seymour Hare. There was something dirty about him. He knew about girls. He was older. Crown Prince von Mocassin wasn't supposed to play with him because Stillmore Hare his father liked Hitler. Also he was stupid that was clear even then Crown Prince von Mocassin thought he was stupid because he was older. There is always the possibility that children are little geniuses and it's all down hill from there. The greatest tides of stupidity sweep in with adolescence we never recover. Maybe that explains why I. Seymour Hare was so slow maybe it explains Queenmother's hurry in any case the tree was growing. Shaky warped and scarred where branches had been torn off during close decisions at first base but still alive. What is this story about? It's about a prince. It's about a tree. It's about standing up straight. It's about a cemetery. It's about a Kingdom coming it's about a Kingdom come. And there's a counterplot involving light and time. You see what's happening here you take a few things that interest you and you begin to make connections. The connections are the important thing they don't exist before you make them. This is THE ENDLESS SHORT STORY. It doesn't matter where you start. You must have faith. Life is whole and continuous whatever the appearances. All this is rather coarse you say that may be but remember coarse is the opposite of slick and the coarser the texture the more it can let in. So. Pussy Hare. The little sister of Seymour Hare. Crown Prince. The Kingdom. Pickles. The cemetery. The tree. Standing up straight. The counterplot involving light and time. Now.

Outbreak of war between the Kingdom and Neckstore. One day Pickles Pecker pulls Crown Prince von Mocassin into the alley. Hey yuh wanna hear a doity joke? he says.

Wha's a doity joke?

You ain't never hoid a doity joke?

Nah.

My fadder tole me it.

Oh. Actually Crown Prince von Mocassin didn't want to hear a dirty joke but there didn't seem to be any way of getting around it. The joke involved a girl from Brooklyn who used the phrase tin bloomers. The punch line was "Whaddya tink my prick is, a can opener?" Crown Prince von Mocassin didn't understand why any girl would want to wear tin bloomers. He didn't understand the joke on Brooklyn accents since they all spoke in Brooklyn accents so what was the joke. And he didn't understand that a prick is in a sense a can opener. He laughed anyway. That was the beginning of it. The next thing was Hey yuh know Pussy Hare?

Yeah.

Yuh wanna see huh bloomuhs?

Wha do I wanna see huh bloomuhs for?

Cause it's doity yuh joik. Crown Prince von Mocassin never remembered exactly what happened after that. Even right after it happened. Even while it was happening. It seems that at that time Pussy Hare was showing boys her bloomers. They called for her and she came over to the alley. Something was happening but Crown Prince von Mocassin wasn't sure what it was. Pussy Hare was lying down and Crown Prince von Mocassin was standing up. Straight. The Kingdom was coming. The Kingdom came. After lunch Crown Prince headed Neckstore. Pickles Pecker was standing in front of his stoop Yuh can't go past he said.

Why not?

Cause yuh joosh. Wham. Pickles lying on his back on the sidewalk Crown Prince didn't even remember hitting him. He went back to his Kingdom.

That happened on a Saturday. The next day was Sunday, December 7, 1941. The day Queenmother had an attack and dispersed. Crown Prince was not at the burial they said he was too young to go to the cemetery. He thought of her as horizontal himself as vertical. Her grave is the subplot of this story. The Kingdom Come. That's when time began to change it started moving faster so fast it got hard to remember things light thickened and congealed in stilted snapshots that left you wondering what happened before and after. By the time the War was over I was thirteen. Bar Mitzvah time. The ceremony was during the winter that night it snowed it started snowing the famous blizzard of 1946. The snow covered Brooklyn it covered Hitler covered the four years of the War the camps it covered everything. Recently I went back. The tree is there the house the house next door the neighborhood all much the same. Still. The people gone. An old house a crooked tree. The glassy surface of a lake beneath which old timbers sway while on the shore faster and faster the Kingdom

comes
and
goes
and
comes
and
goes

Born Dec. 2, 1936, New York City. Ph.D. New York University, 1971. Assistant Professor of English, The City University of New York. Guggenheim Fellow in Creative Writing, 1973–1974. Novel: *The Adventures of Mao on the Long March,* 1971.

from *Jean Lambert Tallien: A Brief Romance*

For Raymond Queneau

Must I not serve a long apprenticeship
To foreign passages, and in the end,
Having my freedom, boast of nothing else
But that I was a journeyman to grief?

"Tallien, Jean Lambert (1767–1820), French Revolutionist, was the son of the *maître d'hôtel* of the marquis de Bercy, and was born in Paris. The marquis, perceiving the boy's ability, had him well educated, and got him a place as a lawyer's clerk. Being much excited by the first events of the Revolution, he gave up his desk to enter a printer's office, and by 1791 he was overseer of the printing department of the *Moniteur.* While thus employed he conceived the idea of the *journal-affiche,* and after the arrest of the king at Varennes in June 1791 he placarded a large printed sheet on all the walls of Paris twice a week, under the title of the *Ami des Citoyens, journal fraternel.*

"On the 8th of July 1792, Tallien was the spokesman of a deputation of the section of the Place Royale, and he was one of the most active popular leaders in the attack upon the Tuileries on the 10th of August, on which day he was appointed secretary or clerk to the revolutionary commune of Paris. In this capacity he exhibited an almost feverish activity. At the close of the month he resigned his post on being elected, in spite of his youth, a deputy to the Convention; he began his legislative career by defending the conduct of the Commune during the massacres."

He rose, his slender body erect, and brushed aside the black curls furled about his forehead.

"The brow of Shelley," remarked a tanner on seeing Tallien rise to the dais.

"The fervent eyes of Rimbaud," added another as the youth commenced his address:

"Citizens, brothers, children of the Revolution, our sacred mother, and of France, our fierce father, be assured: the Revolution is soon lost. [Murmurs, coughs, the start of an upcry in the balcony.] Soon lost, I say, but no loss for some among you, perhaps. But as we glance back over our recent history, let us recall with some degree of pleasure—egotism even—our accomplishments. 'We had left the rusty iron framework of society behind us; we had broken through many hindrances that are powerful enough to keep most people on the weary treadmill of the established system, even while they feel its irksomeness almost as intolerable as we did. We had stepped down from the pulpit; we had flung aside the pen; we had shut up the ledger; we had thrown off that sweet, bewitching, enervating indolence, which is better, after all, than most of the enjoyments within mortal grasp. It was our purpose—a generous one, certainly, and absurd, no doubt, in full proportion with its generosity—to give up whatever we had heretofore attained, for the sake of showing mankind the example of a life governed by other than the false and cruel principles on which human society has all along been based.

" 'Therefore we built splendid castles . . . and pictured beautiful scenes, among the fervid coals of the hearth around which we were clustering, and if it all went to rack with the crumbling embers and has never since arisen out of the ashes, let us take to ourselves no shame. In my own behalf, I rejoice that I could once think better of the world's improvability than it deserved. It is a mistake into which men seldom fall twice in a lifetime; or, if so, the rarer and higher is the nature that can thus magnanimously persist in error.'

"And my nature is no higher than yours, brother and citizens. For nature needs instruction from models higher than itself, from natures pure, incorruptible, indefatigable, bound only to Reason, swayed only by Reason, in love only with Reason.

"Thus, if my brothers say: halt this excess, stanch the bloodflow, return us to peace; if they should say: return us to Chardin, Boucher, Fragonard, give us our serene, unbloodied landscapes; if they should cry: In the name of heaven! Give us a restful night in bed! Why then, should I find in my brothers the higher Nature which I long to follow?

"No, I may only say, with my brothers: open the dungeons, usher out, and escort the nobles into the light of Paris day, let them share our bread, give them our seats, here, in the Assembly, so they may discourse with us the way to Justice. Let us beg their pardon and, like penitent children, implore their love. Yes, summon our best tailors to sew back necks to bodies, let our revolutionary breath inspire their wronged bodies to life, and all will be sweet again." [Shouts: "No! No! Forward the Revolution! Forward the Commune!"]

"He took his seat upon the Mountain, and showed himself one of the most vigorous Jacobins, particularly in his defense of Marat, on the 26th of February 1793; he voted for the execution of the king, and was elected a member of the Committee of General Security on the 21st of January 1793."

Piccolomini, A., De la Sfera del Mondo; De le Stelle Fisse. Eighteen full-page star maps, and a number of text woodcuts. Said to be in the private library of Pico della Mirandola; text frequently cited in the writings of Brunetto Latini; 4to, modern boards. Venice: N. de Bascrini, 1548. $110.00.

"Tallien showed himself one of the most vigorous of the proconsuls sent over France to establish the Terror in the provinces; though with but few adherents, he soon awed the great city into quiet.

"It was at this moment that the romance of Tallien's life commenced. Among his prisoners was Thérèse, the divorced wife of the comte de Fontenay, and daughter of the Spanish banker, François Cabarrus, one of the most intriguing women of her time. Tallien not only spared her life but fell in love with her."

"In the dimness of this cell, Madame, you radiate. A glittering serene star, even in this dusky atmosphere."

"I greet you, Citizen Executioner. Oh! Forgive me, perhaps you are just the cart-man come to carry me to oblivion."

"Neither, my dear woman. Your friend."

"Is the blade my friend then?"

"Not the blade, my bosom."

"My dear man, save your charm for the living, they are quick to respond."

"You are the most sentient animal in all of Paris, witty too, I should say by the measure of your costume."

"Short measure, you mean."

"One gorgeous breast bared in the style of Mother Republic is ample measure, my darling."

"Are you a suckling then?" Thérèse slips down from her left shoulder the slender band supporting the slashed shift.

"The cell grows brighter still, Madame. I'm nearly blinded by the creamed whiteness of your orbs."

"My dear Sir, if I am hanged to the lamp-post will you see the better for it?"

"Put up your sash and restore me to reason, I implore you. Let me think out the nature of this question in peace."

Scene: a large apartment of a *hôtel particulier* recently commandeered by the Revolution, now the headquarters of Tallien and Thérèse, his mistress.

"Jean Lambert, this must not be. Others are left to flee to England, to the Swiss, while my friends are persecuted and brought to the Machine. Boors! You and your accomplices! Send my friends to America—there is sufficient punishment in that for delicate and sensible people."

"My darling, why plague those forest virgins with such breed. In two years Mme Lafite and her circle will transform such men as Franklin and Jefferson into frontier fops. Perfumed saddles, gilded carriages, birdcages in the coiffures, truffles in the savage venison. I have nothing against your friends personally, but we can't afford a politique of favoritism."

"As you wish, murder them."

"Murder? A basketful of wigs only: the trunks may go their way."

"Oh! How gallant your abstractions. Give me up too, then. Better the scaffold than to suffer you and your speaking triangles, those constipated Platonists of the Revolution, of the riot, I mean."

"Enough! Hold. Let your lips form a kiss. Give your mouth to love, not anger. Should not beauty triumph over reason?"

The dress undone. A clump of blue silk on the polished parquet beside the marble fireplace. Cloth breeches draped over the velvet sofa. Tallien's sighs; his agitated lovetwitch; his calm, spent body.

"Tallien was even elected president of the Convention on

the 24th of March 1794. But the Terror could not be maintained at the same pitch: Robespierre began to see that he must strike at many of his own colleagues in the committees if he was to carry out his own theories, and Tallien was one of the first men condemned with them. They determined to strike first, and on the great day of the Thermidor it was Tallien who, urged on by the danger in which his beloved lay, opened the attack upon Robespierre. The movement was successful; Robespierre and his friends were guillotined; and Tallien, as the leading Thermidorian, was elected to the Committee of Public Safety. He showed himself a vigorous Thermidorian; he was instrumental in suppressing the Revolutionary Tribunal and the Jacobin Club. . . ."

Tallien himself could not wait until he returned home to Thérèse who, he knew, would still be sleeping or idling in bed, although it was nearly eleven in the morning. Before the Revolution she had exercised the luxurious habits of her class, and now, scarcely two weeks after her release from prison, she had resumed them without reference to the hardship of her captivity. Tallien marveled at her resiliency and ability to continue life precisely in her accustomed mode. The periodic riots and lootings, the pockets of angry rabble menacing the streets, the constant threat to her and her friends' lives, the upheaval of all she had known, appeared to leave her unaffected. She complained only once, when Tallien's housekeeper, Tartuffe, refused to serve her breakfast in bed and had addressed her, sardonically, as Citizeness. But Thérèse weathered the insult, managing even, eventually, to win the housekeeper to her side.

"She is an aristocrat, but she is a great lady," Tartuffe told Jean Lambert one morning, as he was on his way to supervise the interrogation of several men thought to be spies for the English. He felt uneasy at that declaration, an instant of jealousy. Here was Thérèse, just recently surfaced from her cell (literally blinking her way through the street and into Tallien's carriage), formerly reviled and in disgrace—the lowest beggar having more status than she, by virtue of the new order—and yet people continued to respect that which by all rights they should have despised. Period of transition, he reflected, adjustments come slowly, people's habits are too ingrained to die off quickly, generations would have to pass before men were esteemed for their merit, for their earned virtues.

"In all these months he was supported by Thérèse, whom he

married on the 26th of December 1794, and who became the
leader of the social life of Paris. His last political achievement
was in July 1795, when he was present with Hoche at the
destruction of the army of the *émigrés* at Quiberon, and ordered the executions which followed. After the close of the
Convention Tallien's political importance came to an end, for,
though he sat in the Council of Five Hundred, the moderates
attacked him as a terrorist, and the extreme party as a renegade. Madame Tallien also tired of him, and became the mistress of the rich banker Ouvrard.

"Bonaparte, however, who is said to have been introduced
by Tallien to Barras, took him to Egypt in his great expedition
of June 1798, and after the capture of Cairo he edited the
official journal there, the *Décade Egyptienne*. But General J. F.
Menou sent him away from Egypt, and on his passage he was
captured by an English cruiser and taken to London, where he
had a good reception among the Whigs and was well received
by Fox. On returning to France in 1802 he was divorced by his
wife (who in 1805 married the comte de Caraman, later prince
de Chimay), and was left for some time without employment."

Thérèse, he wrote, do you recall how you had me confiscate
several of Boulle's pieces from the Bouchard family, how you
said you would suffer should they fall into the hands of the
mob, and thus into their midnight bonfires. Recall the *bonheur
de jour*, the one inlaid with marqueterie and edged with ebony
and ivory, the one in whose little secret drawer you kept my
letters. I ask only that one. Keep the armoirs, the commodes,
the cabinets, the gilded bureau mounted on brass feet and set
in blue enamel.

"At last, through Fouche and Talleyrand, he got the appointment of consul at Alicante; he remained there until he lost
the sight of his left eye from yellow fever. On returning to
Paris he lived on his half-pay until 1815, when he received the
favour of not being exiled like the other regicides; nonetheless,
his pension was suspended. His latter days were spent in poverty; he often had to sell his books to buy food. He died in
Paris on the 16th of November, 1820."

Cunt was selling as cheaply as hot piss. Lucie-Marie and
Sally, the chestnut vendor's daughter, peddled their asses extra hours, but it grew so cold that even their usual customers
rejected them.

"I'd rather dip it into the Seine than stick it into that hairy tundra," shouted Marcel the flourman to a band of roving whores who, driven by the freeze, found themselves in ever alien streets and parks.

Freezing sparrows perched stolidly on window sills; nervous pigeons padded about little frozen puddles along the quay: the winter was severe, the flats frozen, the streets coldgrey; beggars and the poor crowded about cratefires in the open squares. Bundled men fished eels through broken plates of the ice-sheeted Seine.

Through the month of the great freeze Tallien dreamed of Egypt, her tombs and tepid sands, the pyramids on which soldiers of the Grand Army had scratched their perishable names. He dreamed of how, when he returned to Paris, he gave Thérèse a pouch of golden scarabs. Now she would not see him nor answer his accusatory, self-pitying letters. She found the style wanting, she wrote him in her only reply. He reviled her infidelity, boasted of high positions that would be offered to him shortly, that very hour. He begged her to intercede for him, to plead with Talleyrand, with whom he learned she had dined a fortnight past.

All Paris knows he adores you and would favor my petition should you favor it. Let me be sent to Brazil; even to live among marshes and monkeys is welcome. May I tell my creditors you are arranging my safe-conduct through these bitter days? My god! I should have let them take your head when I had a chance, you charmed bitch.

Commerce eventually would return to optimum levels; expectations on the Bourse were high. But, in the countryside, peasants still hoarded grain and potatoes in earthen cellars. Painters opened their studios to merchants and their families; portraits went by the square foot, but rates were negotiable, some barter tolerated. Laces and silks, chambray and velvet returned to the salons, although there still was uncertainty as to what was *de rigeur* for balls and late suppers: since the Egyptian campaign some detected an oriental trend, especially in the brocade sashing of housecoats, and during the Peninsular War, a Spanish influence—several fashionable women wore castanets in their hair—but neither mode took on. Morning coats and beaver hats were prominent in the custom offices along the coast, except in Marseilles, where no one seemed about to set a standard and a rather free style flourished.

Mme Volvaney's large flat near the Bois de Boulogne was

the scene of midnight suppers once again, but it was her daughter, Marie, who presided over them now. Recently arrived from London, Marie established the social pace for the second generation of *émigrés* finally come home.

Once or twice during the course of the season, Princess de Chimay, formerly Mme Tallien (née Cabarrus), stopped by for wine and oranges after dinner, her carriage posted by the *hôtel*. She enjoyed seeing young people, she said, "so gay, as they are, so new." Radiant still, she enchanted the young of both sexes. Her husband, the Prince, beams in her presence. He speaks of her only. Her energy, her passion and curiosity.

"She will go to the Americas yet, I am certain, yes, even to the pampas and the prairies, but first she will recivilize Paris and make us forget what we have endured as a people and a nation."

"My husband is a dreamer, that is why he is so charming. He still believes in women, in their magic."

"To know you, Princess, is to have cause to believe."

"Believe then in life, trust it as I have. And to you, my fresh young souls, an old woman asks only that you return us to grace and gorgeous repose."

A bow, embraces exchanged, the kissing of her hand, the swift rush of servants and opening doors, her voice in the foyer, the hoofsteps in the street below, the reverent remarks by those at the window following the carriage ease away into the vacant night, the conversation softly, then volubly returned to.

Cooper, James Fenimore, The Bravo: A Venetian Story. 3 vols. 12mo. Bound in original grey boards; uncut, with paper labels. Cooper's first of three European novels deals with political and moral corruption of 18th-century Venice: A cautionary tale. London: Colburn and Bentley, 1831. First British edition. $150.00.

Tallien's life grew ever solitary, embittered. No one visited his tiny flat; there was no one in his life left to visit. He was not known in the cafés and was on no one's invitation lists—doors were not *closed* to him, he was simply not beckoned to enter. Even so, should he have been asked to dinner or to a party he would have been hard-pressed to find a proper outfit to wear. What costumes he possessed were out of mode; perhaps worse, they were threadbare, spotted and soiled. He stuffed cardboard in his shoes until some coins came his way to have them mended.

There were times he thought he would not last out the year: stronger than hunger, than need for warm, suitable clothes, was his loneliness. His marrow felt lonely, his cells too—that's how deeply it penetrated him, he said to himself. He had once believed himself adored by a beautiful woman, had lived passionately in the radiance of her looks and charm (of greater meaning to him now than the Revolution and all its works, as he now came to understand), but all that had been taken from him, leaving him emptier than the spaces between the stars—his own metaphor. He recognized that destiny had dealt him mocking cards, several rounds of full houses and royal flushes, followed forever by empty hands. It might have been better for him had the Revolution never occurred, that he had remained a printer's apprentice and gone to the dogs in the way natural to his class. What mattered now those honors and medals, the handshake of the great; the excitement of having helped divert, even if only temporarily, the stream of history; his name presently was a sullied relic of the Terror whose history, at that very moment, was being revised by alien pens.

Carriages passed in the night bringing people to festivities, to brilliantly lit capacious rooms, while he sat alone by the window reading. Once a barouchet paused in the street below; Tallien's heart quickened; perhaps, he thought, it was Thérèse, contrite, loving, finally come to rescue him from his life. She would mount the stair, enter his room—filling it with her brilliance and warmth—kneel before him, her eyes tear-brimmed:

"I have wronged you, my love," she would begin; "I've led a venal life with soulless people. I want you, only you, forever you."

Joyously, they would reunite, recommencing the great collaboration of their youth. His heart would be warm again, after so many frozen years.

But there was no sound on the stair, no knock at the door, only the clattering of hoofs and the rumble of wheels as the carriage continued on its way. Tallien sighed, relapsing once again to familiar misery. To distract himself from his shattered expectation, he resumed reading Washington Irving's tale, "The German Student":

Gottfried Wolfgang was a young man of good family. He had studied for some time at Göttingen, but being of a visionary and enthusiastic character, he had wandered into those wild and speculative doctrines which so often bewildered German students. His secluded life, his intense application, and the singular nature of his studies, had an effect on both mind and body. His health was impaired; his imagination diseased. He had been indulging in fanciful speculations on spiritual essences, until, like Swedenborg, he had an ideal world of his own around him. . . .

Wolfgang arrived at Paris at the breaking out of the revolution. The popular delirium at first caught his enthusiastic mind, and he was captivated by the political and philosophical theories of the day: but the scenes of blood which followed shocked his sensitive nature, disgusted him with society and the world, and made him more than ever a recluse. He shut himself up in a solitary apartment in the *Pays Latin*, the quarter of students. There, in a gloomy street not far from the monastic walls of the Sorbonne, he pursued his favorite speculations. Sometimes he spent hours together in the great libraries of Paris, those catacombs of departed authors, rummaging among their hoards of dusty and obsolete works in quest of food for his unhealthy appetite. He was, in a manner, a literary ghoul, feeding in the charnelhouse of decayed literature.

Wolfgang, though solitary and recluse, was of an ardent temperament. He was too shy and ignorant of the world to make any advances to the fair, but he was a passionate admirer of female beauty, and in his lonely chamber would often lose himself in reveries on forms and faces which he had seen, and his fancy would deck out images of loveliness far surpassing the reality.

While his mind was in this excited and sublimated state, a dream produced an extraordinary effect upon him. It was of a female face of transcendent beauty. So strong was the impression made, that he dreamt of it again and again. It haunted his thoughts by day, his slumbers by night; in fine, he became passionately enamoured of this shadow of a dream. This lasted so long that it became one of those fixed ideas which haunt the minds of melancholy men, and are at times mistaken for madness.

He was returning home late one stormy night, through some of the old and gloomy streets of the *Marais,* the ancient part of Paris. The loud claps of thunder rattled among the high houses of the narrow streets. He came to the Place de Grève, the square where public executions are performed. The lightning quivered about the pinnacles of the ancient Hôtel de Ville, and shed flickering gleams over the open space in front. As Wolfgang was crossing the square, he shrank back with horror at finding himself close by the guillotine.

Wolfgang's heart sickened within him, and he was turning shuddering from the horrible engine, when he beheld a shadowy form, cowering as it were at the foot of the steps which led up to the scaffold. A succession of vivid flashes of lightning revealed it more distinctly. It was a female figure, dressed in black. She was seated on one of the lower steps of the scaffold, leaning forward, her face hid in her lap; and her long disheveled tresses hanging to the ground, streaming with the rain which fell in torrents. Wolfgang paused. There was something awful in this solitary monument of woe. Perhaps this was some poor mourner whom the dreadful axe had rendered desolate, and who sat here heartbroken on the strand of existence, from which all that was dear to her had been launched into eternity.

He approached, and addressed her in the accents of sympathy. She raised her head and gazed wildly at him. What was his astonishment at beholding, by the bright glare of the lightning, the very face which had haunted him in his dreams. It was pale and disconsolate, but ravishingly beautiful.

Trembling with violent and conflicting emotions, Wolfgang again accosted her. He spoke something of her being exposed at such an hour of the night, and to the fury of such a storm, and offered to conduct her to her friends. She pointed to the guillotine with a gesture of dreadful signification.

"I have no friend on earth!" said she.

"But you have a home," said Wolfgang.

"Yes—in the grave!"

The heart of the student melted at the words.

"If a stranger dare make an offer," said he, "without danger of being misunderstood, I would offer my humble dwelling as a shelter. I am friendless myself in Paris, and a stranger in the land; but if my life could be of service, it is at your disposal."

There was an honest earnestness in the young man's manner that had its effect. His foreign accent, too, was in his favor; it showed him not to be a hackneyed inhabitant of Paris. Indeed, there is an eloquence in true enthusiasm that is not to be doubted. The homeless stranger confided herself implicitly to the protection of the student.

All Paris was quiet; that great volcano of human passion slumbered for a while, to gather fresh strength for the next day's eruption. The student conducted his charge through the ancient streets of the *Pays Latin*, and by the dusky walls of the Sorbonne, to the great dingy hotel which he inhabited.

On entering his apartment, the student, for the first time, blushed at the scantiness and indifference of his dwelling. He had but one chamber—an old-fashioned saloon—heavily carved, and fantastically furnished with the remains of former magnificence, for it was one of those hotels in the quarter of the Luxembourg palace, which had once belonged to nobility.

When lights were brought, and Wolfgang had a better opportunity of contemplating the stranger, he was more than ever intoxicated by her beauty. Her face was pale, but of a dazzling fairness, set off by a profusion of raven hair that hung clustering about it. Her eyes were large and brilliant, with a singular expression approaching almost to wildness.

In the infatuation of the moment, Wolfgang avowed his passion for her. He told her the story of his mysterious dream, and how she had possessed his heart before he had even seen her. She was strangely affected by his recital, and acknowledged to have felt an impulse towards him equally unaccountable. It was the time for wild theory and wild actions. Old prejudices and superstitions were done away; everything was under the sway of the "Goddess of Reason." Among other rubbish of the old time, the forms and ceremonies of marriage began to be considered superfluous bonds for honorable minds. Social compacts were the vogue. Wolfgang was too much of a theorist not to be tainted by the liberal doctrines of the day.

"Why should we separate?" said he: "our hearts are united; in the eye of reason and honor we are as one. What need is there of sordid forms to bind high souls together?"

The stranger listened with emotion: she had evidently received illumination at the same school.

"You have no home nor family," continued he; "let me be everything to you, or rather let us be everything to one another. If form is necessary, form shall be observed—there is my hand. I pledge myself to you for ever."

"For ever?" said the stranger, solemnly.

"For ever!" repeated Wolfgang.

The stranger clasped the hand extended to her: "then I am yours," murmured she, and sank upon his bosom.

The next morning the student left his bride sleeping, and sallied forth at an early hour to seek more spacious apartments suitable to the change in his situation. When he returned, he found the stranger lying with her head hanging over the bed, and one arm thrown over it. He advanced to awaken her from her uneasy posture. On taking her hand, it was cold—there was no pulsation—her face was pallid and ghastly.—In a word she was a corpse.

Horrified and frantic, he alarmed the house. A scene of confusion ensued. The police were summoned. As the officer of police entered the room, he started back on beholding the corpse.

"Great heaven!" cried he, "how did this woman come here?"

"Do you know anything about her?" said Wolfgang, eagerly.

"Do I?" exclaimed the officer: "she was guillotined yesterday."

He stepped forward; undid the black collar round the neck of the corpse, and the head rolled on the floor!

The student burst into a fenzy. "The fiend! The fiend has gained possession of me! " shrieked he: "I am lost for ever."

They tried to soothe him, but in vain. He was possessed with the frightful belief that an evil spirit had reanimated the dead body to ensnare him. He went distracted, and died in a madhouse."

Perhaps Tallien would have said of this simple tale that its author little understood passion and comprehended even less the nature of revolution. Tallien might have suggested that only two elements of the story deserved attention: the idea of conjugal ties predicated on the wants of the moment and the theme of youth's penchant for transmaterial speculation, the rest of the story dependent on worn Gothic and supernatural conventions for its not too remarkable effects. Poe would have managed it better, certainly. In Poe, tone, mood, imagery, rhythm would have been as central to the matter and to the effect of the tale as its weird dénouement. Of course, the young German of this story does share with Poe's character, Roderick Usher, the metaphysical craze, although Usher's manias are, decidedly, cast in a more sensual mould than are our student's, and Usher's transcendental perceptions have wider boundaries, extending to the use of music in attaining and heightening cosmic receptivity. Be that as it may, in point of fact, there is only one interesting facet of the student, his *premonition* of love. His *predisposition* to it. Love prior to the sighting of the object of love. We each have in our consciousness, in the very tissue of our being, an anticipation of the object to be loved. This is not suggested in a Platonic way. For the love-object is not rooted in some intimation of its presence in an other-worldly sphere of forms but in the manner in which the psychic genes are stamped from childhood.

In this regard, Tallien's psychic destiny was cut to a rigid pattern. First, the woman to be loved must be of an elevated station, that he must feel abject in her presence and in the very thought of her. Second, that in its initial stages, Tallien must feel power and mastery over the one to be loved; thus making all the more poignant and painful the fall from master to slave. How else to explain his irrational, antirevolutionary behavior when encountering Therèse, the victim, in her final dungeon. By instinct he must have understood that she was his ideal tyrant, his lamentable destiny. That by plucking her from under the revolutionary blade, he would organize his own fate, one as interesting and necessary (to himself) as that then being pursued by his nation. The psychic genes are stronger than the pull of ideas, stronger than history. (May one explain the sea to a man by showing him a glass of tap water? Let's admit,

finally, that the psychic genes are minted in heaven. Let's
leave it at that. Heaven.) So, perhaps Tallien would have said
of the meaning of this tale that we have so little comprehension
of the world that we regard it as enemy or friend, while it is
neither. We speak of bad and good men, while there are neither. We form ties in order not to drift, yet whoever forms a tie
is lost. Whoever is tie-less is also lost. Our experience mocks
our dreams; still, we dream. I do wonder, however, whether
Tallien's exegesis has any base in the text, or whether, as with
so many men of action, themes in the text of one's own life are
not unknowingly projected into the fabric of the art-work experienced. We tend to seek in literature mirrors or explanations of our Self, unless we skill ourselves to separate our own
blood from another's text. This one sings dirges over his mis-
fortune one day and makes rhapsody over his life-joys another: he lets out his song full stop and leaves off empty, spent,
the shell of a revolution. What have we to do with one another? Why these dreams and songs? Why wish to mean?

(My darling, you touched my readied disquietude. How did I
know during those many years spent in libraries [long, heavy
oak tables] and in rare-book reading rooms, during those hours
my eyes surveyed manuscripts [my mind bent on creating definitive texts], hours of abstract silence—only the sounds of
pages turned, of pencil on pad, of my watch ticking—when the
day went so peacefully fast that I often forgot to smoke, to
lunch [librarian in the Berg Collection, N.Y. Public Library,
would have to alert me to closing time, and I had to recompose
my senses, walking out in a reverie of printed and scripted
words, out into a late winter afternoon of streets, taxis, buses,
shoppers, and myself, off for an aimless stroll or directly to my
apartment and a cheese sandwich and beer, to the reading over
of my notes, or perhaps a brief scholarly chat with a colleague
on the phone, bibliographic details, ideas for an article sorted
out], how was I to know in all those years spent in unremarka-
ble ordinariness, that you one day would strike my reserved
soul and spark this urgent passion.

Sweetheart, let's be together on misty days such as this,
when the parks drip mist from their tame leaves and branches;
we'll stop for kir at the Hotel Plaza in New York, or order
mutton chops [rare for you] and ale in some Lake Country inn,

or have porridge and hot coffee in September in Scotland—you
must wear cashmere pullovers and thick socks under your
walking shoes.

Or, let's burn together in burning climes—Bahia, maybe,
where we'll sweat and slide on hot sheets and wait out the
steamy afternoons to make love again in the palmy, bright-
starred night breeze smelling of slaveships and sex. I tell you
my young darling, there is only you, forever you.

Or, just us two, in an Arabian oasis, under a puffy lavender
silk tent; the stars pink dots against a flat aquamarine sky: one
lone, drooping date tree. I'll nudge your small hard ass with
the butt of my braided, thin whip. You'll drop to your knees on
the carpeted sand and clasp your arms behind you, your bow-
mouth open, your eyes cast downward. Perhaps a golden desert lion will visit us in our afterlove sleep.)

Oh, Tallien! You in your coldbareroom, you in the narrow
bed and stiff, unchanged sheets, your sooty windows and mot-
tled dank walls, the fireplace cold, like a dead star, you Tallien,
regicide and cuckold, the wolf at your door, we watch you
sortie out to the rue Bonaparte to hawk your early wallposters
to a buying crowd ready for revolutionary relics and souve-
nirs. Jean Lambert Tallien, sing our delusions. Sing, sanguine
dandy, the song of the Blade and bloodrunning streets, the
regulation of the price of bread, the execution of the blackmar-
keteers and hoarders, the masques of Reason at the guillotine
steps, sing of Louis' gurgling head sliced into the sticky wick-
er. Sing, you ambiguous terrorist the *chant d'amour* as you
stuff your radical cock into her perfumed crotch. Spring days
of the year One.

Tallien, widower of the apocalypse, yours is the best porny
show since Batista's Havana, 1957. You give us plenty of hot
nights to mull over. We could almost jerk off in our seats
stewing over your Rococo Dumb Show. Here's how we'll
block it: Tallien, you enter, stage left; naked guys and girls
bound to posts are getting whipped by perfumed wigs and
powdered pantaloons, then you and your buddies scare off the
perverts of the *ancien régime* (exit right) and cut down the
flogged sexobjects, who in turn start grabbing for your cock:
you are offended and keep your pants on but one or two of
your chums go off into a corner and get blown. You cross
center stage and meditate a bit, keeping your hand over your

fly, just in case. Then you decide this is all jive and things must come to order presto-quick. You put on a tricornered hat and march about a bit (the Marseillaise is meanwhile being whistled by those few of your chums who still haven't gotten it up). This ends Act I—you just stay on stage until the curtain is drawn.

Now, in Act II, when the curtain rises, you are standing in a gilded dungeon, center stage, lights dim.

EUGENE WILDMAN

Born, school, love, no love, travel, work, down, up. Any order. Faculty, Program for Writers, University of Illinois Chicago Circle. Edited *Chicago Review*. Two anthologies *Anthology of Concretism, Experiments in Prose*; two novels *Montezuma's Ball, Nuclear Love* all Swallow Press. Magazines, anthologies.

If I could, combine the cleanness, the simplicity of story with the immediacy of theater. Closeness to speech, closeness to real rhythms (structures, organization) of experience as experienced. Not so mechanistic as heretofore.

This country was made by people who were busy losing a language. The result has been a kind of affectless, musicless school English. One of the things going on is the struggle to discover our language.

Not style, use of language. Something about energy, about knowing.

You always mean to tell the truth. People who speak no-language *cannot* tell the truth. Or know it probably. Politicians, executives. Anbody who quotes any rulebook.

The Two Exemplary Deaths of Angel Face

The first exemplary death was on a Tuesday, a coincidental day with a flaring pollution sunset; the kind that makes you stop worrying about the reasons it got to be that way. Pollution beats El Greco for visuals as far as I'm concerned. That might sound gross but it's how I feel. It's a now thing, it's far out. What the hell I live in the world. I never saw sunsets like these before, not coming up I didn't. So much for those who worry about reasons. I'd rather worry about my connections.

This is about coincidence on Morningside Heights and the mathematics of the end.

It was Tuesday because David Himmel was my friend. Insinuated himself as my friend that day. I knew straight off that's what was happening, and that I would have to pay the price for it too. I walked into a class and there were those "darkappraisingeyes." It felt like breath on glass when he changed seats and sat behind me.

I'm a poet how about coffee he said to me after class.

Not really. Actually he only told me he was a poet after we ordered the coffee.

If you were a poet David Himmel what the fuck was Angel Face?

Maybe it's something about any Tuesday. Maybe you just have to watch out on Tuesdays. Or did then. Now it's Here, or the other way around. Hard to stay plugged in but advisable. Like after a whole string of 13s coming up, seeing Jimi Hendrix at an airport 13 days before he died.

It was a year later on a Tuesday when D. T. Suzuki tried and failed to enlighten me. He was demonstrating with arrows crisscrossing over the blackboard that total determinism and total free will could exist simultaneously. That's *total*. I said I didn't understand. You're free or you're not free. He drew more arrows and looked at me hopefully. I still didn't understand. He drew some more arrows. Two more rounds of this. Suddenly he lunged and gave me a good vigorous shaking. *Now* you understand he said, smiling very confidently. Nope. He put all his books in his large handkerchief, folded it, walked right out of the room.

Also some days are frayed. You don't push. You have to respect life, it hangs by a thread sometimes.

Angel Face was a bum. His breath stank, clothes filthy and torn, tangled hair, piss, the works. You could see his ass where the seat of his pants had been worn through. He could hardly walk most of the time. We're talking about rock bottom now. Angel Face wasn't even there anymore. Zero blank rubbed out erased.

Except for one unexpected touch. What was special about him was his face. It was beautiful. Not handsome—beautiful. It was so beautiful it was unsettling. That's how come Angel Face. He did have one thing.

It was like some kind of mixup, a mistake. That's what let Angel Face exist.

Like the wicked witch, waving her magic wand and muttering her incantation, stumbled over the absolute last syllable and couldn't completely pull the transformation off.

David Himmel, on the other hand, was quite unusually ugly, as if the witch that time had played her changes backward. Now obviously this setup requires the unexpected touch again. It's those little details that give the zeitgeist away. David Himmel had, in fact, no soul at all. That poor witch just couldn't keep from goofing.

I remember Angel Face the first day he came around. He startled everybody with that face. We kept waiting for some ole lady tramp to come mooning after. Nobody showed, it was always just him. Contrast that with David Himmel, who was ugly in a way that women positively could not resist. Super Fly? That dude was Spanish Fly and somethin else!

Who said fairy tales are supposed to be edifying, and when do they ever have happy endings?

What David Himmel did for me was invite me to come and watch while he made it with the girl I couldn't even begin to *imagine* being alive without. And me there, scheduled to go into a locked ward the next day, shivering, totally unable to stop crying, running head down into brick walls, trying to smash my skull open, so that maybe maybe maybe maybe all that horrible shit would come running out.

Yeah, he knew exactly what was going down.

I can't be sure what day that was on but it was definitely Tuesday a month later when I came back out of that hospital. How everybody's story gets into sync. Sooner or later we all come together.

Angel Face? He became a wino to get off being strung out on smack.

It was a few hours later on that same coincidental day we started out with. Naomi and I were on Broadway, across the street from Julliard. There's this cop he's punching Angel Face. Actually punching him. We get closer and we hear the

cop is yelling at him. Talk you sonofabitch he's saying, and
Angel Face is just looking blank, stupefied. Say something you
filthy bastard, and he smashes him in the face. This cop is
disturbed. Unsettled. Angel Face just mumbles, it's the most
he ever does. You rotten lousy bum, he punches him again.
Then again. Neutrino, Angel Face says. What! the cop says
astonished. Kinesis, Angel Face says. The cop hits him again.
Neuron, dendrite, eros.

And now it's gone too far to stop. Whatever kind of energies
have met, whatever friction, whatever invisible line has been
stepped over, there is nothing on earth that can deflect this
thing now. *The cop takes his gun out. He shoots Angel Face in
the head. Blood spurts.* The unified field theory, Angel Face
says. He is standing there with blood running from a hole in his
head. The cop puts another one through the head. Although
the Incas were highly organized, viz. their system of roads,
they nonetheless do not seem to have been a true socialist
state. The cop knocks Angel Face to the ground and empties
his gun into his head. Angel Face still keeps on talking.

We are just about at the absolute edge of the silent '50s. You
win Dr. Suzuki. Dave Himmel you lose. You will not be the
singer of your age.

Blood is gushing from his head and Angel Face will not stop
speaking. The observer has the following visual experience of
the relativity of the mutual enclosure of the shells, he says. At
one time he sees shell 1 inside shell 2, he says. The cop is in a
frenzy. He kicks him in the head again and again and again. He
fires bullet after bullet into Angel Face's head. Angel Face is
dying. The lips barely move, the voice is soft as Angel Face
continues his discoursing on every subject known to man. Ex-
tension is a topological concept are the last words I can hear
him say.

The cop has sent for reinforcements. The crowd that had
gathered slowly drifts away. I take Naomi's hand and we walk
quietly back toward my place. By now it is dark out. Neither
of us says anything. In bed that night she is almost
uncontrollable.